"Hope *is another fun, inspir* ████████████████ *Lori Copeland. Who else bu* ████████████████ ~~acters an ornery goat, a stolen~~ ████████ *a man named Frog? It's easy to s* ████ ~~~ders~~ *are circling their wagons around the Brides o* ████ *st series!"* **Liz Curtis Higgs,** author of Mixed Signals

"*I just loved this book! Only Lori Copeland could weave a knee-slapping tale with such a beautifully redemptive message. Her characters are delightfully funny and unpredictable, and her plot is full of refreshing twists and turns. I can't wait for her next book!"* **Terri Blackstock,** best-selling author

"*Lori Copeland concocts just the right mix of faith, romance, and humor in Hope. I started chuckling right away and didn't stop till the end. A cheering, uplifting story of God's wisdom and love."* **Lyn Cote,** author of Whispers of Love

"*Lori Copeland's third book in the Brides of the West series,* Hope, *is such a delight! I laughed, I cried, but most of all I thrilled to see how spiritual truths could be woven into a rollicking good story! Lori's light and lively voice makes for good storytelling! This one's a keeper!"* **Angela Elwell Hunt,** author of The Silver Sword

"*This tender and funny page-turner will tug at your heart from start to finish. Hope's journey to love kept me cheering, sighing, and chuckling as I read. Hope is Lori Copeland at her very best!"* **Diane Noble,** author of When the Far Hills Bloom

romance the way it's meant to be

HeartQuest brings you romantic fiction
with a foundation of biblical truth.
Adventure, mystery, intrigue, and suspense
mingle in these heartwarming stories of
men and women of faith striving to build
a love that will last a lifetime.

May HeartQuest books sweep you
into the arms of God, who longs for you
and pursues you always.

Hope

LORI COPELAND

Brides of the West 1872

Romance fiction from
Tyndale House Publishers, Inc.
WHEATON, ILLINOIS

www.heartquest.com

Visit Tyndale's exciting Web site at www.tyndale.com

Check out the latest about HeartQuest Books at www.heartquest.com

Copyright © 1999 by Lori Copeland. All rights reserved.

Cover illustration copyright © 1998 by Michael Dudash. All rights reserved.

Author photo taken by Sothern Studio © 1998. All rights reserved.

HeartQuest is a registered trademark of Tyndale House Publishers, Inc.

Edited by Diane Eble

Designed by Melinda Schumacher

Scripture quotations are taken from the *Holy Bible,* King James Version.

ISBN 0-8423-7438-8 (sc)

Printed in the United States of America

05 04 03 02
5   4   3   2   1

To my family,
the source of
my greatest earthly joy.
I love you all so very much.

Preface

This book is a work of fiction. Thomas White Ferry
(1827–1896) of Grand Haven, Michigan, had a long career
in politics. He was a member of the Michigan House of
Representatives from 1851 to 1852; a member of the
Michigan Senate, 31st District, from 1857 to 1858; a U.S.
representative from Michigan's 4th District from 1865 to
1871; and a U.S. senator from Michigan from 1871 to
1883, when this story takes place. I'm not sure the senator
had a daughter; she's as fictional as Big Joe Davidson.

Prologue

"You're a Christian, Dan."

At the odd remark, Dan Sullivan looked up. Franklin knew Dan had accepted the Lord several years ago. It had taken a lot of hard knocks to get to that point, but now his convictions were strong.

Franklin chuckled. "You're going to need the patience of Job for what I'm about to ask you to do." The general reared back in his chair, his scruffy boots propped on the scarred desk. The smell of reams of periodicals wedged in the floor-to-ceiling bookshelves permeated the room. The office was cramped and perfectly reflected Franklin Talsman. The old gentleman absently drummed his stubby fingers on the belly of one who'd partaken of too many of his wife's biscuits.

Dan studied the man who'd been more like a father to him than a commanding officer. There wasn't much Frank could ask that Dan wouldn't try to oblige. One more job wasn't going to hurt. God had been good, kept him alive all these years. One last favor for the general wasn't out of place.

"I'm not sure I like the sound of that. What do you need, General?"

"Oh . . ." Franklin pretended sudden interest in his ink

blotter as he fidgeted with the inkwell. Dan frowned. Then again, maybe he shouldn't be so quick to offer his services.

"Just a small job—shouldn't take more than a week or two at the most." Franklin kept his eyes on the blotter. "Maybe three."

Two or three weeks. Not much of a delay for an old friend. Still leaves plenty of time to buy that farm, get a small crop into the ground before summer hit.

Leaning back in his chair, Dan recalled the time he first met the general. Had it been fifteen years ago? Frank had waded into a rowdy New Orleans street brawl to save his neck. Dan would never forget the favor.

He'd been a headstrong, cocky nineteen-year-old spoiling for a fight and never had trouble finding one. He was lucky that the general liked that in a man. He took Dan under his wing, drew him into the military, and became both friend and mentor. By the end of Dan's military stint, Franklin bragged openly that Dan Sullivan had matured into one of the army's most prized possessions.

Three years ago Franklin had formed a small but elite group of men for high-risk jobs like the recent rash of government payroll robberies. Dan was part of that unit—at least until he retired at the end of the month.

"Interested?"

"As long as it's no more than two to three weeks."

No one was more surprised than Dan when he recently came to the realization that he wanted out of the service. Two years ago, he'd have laughed at the idea. But he was thirty-four now, long overdue for roots—somewhere to call home. Last month he'd informed Franklin he was leaving. He planned to go back to Virginia, buy a piece of land he'd had his eye on, and start a new life. Both parents were dead, and his one sister lived in England. All of a sudden he needed something other than a cold bedroll and a lonely campfire.

Franklin pushed away from his desk and stood up. "It's the Davidson gang. They're on the move again. They've robbed three government payrolls in the past six weeks. You've got to find these men and stop this piracy."

Dan frowned. "The Davidson gang? Aren't they—"

"Nuts?" Franklin shoved a sheaf of papers aside. "Nuttier than Grandma Elliot's fruitcakes. But they're smart enough to rid the government of a good deal of money lately."

Getting out of his chair, Dan moved to the window. Outside, twilight settled over the barren ground. In another few months, Washington, D.C., would come to life. Ugly patches of snow would give way to tender blades of new green grass. Crocuses and lilies would push their heads through rich, black soil. Tulips and daffodils would bloom along the walks and roadways.

"You know, Dan, Meredith and I have been hoping you'd reconsider your resignation. Why not take a few months off—take a well-deserved break, then come back." The old man chuckled. "After the assignment, of course. The army needs men like you."

Dan watched the streetlights wink on in the gathering dusk. Carriages rolled by outside the window, men going home to families. Six years ago he'd stood at this window

and watched the Union army parading up Pennsylvania
Avenue in a final Grand Review. That same month, April
1865, he'd watched the funeral cortege of his beloved presi-
dent, Abraham Lincoln, led by a detachment of black
troops, move slowly up the avenue to the muffled beat of
drums and the tolling of church bells. Dan had stood in the
East Room of the White House earlier that day and said
good-bye to his old friend. Mary had pressed a large white
linen handkerchief with A. Lincoln stitched in red into his
hand as he'd offered his condolences. Most of his life had
been here in Washington. It wasn't going to be easy to
leave, to start over. "Thanks, Frank, but it's time to go.
Move on with my life."

The older man moved beside Dan. "Next thing I know,
you'll be getting married."

Dan didn't have to look up to know humor danced in his
friend's eyes. Married? For the past fifteen years there hadn't
been time for a wife. There was no time for a personal life
at all. Besides, he'd been in love once. The brief episode
had ended in dissatisfaction and heartache. He wasn't interested in marriage; he planned to live the remainder of his
life in peaceful solitude.

"Right now I'm more concerned about buying a few
head of good beef cattle." Dan sank back into the hard
wooden chair in front of Frank's desk. "Exactly what is it
you want me to do, Frank?"

Franklin sat down again, shuffling more papers and handing them to Dan. "Wouldn't be our kind of thing except
that military payrolls are involved. Seven total, to be exact."

Dan frowned. "Seven?"

"Seems this gang of three scruffy ne'er-do-wells has been able to intercept seven payroll shipments—three in the past six weeks. Witnesses say the gang is a bunch of inept fools—don't seem to know what they're doing—but that could be a cover." He pushed a sheet of paper across the desk. "We've tentatively identified them. One is Big Joe Davidson. Spent some time in Leavenworth for armed robbery. A bank. Tall, strong as an ox, got one eye that wanders. Isn't known to be real bright, but that could be a cover, too. The second is Boris Batson—don't know much about this one, just that he's ridden with the gang two years.

"The third one is called Frog. He sustained a bad throat injury in a fight several years ago. Ruined his voice." Frank leaned back in his chair. "He's been in prison once that we know of. Apparently he doesn't talk much. At least hasn't during a holdup, and from what we've heard, never spoke while he served his time."

Dan studied the wanted posters. The three faces that stared back at him didn't appear to be overly bright.

"I want you to hook up with them. Gain their confidence, find out where they're getting their information. We'll put the word out on you." Frank grinned. "In fact, you'll be one dangerous character. Name's Grunt Lawson, and you're lightning fast with a gun, even faster with women, and mean as a woodpile rattler. We hope the Davidson gang gets wind of you, so that when you meet up, they'll be begging you to join them."

"You think someone on the inside is feeding this gang information about the payroll shipments?"

"That's what we think. Only two or three people know when those shipments go out and how much. So far, the gang has hit the three largest ones. Someone has to be filtering information. Your job is to find out who and make the arrest."

It was a standard request. Dan had followed the procedure more than a dozen times over the years. But he was tired. Tired of being someone else, tired of cozying up to outlaws, then moving in for the arrest. Tired of living a lie. He tossed the flyer back on the table. "Where's the next shipment?"

"Kentucky."

"When do I leave?"

"First light. You accepting the job?"

Dan pushed out of the chair and stood up. "For you, yes. But it's my last one, Frank."

Frank's smile widened as he rounded the desk to walk Dan to the door. "Your orders will be ready in the morning. Be careful, Son. This gang may be stupid, but they're also dangerous. I'd hate to lose you over something foolish."

"I'm always careful, Frank. You know that."

The general clapped him on the back affectionately. "Gonna miss you, boy. Sure you won't reconsider and stay on? I can arrange for a desk job if that's what you want."

"No, thanks. I'm going to simplify my life."

"Simplify your life, huh?" Franklin grinned.

Dan didn't know what the general found so amusing. One last job, and Dan Sullivan's life was going to be dull as dishwater.

"I'm tired of moving around, Frank. From now on, I'm going to live a quiet, uncomplicated life, alone—with a few head of cattle on my own piece of land with nobody telling me where to go or what to do."

Franklin's grin widened.

Dan eyed him sourly. "What's so funny?"

"You."

"Me?"

"Got your life all planned out, do you?"

"Sure. Why not?" Dan prided himself on control. Control of his life and his actions. God took care of the big picture; he took care of the details. "What's so odd about that?"

Franklin shrugged. "My mother, God rest her soul, had a saying: 'Want to hear God laugh? Tell him what you got planned for your life.'" He winked. "You take care of yourself, Son. It's going to be real interesting to see if God agrees with you."

Chapter One

Hope Kallahan pressed a plain cotton handkerchief to her upper lip and shifted wearily on the hard wooden seat, bracing herself against the wall of the coach.

Her bones ached.

She'd have given all she owned for a pillow to cushion her backside. Never had she sat for so long on such a hard wooden bench, not even in church. The pews in Papa's house of worship were softer than this device of torture.

"Are you feeling poorly, Miss Della?"

The young woman sitting opposite Hope peered anxiously into the sickly face of her elderly companion.

"I'll be fine, dear. Just having some mild discomfort. Don't worry your pretty head, Miss Anne. I'll be just fine."

Della DeMarco, the young woman's escort, fanned her flushed face. The poor woman had taken ill the moment she boarded the coach, but she insisted on continuing the journey. Her charge, Miss Anne Ferry, daughter of Thomas White Ferry, U.S. senator from Michigan, was traveling to Louisville to visit friends.

Pressing back against the seat, Hope counted the tall trees lining the road. Miles of countryside rolled by, bringing her closer and closer to her new home.

And a new husband. To think that a man like John Jacobs wanted her as a mail-order bride—well, it was answered prayer. After Papa died, Hope and her sisters, Faith and June, were in desperate straits. They knew Aunt Thalia couldn't afford to feed another mouth, much less three. With no resources of their own, the girls felt they had no other choice but to find suitable mates. And since Cold Water had no likely prospects, they were forced to look elsewhere.

Faith had moved to Texas to marry Nicholas Shepherd, a fine upstanding rancher; June would soon travel to Seattle to marry Eli Messenger, an understudy to the powerful evangelist, Isaac Inman of the Isaac Inman Crusade.

Of course it was too soon for Hope to have heard from either Faith or June, but she hoped to very soon. She was anxious to see how each sister fared with her new husband.

Ordinarily, Hope would be frightened by such a long and perilous journey undertaken without the security of her sisters' companionship, but she was resigned in the knowledge that she was doing the right thing. She simply had to trust that God had ordained this marriage. Soon she would marry John, and they would live happily ever after.

Would she be a good wife, one John would be proud to claim? Papa had spoiled her shamelessly, but she was perfectly capable of being a dutiful wife. She reached up to pat her ebony hair into place.

If matrimony wasn't too demanding—and Medford had a decent hairdresser.

Anne Ferry edged forward in her seat. Large brown eyes saved the petite blonde from being plain. "I just don't know what to do. Miss Della shouldn't be traveling, but she insists."

"Well—she's the best judge of that," Hope murmured, but she uttered a silent prayer for the woman's impediment anyway. Papa always said that folks sometimes weren't the best judges of their own resources, meaning that they depended upon themselves far too much and not enough on the Lord.

Papa. She sighed, still feeling his loss. So much had changed since his death. One moment he had been preaching a fiery lesson, and the next, he was lying cold and unresponsive in the pulpit. Now she was leaving everything and everyone she knew to marry a man she didn't know.

She closed her eyes, her forced enthusiasm waning. From now on her life would be just plain dull. She'd be a tired old married woman with three or four young ones hanging on her skirts. She sighed.

She knew little about this man she was about to marry. They'd become briefly acquainted through letters exchanged over a few short weeks. John's picture depicted a rather plain face, dark hair neatly trimmed and parted on one side, a handlebar mustache. She'd never cared for mustaches, but then perhaps she'd learn to like one. John looked a bit uncomfortable in the photo, as if his collar were too tight or his britches too snug in the get-a-long.

Sitting up, Hope opened her compact and peered at her image in the mirror. Everyone said she was beautiful, but Papa said that was the Lord's doing, not hers. She studied her violet-colored eyes and dark hair gleaming like black coal in the sunlight. Indeed, she had been given high cheekbones and a rosy, full mouth. Lots of people were pretty . . . but maybe she was extraordinarily blessed. . . . She snapped the compact closed. Papa had warned her about being vain.

"Ohhhh, who would have ever thought this would happen?" Anne glanced at her chaperone. "Miss Della was in blooming health when we left."

"One can't always anticipate these things." Hope was more concerned about the slightly green tinge that had come on Anne's companion than about her persistent cough. The old woman was dozing, her head bouncing against the rolled upholstery.

"Have I told you that I'm visiting old friends from the Ladies' Seminary?" Anne asked. "We share such wonderful times together in Bible study and discussion." She leaned closer. "There are very few, you know, who can discuss the Scriptures intelligently. Most are inclined to frivolous things, parties and such. Even Father. Why, there's this one man on our staff who is positively decadent. He dresses well, but his hair is much too long and he has this, well, this 'look' to him." She shivered. "He's taken a shine to me, but I fear he hasn't much interest in Scripture." She glanced at Miss Della, whose dry snores resonated off the coach walls.

"I've wanted to visit friends for some time now, and now Miss Della has taken ill." She fanned her face with a small fan she kept in the turquoise bag in her lap. She glanced back, her pretty blonde curls bobbing with each jolt. "But it's been a joy to travel with you. I do hope that your Mr. Jacobs isn't too far from Louisville, so that we might see each other often while I'm in Kentucky. I want you to meet all my acquaintances, perhaps even join our Bible studies."

"That would be nice, but Mr. Jacobs said Medford is some fifty miles from Louisville." Hope shifted, trying to get more comfortable. The miles seemed endless now. She'd been traveling for over a week, and she was anxious now to reach her destination.

Though she had little in common with Anne, she had been excited to have someone her age on the long journey. Papa had been a preacher, and she'd heard whole chapters of Scripture every day of her life, but she wasn't as dedicated to Bible study as Anne.

And her memory was just awful. She couldn't remember a thing she read.

June was more to Papa's liking when it came to spiritual matters—and Faith, too. They recalled every single thing they read. It seemed a natural thing for her sisters to accurately quote Scripture, but though she tried, she got hopelessly confused.

Blessed are the peacemakers for they shall . . . they shall
. . . find peace? No, they would be called something, but
she wasn't sure what.

She studied serious young Anne Ferry. She bet Anne
would know—she'd quoted the Bible since boarding the
stage, and it all sounded perfectly flawless to Hope.

The coach slowed noticeably, and Hope straightened to
look out the window.

"We're coming to a way station."

"Thank goodness," Anne breathed. "I am so weary of all
this lurching—and the dust. Perhaps a stop will make Miss
Della feel better."

Hope doubted it, but then, as bad as Miss Della was looking, most anything was likely to help. She automatically
braced herself as the stage drew to a swaying halt. Miss Della
jarred awake, looking around dazedly. Her small round face
was flushed with heat. Hope feared she was feverish.

The driver's face appeared briefly in the coach window
before he swung open the door. "We'll be stopping to
change teams and eat a bite, ladies."

Hope settled her hat more firmly on her head. "Thank
you, Mr. Barnes." She clambered out of the coach, then
turned to assist Anne with Miss Della.

"Oh, my," Miss Della whispered, her considerable bulk
sagging against the two young women. "I don't feel well at
all."

Hope gently steadied her. "Perhaps you can lie down
until we're ready to leave."

"Thank you—yes, that would be nice. Oh, my. My head is reeling!"

With Anne on one side and Hope on the other, they supported the elderly woman's bulk inside the way station. The log building had a low ceiling and only one window. The interior was dim and unappealing, but the tempting aroma of stew and corn bread caught Hope's attention. Breakfast had been some time ago.

Anne waited with Miss Della while Hope asked the stationmaster if there was a place for the woman to rest. The tall, thin man pointed to a narrow cot that didn't appear to be all that clean. But beggars couldn't be choosers.

When Della was gently settled on the small bed, Anne and Hope sat down at a long wooden table. A haggard-looking woman wearing a dirty apron set bowls of steaming hot stew and squares of corn bread before them.

Hope cast glances at the cot, concerned for Della's comfort. "She seems very ill."

"Yes—if only she could see a physician. . . . Sir!" Anne called.

The stationmaster paused in the middle of refilling the drivers' coffee cups.

"Is it possible that a physician might look after my chaperone? I fear she's running a fever."

"Sorry, lady. Ain't no doctor around here."

"How far is the nearest one?"

"Twenty miles—maybe more."

Anne met Hope's eyes anxiously. Picking up her spoon, Hope began to eat.

It seemed like only moments had passed when the two drivers pushed back from the table and announced they would be leaving shortly.

Della thrashed about on the cot, moaning.

"She isn't able to go on," Anne said. "We'll have to return home."

"Might be for the best," one of the drivers observed. "I got to stay on schedule."

"Don't worry about me," Hope said quietly. "You just see to Miss Della. I suggest that you send for a doctor immediately."

Anne looked uncertain about her new role—that of caregiver rather than receiver. "Yes—I'll have to forego my trip—but there will be others. I would never forgive myself if anything happened to Della. The moment she's able, we'll return home and have our family doctor assume her care."

"Got to get back on the road." Mr. Barnes picked up his hat and left.

"I'm coming." Hope rose and embraced Anne, then touched Miss Della's unresponsive hand. With a final glance over her shoulder, she returned to the stage.

Dear Lord, please restore Miss Della to health. And please watch over Anne and keep her from harm.

The coach lurched forward, and Hope's gaze fell on Anne's turquoise bag lying on the seat. Picking it up, she moved to call out the window for Mr. Barnes to stop the stage but then realized that she could arrange for the purse to be returned. The driver had made it clear that he intended to stay on time. Hope opened the turquoise tote.

Inside were a few of Anne's calling cards, some spare hair-pins, a gold locket engraved with Anne's initials, and a small mirror, also engraved. Valuable treasures, but nothing Anne couldn't do without for a few weeks.

The day seemed endless without the senator's daughter's conversation to break the monotony. Hope's clothing was covered in dust, and she'd have given nearly everything she owned to be able to take her hair down and brush it out. A headache pounded between her eyes.

In spite of the discomfort, she finally dozed, dreaming of Kentucky, a hot bath, and a bed that didn't rock.

Dan Sullivan wearily urged his horse down the steep incline. Up ahead, the Davidson gang wound their way through the narrow pass. Four months. He never planned on this assignment taking four long months. Was Franklin nuts, sending him on this wild-goose chase? The Davidson gang was a threat, all right—to anyone who came near them. How they'd managed to lift twenty thousand dollars in army payroll he'd never know. They moved at a whim, choosing a target by chance, never with apparent forethought. Yet their luck was uncanny. Or else someone was feeding them information. But if this was the case, Dan had been unable to identify the source.

Joining up with the gang had been easy. Frank had done an admirable job spreading the word about the legendary Grunt Lawson. Grunt was accepted into the gang and given the job as lookout.

But Dan was tired.

Tired of cold food and sleeping on hard ground. Tired of washing in cold streams and tired of watching his back.

Weary of living with imbeciles.

This case had no apparent end in sight. The gang had hit several payrolls, but Dan considered it blind luck. If something didn't happen soon, he was going back to Washington and tell Frank he was through. Spring was here, and he didn't have a potato in the ground. The thought irked him. His plans were made, and he didn't like interruptions.

Big Joe drew his bay to a halt at a wide place in the trail. "This is it."

Boris and Frog reined up short. Boris's mare jolted the rump of Big Joe's stallion. Big Joe turned to give the outlaw a dirty look.

Boris blankly returned the look. "This is what?"

"This is where the stage'll be comin' through. We wait here until we see the dust on that second rise over there. Back yore horse up, Boris! Yore crowdin' me."

Boris grudgingly complied.

Dan studied the road below. It was the third stage the gang had attempted to rob in as many weeks. Somehow, their luck had soured lately. Yesterday Boris broke a stirrup. He rode it to the ground, and the stage flew past before he got the horse stopped and his foot untangled.

The week before, Frog had burst out of the bushes and had ridden straight into the oncoming coach. He was thrown fifty feet into the air and was lucky he hadn't broken his neck. His horse ran off, and they still hadn't found her. Frog had to steal a horse to replace the missing one; he also nursed some pretty ugly bruises for days, vowing that from now on Boris was leading the charges. A heated disagreement erupted, with a lot of name-calling Dan didn't appreciate.

"I'll wait here." Reining up, Dan settled back into his saddle to wait. With any luck, they'd botch this one, too.

"Nah, you ride with us. Don't need no lookout for this one. Ain't nobody around these parts for miles." Big Joe's left eye wandered wildly. "The drivers usually whip up the horses when they come through this pass, so be ready."

Dan shifted in his saddle. "What if the stage isn't carrying a strongbox?"

"Don't matter. This one's carryin' somethin' better." Boris leaned over and spat. A grasshopper leapt clear of the sudden onslaught.

Better? That was a strange statement. What did this stage carry that the men wanted more than army payroll?

The four men waited in silence. A dry wind whipped their hats, and the horses grew restless.

Dan shifted again. "Maybe it's not coming."

"It'll come," Big Joe said. "Somethin' must be keeping it."

"Yeah, somethin's keeping it," Boris echoed.

"Shut up, Boris."

"Can talk if I want to."

"Shut up."

"Can't make me."

Dan shifted again. "Both of you dry up."

Frog hunched over his saddle horn, staring at the horizon. Dan decided Frog didn't speak much because it wasted too much effort. Frog was lazy. Lazy, and he smelled like a skunk. The only time Dan had seen him take a bath was when his horse fell in a river and Frog was sucked under. Dan had begun to pray for river crossings.

He studied the motley group. Big Joe was questionably the brain of the outfit. Joe had difficulty deciding which side of his bedroll to put next to the ground. Frog was like his namesake, easily distracted, his attention hopping from one thing to another so quickly that it was impossible to follow his reasoning—if he had any. If this was the dangerous gang that was so adept at robbing the army-payroll coaches, their success had to be more fluke than finesse. These three had a hard time planning breakfast.

Big Joe suddenly sat up straighter. "There she comes!"

The others snapped to attention. Boris craned his neck, trying to get a better look.

"Where?"

"There."

"Where?"

"There!"

"Wh—" Boris winced as Big Joe whacked him across the back with his hat. Dust flew.

"Oh yeah. I see it."

Flanking the stallion, Joe started down the narrow trail. The others followed, Dan bringing up the rear. This had better be resolved soon.

Dan had had just about enough of this job.

Hope was dozing, her body automatically swaying with the motion of the coach. The sound of pounding hooves pulled her into wakefulness. One driver shouted and the reins slapped as the team whipped the coach down the road.

Scooting to the window, she peered out, wide-eyed.

A sharp crack rent the air. Clamping her eyes tightly shut, she swallowed the terror rising in the back of her throat. The crack sounded again and again. Gunshots! Someone was firing at the coach!

Horses pounded alongside the window. Hope's fingers dug into the crimson upholstery, gripping the fabric. She craned, unable to see who was chasing the stage. Then four men rode alongside the coach, hats pulled low. Her heart hammered against her ribs. Robbery. The stage was being robbed!

"Stop the coach!"

The harsh yell was accompanied by another gunshot. Hope's lips moved in silent prayer. *Don't let this be a holdup. Let me get to Medford safely. Protect the drivers. Oh dear—if only I could accurately remember the Lord's Prayer . . . the part about walking the fields of death . . .*

The coach came to a shuddering halt, dust fogging the open windows. Hope sat still as a church mouse, terrified to move. She heard the sound of someone cocking a rifle, and her heart threatened to stop beating. Dear Lord, what if she were killed before she reached John Jacobs? Would anyone find her? Faith? June? Aunt Thalia?

Our Father, who art in heaven, how now be thy name. Thy

kingdom come, thy . . . thy . . . something or other be something or other . . .

"Stay where you are!" a hoarse voice called out.

"You ain't gettin' the box!" Mr. Barnes yelled.

Another harsh laugh. "You totin' cash money? Throw it down!"

"Stay back, Joe! Yore horse is gonna—"

A gun exploded and a horse whinnied. Hope carefully edged back to the window. One of the bandits was now lying spread-eagle on the ground, rubbing his noggin.

"Git back!" the grating voice yelled to the drivers who'd gone for their guns.

The drivers stepped back, still shielding the strongbox.

The second rider eyed the outlaw sprawled on the ground. "Git up, Joe. This ain't no time to be foolin' around."

The man sat up, nursing his head between his knees. "Fool horse. Pert near knocked the thunder outta me."

A third man rode in, his gun leveled on the drivers. His voice was steady, unyielding. "Throw down the box, and no one gets hurt."

Hope shivered at the sound of the strong, confident tone. It was nothing like the others. She timidly poked her head out the window, her heart skipping erratically. The outlaw with the calm voice wore a mask across his face, but the disguise couldn't hide his dark good looks.

The heavy metal box bit into the dirt beside the coach.

"Whooeee! Look at that!" The big man on the ground

shook his head to clear it, then got to his feet. "We got us another U.S. Army money box!"

The second outlaw climbed off his horse and approached the cache. "Yes sirreeee. That's sure nuff what it is, all right—got us another army payroll! Money and the woman too! This must be our day!"

"Lemma have it."

"No way. Frog's gonna carry it. You cain't even stay on yore horse."

Frog urged his animal forward, and the outlaw slid the cash box across his lap.

"Now, let's see what we got inside here." The big man, undaunted by humiliation, walked over to the coach and yanked the door open. Hope stared into the face of one of the strangest-looking men she'd ever seen. Thick body, bowed legs, square face. It appeared as if someone had fashioned a seven-foot man, then pushed him down into a six-foot-three body with a wandering eye.

"Well, howdee do! Here's what we're lookin' for!" Big Joe's mouth split into a tobacco-stained grin. "It's Thomas Ferry's daughter! And ain't she pretty."

Dan's eyes switched to the frightened girl. "Senator Thomas Ferry's daughter?" He urged his horse closer to the coach. "What are you doing?"

Joe looked back at him. "This here is the daughter of the big politician from Michigan. Read in th' paper that she was on her way to visit friends in Louisville—"

"You cain't read!" Boris accused.

"Oh, all right! I had someone read it to me! What's the

difference?" Joe's good eye rested on the prize. "Bet her daddy will pay a fine ransom to get his little girl back. A fine ransom."

The young woman drew back, slapping the outlaw's hand when he reached for her.

"Now don't be spunky, little gal. Come on out here and let us have a look-see at what's gonna make us rich."

Boris grinned. "Yeah, rich—even if we cain't spend any of the money."

"Not yet, we cain't. But in a few months, when we got all we want, we'll lie back and let the stink die down; then we'll hightail it to Mexico and live like kings."

Big Joe reached inside the coach, but the woman scooted to the far end of the bench. "Why, Boris, she don't want to come out," Big Joe complained. He grinned. "Guess I'll jest hafta go in and git her."

One boot was on the metal step when the occupant apparently decided it would be better to exit the stage herself than have him inside with her.

"I'm coming out!"

"She's coming out," Joe repeated loudly.

"Could be she don't want anywhere near you!" Boris laughed.

Dan backed his horse away from the coach as a bronze-booted foot searched for the stage step.

Dressed in a brown traveling dress with a straw hat perched atop her ebony hair, the young woman slowly exited the stage. For a moment, Dan couldn't take his eyes off her. He'd seen his share of good-looking women in his day, but this one was a rare jewel. Safe on the ground, she brushed at her skirt, glancing from one gang member to another, her gaze finally fastening on him.

Dan drew a resigned breath, looking away.

There was only one problem: This woman wasn't Anne Ferry.

Chapter Two

The dark-haired beauty struggled against the burly outlaw who had slung her over his shoulder like a sack of feed. Dan watched the exchange, helpless to intervene. If he tipped his hand, he and the girl would both be shot.

"Stop fighting me, girlie!" Big Joe dragged Hope toward his waiting horse. "Frog, tie up that driver and guard!"

"Hold it a minute." Joe whirled at the sound of Grunt's voice. Dan met his eyes with a grave warning.

"How do we know she's Thomas Ferry's daughter?"

Dan had met Anne Ferry at a social event at the senator's mansion in Lansing a couple of years back. While Anne was an attractive young woman, she couldn't hold a candle to this dark-haired beauty pummeling Joe's back.

Slim and fine boned, she was a striking enchantress. A

cloud of black hair framed her pretty heart-shaped face. Eyes—an unusual shade of violet—were wide beneath her flowered straw hat, but not with fear. Stubbornness. Dan could spot obstinacy a mile off. This woman was going to fight Joe Davidson every step of the way.

"It is Miss Ferry—paper said so," declared Joe.

Dan met the girl's headstrong gaze as Big Joe let her down off his shoulder. "Are you Anne Ferry?"

"Certainly not!"

"She is too!"

Dan shot Boris a short glance. "She says she isn't."

"Well, she's lyin' through her teeth. Look here." Boris picked up the turquoise purse lying in the coach seat and rummaged through its contents. Holding up a gold locket, he asked smugly, "What's this say?"

Dan frowned when he read the initials: *A. F.* How did this young woman come to be in possession of Anne Ferry's personal effects?

Hope watched the spectacle, tapping her foot. "Anne was on the stage, but she had to leave when her chaperone fell ill and—"

"She's lyin'!"

"I am not!"

"Are too! You'd say anythin' to save yore hide!"

Dan's sharp command broke up the spirited debate. "We can't just take a woman hostage without knowing her identity." That's all Dan needed—a woman thrown into this insane mission to up the ante.

The girl wasn't Anne Ferry, but he had little choice but to

play along and stay close enough to keep her from harm. Thomas Ferry wasn't going to pay money for a daughter who wasn't missing.

"Well, well." Big Joe rubbed his beefy hands together, studying his prize. "Yore a purty little dish. Papa's gonna pay a handsome sum to get you back."

Crossing her arms, Hope glared at him. "I can't imagine why. I'm not Anne Ferry. My name is Hope Kallahan."

Big Joe snickered. "Is not."

"Is too."

"Is not!"

"I am not Thomas Ferry's daughter!" Hope stamped her foot.

"'Course you'd say that!"

Dan shook his head, turning his horse. Now he had four of them on his hands.

"Frog! Get Miss Ferry's valise," Big Joe ordered. "She'll need duds."

The silent outlaw climbed atop the stage and started rifling through the baggage. Grinning in triumph, Frog lifted up a green carpetbag a moment later.

Joe nodded. "Says *A. F.* That's hers all right."

Dan watched the exchange. Where was Anne Ferry, and why was her bag still on the stage? Was foul play involved? He studied the young woman, who was engaged in another heated dispute with Joe. Exactly what was going on here?

Frog pitched the valise to the ground, then climbed down. A moment later the gang mounted, and Boris and Frog fired their guns in the air. The sudden explosion spooked Big Joe's horse, and it reared, spilling Joe and the woman to the ground. In a flurry of screeches and petticoats, Hope landed hard on top of the outlaw. The breath whooshed out of him. He lay for a moment, staring blankly up at the sky.

Bounding to her feet, Hope kicked dust at the outlaw. "How dare you!"

Joe's face flamed, and he rolled awkwardly to his feet. "Doggone it."

Brushing dust off the back of her dress, Hope glared at him. "Can't you ride a horse?"

He swore and glared at her. "The fool thing spooked."

Boris eyed the stage drivers warily. "Quit messin' around, Joe. We gotta get outta here."

Joe climbed back on the horse, swung Hope up behind him, and the gang rode off in a boil of dust.

Hope's heart hammered as the horses galloped down the narrow road. Fear crowded her throat, but she refused to give in to its paralyzing effects. She was scared—more frightened than she'd ever been in her life. Were they going to kill her? How soon before someone found her bones that the buzzards had picked clean and shipped them back to Aunt Thalia? *Pray, Hope. Pray!* But her thoughts were frozen.

She quickly weighed her options. She couldn't convince these men that she wasn't Anne Ferry. Perhaps that was good. When they discovered that she *was* Hope Kallahan and not the senator's daughter, they'd have no further use for her. But she could identify them. They would be forced to do away with her in order to save their rotten hides.

She had to pretend to be Anne until she could escape. That's what she had to do. Pretend to be Thomas Ferry's daughter until she could get away from these horrible men.

The men pushed the horses hard, up ravines and through narrow passes. Hope lost track of time. She concentrated on staying astride the animal though her limbs were numb. They rode at a feverish pace, but the one called Grunt controlled his horse effortlessly. He was different from the others. His body was hard and lean. His shirt and denims—even his bedroll looked clean and well kept.

Hope found herself hypnotized by the horse's rhythm beneath her. Surrendering to exhaustion, she lay her head against Big Joe's back and closed her eyes. Her mind refused to rest. She wasn't Anne Ferry. What would happen to her when these men discovered their mistake?

Toward dark, she became aware that the riders were slowing. She sat up straighter, trying to focus.

The sun was sinking behind a row of tall pine trees as they rode into a small clearing. A shallow stream gurgled nearby. Hope peered around the outlaw's shoulder and saw a ramshackle cabin set in the middle of the meadow, the front door sagging half off its hinges. Her pulse quickened, and her arms tightened around her captor's waist.

"Home sweet home, girlie." Big Joe swung out of the saddle, pitching the reins to Boris. The desperado stalked toward the cabin, leaving Hope to dismount for herself.

As she attempted to climb down, a pair of strong arms

grasped her around the waist. Grunt lifted her out of the saddle and onto the ground. His touch was surprisingly gentle.

Yanking free of his grasp, she marched toward the rickety shelter.

"Whooooeeee. Got us a fireball!" Joe stood on the front porch, mock fright on his face. "Hurry along, darlin'. You got to write a note to yore daddy."

"I don't know how to write," Hope said, trying to meet his one-eyed gaze. One eye kept going south.

He managed to focus. "Stubborn, ain't ya?"

"Your effort to extort money from Mr. Ferry is useless."

Big Joe bent forward, and Hope fought the urge to run. His good eye pinned her. "We know who you are, so jest stop sayin' that unlessin you want to get me riled. Your luggage says you are, your purty gold engraved locket says so too. Yore her, lady."

Hope stiffened. "Maybe."

The bowlegged outlaw spit over the porch railing. She saw Grunt back away from the conversation, watching the exchange from beneath the lowered brim of his black felt hat.

"Git on in there." Big Joe grabbed Hope's arm and tried to shove her ahead of him. He kicked the front door open and stepped inside. Frog followed him, carrying Hope's suitcase.

When Hope saw the room's condition, she caught her breath. Stopping dead in her tracks in the doorway, she wrinkled her nose. She'd never seen anything so filthy. Broken furniture, dishes with remnants of dried food still on them. Something furry skittered out of a bowl and raced down the table leg. She shuddered. Surely they didn't expect her to stay here!

"This is unacceptable!"

Cobwebs dangled from the ceiling. The only window was obscured by dirt. The woodstove, used for both cooking and heating she assumed, had rusted from neglect. Trash littered the corners, and the rodents had brought nuts in from the outdoors. Her gaze traveled to the only bed in the room, a single cot with a dirty quilt wadded up on the bare ticking. Her eyes switched to the ceiling, where holes large enough for a good-sized animal to slide through were apparent.

She whirled at the sudden movement in a corner and cringed. The room was infested with rodents and who knew what else? Fear constricted her throat.

Big Joe came back to physically try and pull her into the room. "Come on, git in here, girlie."

Hope planted her feet and refused to move. "Never."

Big Joe peered at her menacingly. "What'd you mean, never? You gotta come in. I say so."

She shook her head, refusing to budge. "I'm not going in there—not until someone removes those—those things."

Frog and Boris exchanged quizzical looks. Boris scratched his head. "What things?"

Joe tried to yank her into the room, but she dug her heels in.

"Now yore rilin' me, girlie!"

Crossing her arms, Hope planted herself in the doorway. If Big Joe wanted to shoot her he could. She wasn't going into that pigsty. They would either clean it up, or she would stand here all night.

Big Joe, hands on his hips, big stomach hanging over his belt, glared at her. "You get yoreself in here, Missy. Right now!"

Hope shook her head. She was scared—she didn't know if Joe would shoot her on the spot, but she wasn't going in that room. "I will not subject myself to that . . ." *They think you're the senator's daughter,* an inner voice reminded her. "My daddy wouldn' 'low it."

That wasn't a lie. Papa wouldn't have allowed her to breathe air in that room, let alone stay in it.

Big Joe grabbed her arm. "You'll do as I say—"

"No," Hope screeched, stomping his foot.

Grabbing his toe, Big Joe did a painful jig.

The two struggled, Hope's boot connecting with the outlaw's shins. He whooped, dancing in circles now.

Grunt calmly stepped in to break up the fray. Grasping Joe's arm, he moved him to safety. "If she wants to stay out here and let the coyotes get her, that's her choice."

Hope shot him a sour look. He didn't scare her. He might act nicer than the others, but he wasn't.

Well, she could stand anything. Besides, they wouldn't want a coyote near the cabin. Their hides would be in danger, too.

Grunt brushed past her. "Leave her alone. She'll come in soon enough."

Ha. They didn't know Hope Kallahan. Papa said she had a one-track mind. No one could make her do anything she didn't want to do. And right now, she didn't want to go into that dirty room. Crossing her arms, she rooted herself in the doorway.

Boris tried to close the door, but Hope braced her weight and refused to budge.

"Git outta the way so I can shut the door. It's gonna git cold in here tonight."

"No."

Boris took a step back, hunched his shoulder, and burst toward the door, his face filled with determination.

Hope calmly stepped aside.

The outlaw shot through the opening and barreled head-long across the porch, slamming into the porch railing. The impact threw him into the air, and he landed flat on his back. Groaning, he rolled to his side and lay there.

Joe and Frog stood on tiptoe, gaping at the standoff.

Hope resumed her position. Recrossing her arms, she stared at them. They just didn't know Hope Kallahan.

Finally Big Joe gave in. "Hang it all! If she don't want to come in, she don't want to come in!"

Frog tossed her suitcase on the cot. A cloud of dust rose and fogged the air.

"What else could we expect from Ferry's daughter? Livin' in that big house with all kinds of servants," Big Joe grumbled. "Have folks waitin' on her, hand and foot. Spoiled rotten, that's what she is."

Hope shot him an impatient glare.

"Spoiled rotten," Boris groused, rolling to his feet. He stretched, and bones popped.

The men dismissed her, going about their business.

Frog walked to the stove and lit it. He cut carrots and potatoes. Before long, he stirred them into a bubbling pot. Hope's stomach knotted with hunger. It seemed like days since she'd eaten at the way station.

Grunt removed his gun belt and hung it over a hook. Her eyes followed him as he moved about the room. There was something different about him. He seemed more in control, less volatile. Miles smarter. Why would he choose to ride with these miscreants?

The men ate—a thin watery stew with crusted slices of buttered bread. The smell of coffee made Hope faint. The men's spoons mesmerized her. She could almost taste the potatoes, carrots. . . .

"Hungry?" Boris asked without looking up.

"No." She looked away.

"Hummm, mighty tasty vittles, Frog." Joe dipped up a large spoonful of stew and held it out in front of him. Steam rose off the food, the heavenly smell wafting across the room. Hope swallowed and looked at the ceiling.

Minutes ticked slowly by. The wind picked up, blowing a gale through the open doorway. Her thin cloak fluttered. Goose bumps welled on her arms.

The men gulped down their food, shooting resentful glances at her and huddling deeper into their jackets as the wind whistled around their ears. Their breath formed frosty vapors in the air.

An hour passed, then two. Hope couldn't feel her legs now. The men were getting ready to bed down for the night, their teeth chattering as they rummaged for blankets.

"Cold enough to hang meat in here," Boris grumbled.

"Leave her alone. She cain't stand there all night." Big Joe jerked a rug off the floor and wrapped it around his shoulders.

Hope's chin rose a notch. She could stand here forever or until she froze stiff. Whichever came first.

"We take shifts watching her." Big Joe unrolled his bedding. "Grunt, you and Frog take first shift. Me and Boris'll take second. I want her watched ever' minute until we get that ransom."

"She'll have to have privacy, Joe." Grunt pitched the remains of his coffee into the fire.

"We'll string a blanket—she'll hafta make do. This ain't no fancy hotel."

Grunt stared into the fire. "No one touches her. Is that understood?"

When Big Joe opened his mouth, Grunt reiterated the order. "No one touches her. She's to be treated like a lady at all times. We don't want Ferry accusing us of hurting his little girl."

Boris bent down, trying to coax more heat from the old stove. "Maybe we ought not to ask so much for her. She's mean—real mean. Her daddy might not want her back."

Big Joe grunted. "He'll want her—he has to want her. She's his daughter."

Hope choked back an angry response. If they thought the

ransom wouldn't be met, they might easily abandon her here alone, without food or water. She'd die in this filthy hole. She swallowed her complaints.

"Cat got your tongue, Miss Ferry?" Boris grinned, rolling deeper into his blanket.

Hope refused to look at him.

Getting up from his chair, Joe stretched, then scratched in places a gentleman didn't scratch in front of a lady. Stretching out on the cot, he lifted his head off the dirty ticking and grinned at Hope. "Yore welcome to the best bed in the house, Miss Snooty Ferry, if yore a mind to sleep tonight."

Eyes of violet steel chilled him. "I'd sooner eat dirt."

"That can be arranged, too." Joe yawned, then sank back on the pillow. "Nighty, night."

Grunt took up watch beside the fire, huddling deeper into his coat. "Leave her alone, Joe."

Arms akimbo, Hope stood in the doorway.

Soon the only sounds were the groan of the cooling stove and Big Joe's snores.

Grunt sat beside the fire, his dark eyes trained on Hope. Frog kept watch from the table, blowing to warm his stiff fingers.

Lord, Hope prayed, closing her eyes against the sight of four strangers sprawled about the filthy room. *This isn't my fault; I only wanted to get to Medford to meet my future husband. I don't know why you've involved me in this horrible mistake, but please help me.* She opened her eyes, then shut them again. *It isn't fair, Lord. I've done nothing to deserve this. Where are you?* Her feet ached, and she was so hungry she could eat dirt.

What would Faith and June do? They'd pray, just like Papa; they'd pray and trust the Lord to deliver them.

Did she really believe there was a kind, benevolent heavenly Father living in a place with streets of gold, forgiving people of their sins, rescuing them from evil men who kidnapped people?

Did she really, truly believe that?

There'd never been a time when she wasn't aware there was a Lord, a higher being. Papa had made sure of that. But honestly, she'd never thought much about her beliefs. Papa believed—it only stood to reason she did, too. She believed in her own way . . . but belief like Papa had? Tears stung her eyes. She was cold and hungry and alone and scared.

If you're there, show yourself, Lord. Papa was a righteous man. He did enough praying for both of us—have you forgotten? Deliver me from this . . . this travesty.

She reached out to grip the edge of the door frame to steady herself. Grunt and Frog had their eyes closed now. Boris and Big Joe were snoring loud enough to wake the dead. A chair was just three feet from her.

Three short feet away.

The more she looked at it, the more she longed to sit down.

She shifted from one foot to the other. Better. Now if she could just reach that chair without making a noise. She edged one foot forward, then the other, holding her breath. She was nearly there. Carefully, slowly, she lifted the chair, then turned and silently crept back to the door.

Sinking down, she gratefully leaned her head back, closing

her eyes. Glorious. And she hadn't compromised her position one iota. She wasn't exactly "inside" the cabin. She was still at the door.

Blinking hard, she fought to stay awake. She'd be on her feet when the men awoke in the morning. Hummpt. Grunt and Frog were disgraceful guards. They were dozing— sleeping on the job. They'd never know she sat for just a moment . . .

Her eyes flew open. Why, she could stay awake for days if necessary. Everyone knew she was a fighter. She'd stay awake until she escaped these horrible men. Tipping her chair back, she closed her eyes. Ahh. It felt so good. Just for a moment . . .

Her eyes flew open again, and she frantically flapped her arms as the chair upended and hit the floor with a thunderous crash.

All four men sprang to their feet. Hair standing on end, they stared at her, glassy-eyed.

Swallowing, she stared down the barrel of Big Joe's pistol. Oops. Now they'd know she'd sat down.

Picking herself up off the floor, she righted the chair and set it back into place. Stepping back to the doorway, she recrossed her arms, blinking back tears.

Are you there, Lord?

Chapter Three

Somewhere toward dawn Hope heard a rooster crow. Fingers of orange and gold unfolded, then gradually spread a hand the width of the eastern skyline. One by one, the outlaws began to stir. Big Joe sat up on the cot, scratching his head. His mat of tousled hair stood on end.

Hope, arms crossed, swayed with exhaustion. She'd stood for eight hours. Her legs felt like two wooden posts. It had been the longest night of her life. Focusing on her captors, she wondered what would happen next. Would they stick a gun to her head and make her come inside? Physically drag her into the cabin?

Her eyes locked with Grunt's as he stood at the stove pouring coffee. She wasn't stepping a foot into that room unless they cleaned it; they, on the other hand, didn't seem threatened by her stubbornness. That was as plain as the nose on her face. How long could she stand here? Her puffy feet told her not much longer. She'd have to eat—and use the necessary. She hadn't used the necessary in hours.

Her gaze switched to Big Joe, sitting on the side of his cot in a dazed stupor. He seemed to be the leader. Boris and Frog followed orders. Grunt—she wasn't sure what Grunt did.

He robbed stages and abducted an innocent young woman, that's what he did.

The men began moving about. Frog reached for the water bucket and pushed past Hope on his way to the creek. She'd been captive for over fifteen hours, and this man hadn't spoken a word. Could he talk? Did he have a tongue?

Big Joe gave a whining yawn and scratched his belly. He eyed Hope's stance sourly. "You this stubborn all th' time?"

She nodded. More, if the truth were known. One time she'd sat up two nights straight to prove to June that she could do it. She'd wanted to make it three, but Papa had cut a hickory switch and told her he'd use it if she didn't get herself to bed.

Frog returned with the water, his heavy boots tracking mud to the stove. Picking up the poker, he stoked the fire, threw in some kindling, and slammed the lid back in place. She watched as he lay thick slices of bacon in the skillet, wondering how long it had been since he'd washed his hands. If ever. Within minutes, the meat began to sizzle, filling the room with a delicious aroma.

Her stomach ached with hunger. She glanced at Grunt, her eyes sending him a silent plea. *Don't let that bacon burn.*

Grunt finished pulling on his boots and stood up. "Frog, watch that bacon."

Hope closed her eyes. *Thank you, Father.*

The outlaw took a tin cup off a hook beneath the shelf and poured coffee. Hope watched as Grunt approached. He extended the steaming cup to her.

"Drink it."

She might be stubborn enough to stand in the doorway forever, but she had sense enough to know that she had to eat. She was already faint from lack of nourishment. She took the cup, refusing to meet his gaze.

"That'a girl. We can't have our ticket to prosperity gettin' sick on us." Big Joe reached for the coffeepot, his eye shooting west. "We want our little Annie healthy as a horse when her pappy pays us all that money."

"I'm—"

Grunt's eyes sent her a silent warning, and her mouth clamped shut.

I'm not Anne Ferry.

She peered into the cup. The tin cup was burning her fingers. Desperation made her drink the potent black brew. The bitter liquid was scalding and strong enough to walk, but it felt heavenly to her parched throat. Shivering, she took another long drink. Maybe she was being foolish by refusing to eat. A piece of bacon—two pieces. She would eat two pieces of that heavenly smelling bacon and drink one cup of this horrible coffee. She'd need her strength to escape. She sipped and thought.

Anne was a Bible scholar. Would the outlaws know that? Anne had talked of memorizing whole chapters of Scripture. Hope knew Scripture, but she certainly hadn't memorized much. So if the subject came up and she was going to pretend to be Anne, she would have to be careful not to trip herself up. Faith and June knew the whole first chapter of Revelation by heart—she'd heard them recite it once when they were trying to outdo one another. Now that was something—one whole chapter. If anyone asked her to recite verse one by memory, she'd be in trouble. Right now, she was none too proud of that. She sincerely wished she'd been a more dutiful student.

"You gonna just stand there like a mule?" Big Joe asked.

Hope tried to look brave, but her thumping heart told her she had the courage of jelly. Still, she could see her obstinacy was having an effect on the outlaws—it made them uncomfortable.

Boris slammed his fork on the table and got up. Eyes narrowed, teeth clenched, he confronted her. She pressed tighter against the door frame.

"You think yore better than us just because yore papa's in politics and you have all them fancy clothes. But you won't be so uppity if—"

Hope lifted her chin. "You are being most rude."

She wasn't afraid of him—she was terrified, but she couldn't show it. These men understood force. She had to make them see things her way. "I'm not budging until this room is set to order."

"You—" Boris's big hand circled Hope's neck.

Hope dropped her coffee, and the cup rattled across the floor, the hot liquid splashing on the outlaw's trouser leg.

"Leave her alone," Grunt warned from the corner where he sat drinking his coffee.

"She's too persnickety." His fingers sliding off her throat, Boris mocked, "The room's not clean enough, the food's not good enough."

Grunt looked away. "She's got a point."

"You complainin'? Then you do the cookin' and cleanin'," Frog bellowed.

The three men's heads snapped to look at Frog.

Frog's face flamed. "Can talk when I want—just don't want that often."

Grunt got up to refill his cup. "It wouldn't hurt to clean this place up some."

"What? You some girly-girl, want your linens washed?" Boris chided.

"No, but she's going to make herself sick standing in that doorway. So we clean up the room? She comes inside, we shut the door and get warm for the first time in sixteen hours, and she writes the note to her papa. Seems like a fair enough exchange."

Big Joe turned sullen. "I ain't doin' no cleanin'. That's woman's work."

Grunt shrugged. "I don't see any women here, except her. It doesn't seem smart to have her down scrubbing floors, does it?" He stood up, stretching. Hope's eyes involuntarily followed the play of his muscles beneath his heavy shirt. "If you want her papa to pay that ransom, you'd better make sure his little girl's alive and well."

Hope mentally added, *Amen.* Grunt was smarter than the other three put together. She was going to hold out until the cows came home. Grunt could see that.

Boris studied the disheveled room. "Can't say a good cleanin' would hurt."

Big Joe's eye wandered the room. "Nah, guess it wouldn't kill us to clean it up some—knock out a few cobwebs. Ain't like we got anything else to do 'cept wait to collect from Ferry."

The four men looked at each other.

Finally Frog nodded. Then Boris and Big Joe.

Heaving his bulk out of the chair, Big Joe reached for a stack of dirty plates. "Suppose she'll want us to heat water—do this thing up right."

Grunt took a piece of fried bread from the skillet, broke it, and stuck two strips of bacon between the pieces. "Might as well."

He carried a plate to Hope. "You win," he said, extending the peace offering.

She eyed the saucer. It appeared cleaner than the others. At this point it didn't matter. She'd eat anything that didn't eat her first.

The men sat down and began to wolf down their food. Hope dropped into a nearby chair. For a moment she just stared into space. One problem down—a multitude to go.

Bringing the bread and bacon to her mouth, she bit into it, sighing with pleasure. *Thank you, Lord, for sustenance. And forgive me for thinking my troubles are greater than your power.*

Big Joe glanced up from his plate. "Once you eat, girlie, you're gonna write that ransom note."

Boris and Frog grunted their agreement around mouthfuls of bacon.

Closing her eyes, Hope took another bite. She'd write the silly ransom note as soon as they cleaned this cabin.

And not one minute sooner.

Dust smoked the air as Frog wielded a broom. Big Joe took a bucket of hot water, dumped in half a bar of soap, and proceeded to scrub the window. At the sink, Boris and Grunt had their hands in suds up to their elbows.

Hope sat at the table, holding the pencil stub to her mouth pensively, her brow furrowed in thought. What did one say when trying to extract ransom money from a senator for a daughter who wasn't missing? Her thoughts turned to Della, and she wondered if the kindly old chaperone was feeling better. By now, Anne was back home and Della would have proper care. When this ransom note reached Thomas Ferry, his daughter would be safely back in her own room in Lansing.

A bowl slipped out of Boris's soapy fingers, and he let out a string of vehement curses. She flushed at the foul language. Why, Papa would say Boris needed his tongue cut out and fed to the hogs for such blasphemous talk.

Grunt shot Boris a warning look. "There's a lady present."

Boris swore again, dumping more suds into the pan. Bubbles rose up, threatening to overflow the sink. "Don't like doin' woman's work."

Laying the pencil aside, Hope cleared her throat. "I have to use the necessary."

The four men stopped what they were doing and stared at her.

She smiled faintly. "The . . . necessary. Please."

Big Joe flushed a bright red. "Grunt, you take her."

Grunt quietly set his dustpan aside and reached for his rifle.

"While you're out there, see if you can scare up somethin' to eat," Boris grumbled. "I'm tired of stew."

Getting up from the table, Hope preceded Grunt out the door.

"And don't be gone all day!" Big Joe kicked the door shut with his boot. A second later, Hope saw him back at the window, scrubbing the pane.

The morning air was brisk as Grunt hurried her across the clearing toward a row of heavy thickets. She shivered, drawing her cloak tighter around her. Dark clouds skittered overhead, and the wind was picking up again.

Grunt stopped at the first thicket. "This is good enough."

She hurried toward the hedge, turning when the tone of his voice stopped her. There was no humor evident now. His eyes pinned her to the spot. "You understand the situation, don't you? If you attempt an escape, you're a long way from anywhere. It's dangerous—suicidal even—for a young woman to travel these parts alone." His dark eyes refused to release hers. "Do you understand what I'm saying? Now is not the time to show your independence, Miss . . . Ferry."

"I understand you," Hope muttered. She didn't appreciate the sermon. Given a chance, she'd be gone in a second and worry about the consequences later.

As if he read her thoughts, he said quietly, "Don't be foolish. You won't make it alone."

"I'm here to use the necessary. Do you mind?"

Nodding, he tugged the brim of his hat. "I'll wait down by the creek. You might want to wash when you're finished."

She might at that. If she looked half as bad as she felt, it must be scary. Pushing her hair out of her eyes, she straightened regally. "If you'd be so kind as to allow me privacy?"

His eyes sent her a final warning before he pushed his way through a hedge, the sound of his movement evident long after his broad shoulders had disappeared from sight. Releasing a pent-up breath, Hope disappeared behind the bushes.

When she returned, she followed the path to the creek. She found Grunt squatting beside the stream, deep in thought.

"Are you going to hunt before we go back?"

He rose slowly, his eyes assessing her. Apart from the others, he looked like an ordinary man. One Hope might even like, under different circumstances. Might like a whole lot.

"You can't be tired of stew."

"No, but Boris said—"

"You don't want to go back yet."

She didn't want to go back ever. "It is nicer out here." She could breathe again.

"All right. We'll stay for a while." Picking up his rifle, he started off. She fell into step, threading her way through the heavy briars. Anything was better than spending time in that cabin.

She couldn't detect a path, but he seemed to know where he was going. After a few minutes, he paused, gesturing for her to keep her distance. He disappeared into the thicket ahead, and it got very quiet. If he was moving, he was doing it silently.

Suddenly it occurred to Hope that he might leave her out here. He wasn't like the others—what if he had tired of the game and decided to move on? What if he knew—actually knew that she wasn't Anne Ferry and there would never be any ransom money? She'd be hopelessly lost in this thicket, probably be eaten by wild animals. . . .

Her eyes anxiously scanned the area.

Grunt was nowhere in sight. Her heart pounded in her chest. She should run, as fast and hard as she could. She wouldn't be missed for a while. Blood pumped feverishly through her veins.

She jumped as a rifle went off, then again. Gunshots. Grunt had shot something. She closed her eyes, thankful it wasn't her.

A few minutes later she heard something moving back through the brush. Grunt appeared in the clearing, holding two fat squirrels in one hand.

"Dinner."

Feeling faint, she smiled lamely at him. "More stew?"

"Fried, with gravy—if we can find a cow."

She followed him back to the creek and sat on a flat stone while he skinned and cleaned the squirrels. His hands were large and capable, manly hands, tanned dark from the sun.

Hope picked burrs off her skirt, tossing them into the creek. A thin watery sun slid from behind a dark cloud. The air was damp, like it could rain any moment. "You're not like them."

"Um."

"They're not nice men."

"I'm not either."

She studied him, trying to decide what made him different. "You bathe regularly, and your speech is more educated. Did you attend school?"

"Did you?"

"Don't change the subject." If she were Anne Ferry, of course, she would be well schooled. He knew that. It was as if he was testing her—weighing her answers. Well, she was smarter than that. He wasn't going to trip her up.

"Why do you ride with them?"

Tossing a skin aside, he spared her a brief, impersonal glance. "Do you always talk so much?"

Leaning back, she closed her eyes, listening to the early spring morning—the gurgling creek, birds chirping in a nearby tree. Everything seemed so normal, and yet her life was in an upheaval. She was here, with this puzzling man, and almost enjoying it. She should be frightened half out of her mind, but she wasn't. The Lord gave her peace.

"You're doing it again."

"Doing what?"

"Changing the subject."

"Um-hum."

Straightening the hem of her dress, she sighed. For some unfathomable reason, she felt she could be honest with him. If she were mistaken, her fate lay in his hands. "I'm not Thomas Ferry's daughter."

He didn't respond, just went on cutting skin away from the carcass.

"So there won't be any money coming, even if I do write that silly note. Mr. Ferry will read it and think a simpleton wrote it. Anne Ferry is probably home this minute, safe in her own bed."

He rinsed the knife in the water, his eyes meeting hers now. "If I were you, I'd keep that bit of information under my hat."

Her eyes narrowed with suspicion. Who was he? He wasn't a part of those other men; he was too perceptive. Too . . . real.

"The others will find out soon enough."

He tossed the entrails into the stream and rinsed his hands. "The longer they think you're Anne Ferry, the better off you are. Remember that."

"Then you're not—"

His look silenced her. "In any position to help you," he finished her sentence. "Take my advice. Go along with the circumstances for now. Don't cause any trouble."

"I don't understand. Whoever you are, I want you to help me—"

"I can't help you." He stood up, holding the two skinned squirrels. His dark eyes skimmed her coolly. "Write the note and wait to see what happens."

"It's the money, isn't it? That's why you're with them. You want that money as much as they do, but you won't get it. I'm not Anne Ferry."

A mask shuttered his features. "Just do as I say if you want to get out of this alive."

She got up, smoothing the back of her skirt. "What's the profit if a man has the whole world but loses his soul?"

He frowned. "What?"

"The Bible." She repeated the misquoted verse.

"Is that supposed to mean something?"

"It's Scripture. Mark 8 something."

He looked none too happy, and she knew why. The mention of Scripture induced feelings of guilt, as well it should for a man in his profession.

"'What's the profit if a man has the whole world but loses his soul'? That's found in Mark?"

She nodded gravely. "My papa was a preacher."

His eyes narrowed. "Mine is the Lord, and I imagine he'd prefer you get the Scriptures right."

She crossed her arms. "God isn't mocked. What a man sows, he'll get back," she retorted, hoping that was correct.

If a man sows he'll get it back—no, if a sow throws—no, no, there was nothing in the verse about a pig.

Disbelief filled his face. It irritated Hope that he—of all people—challenged her.

"'A fool despises instruction!'" Dear me! Had she misquoted that? Oh, she hoped not—besides, how would he know? Indignant, she paced back and forth.

"I don't understand any of this. I was on my way to Medford, minding my own business. You . . . and those terrible men . . . stopped the stage, dragged me off—"

A clap of thunder shook the ground. Hope glanced up as the first raindrop hit her cheek. "Great. Rain."

"At least you got that right."

Hope planted her fists on her hips. "I don't know who you are or what you plan to do with the money you hope to steal, but I do know that a fool despises instruction—"

"Misquoting again, Miss Ferry."

"My papa—," she began, then gasped as the heavens opened up and poured.

Grunt grabbed her by the arm, and they started running for shelter. He steered her toward a rise with a long outcropping of rock. The ground beneath was dry.

"We'll hole up here until it slacks off." He settled Hope into the cramped space, then crawled in beside her. For a moment she couldn't breathe. She'd rarely been so close to a man—a man this . . . masculine, with such overpowering presence. He was all muscle and brawny strength.

Scooting toward the back, she tucked the hem of her dress around her ankles. Grunt took off his hat and shoved his fingers through his dark hair. The two sat, staring at the falling rain. The minutes ticked by. The space shrank, becoming incredibly small and personal. Her arm brushed the fabric of his shirt, their bodies only inches apart in the tiny space.

She focused on his clean profile. His jaw was firm, not soft and flabby like the others; his nose straight, his mouth well defined. And he had the most incredible dark brown eyes that looked right through her. A sigh escaped her.

He looked over. "Did you say something?"

"No." Such a waste of manhood. He might have made some lucky woman a wonderful husband, been a doting father. Had he implied his "father" was the Lord, or had she imagined it? No self-respecting man would tolerate the likes of Big Joe, Boris, and Frog.

Aunt Thalia's voice echoed in her mind: *Let those without sin hurl the first rock.* She could hear the admonition clearly. Aunt Thalia was a saint; Hope wasn't.

"I'm not without sin, Aunt Thalia, but unlike some people, I don't steal money and terrorize innocent people," she muttered.

Grunt turned to look over his shoulder. "I know you said something that time."

Hope realized she'd spoken her thoughts out loud. Her face flamed. "I was talking to myself, if you don't mind."

The rain came down in blowing sheets. They pressed back into the shelter and huddled as lightning split the sky and the ground rumbled beneath them. *Dear Lord, why must I be a prisoner of a man I find so appealing? Why couldn't Grunt look and act despicable, like Big Joe?*

It might take weeks—months—for the men to recognize

their mistake. The ransom note would have to be delivered. Thomas Ferry would know that someone was playing a cruel trick and strike a match to the absurd request. Then the outlaws would have to wait more weeks before they were sure their demands weren't going to be met. She couldn't survive months here in that one-room cabin! Even if she could keep the men fooled into thinking she was Anne Ferry, when they received no response to the ransom note they'd investigate and discover she wasn't Ferry's daughter. Then what? Fear constricted her throat as another clap of thunder rocked the ground.

Grunt shifted. Was her presence unnerving to him? She hoped so—she sincerely hoped so. It would serve him right.

Settling himself in a dry spot, he tipped his hat over his face and appeared to sleep. Hope's eyes gauged the distance between her and where he rested. It was now or never. Grunt's warning rang in her ears. *It would be suicide for a woman alone in these parts.* But it would be suicidal of her to remain in his custody.

It was pouring rain—she could hide in the bushes, make her way back to civilization under the guise of darkness. It wasn't the smartest plan, but then she'd never been in this situation before. Desperate times called for desperate measures.

Was that Scripture?

No, Uncle Frank used to say that to Aunt Thalia.

Springing from beneath the rock outcropping, Hope ran. As fast and as hard as she could run. Faster than she'd ever run in her life. Her breath came in gasps as she leaped puddles and dodged prickly bushes. Disoriented, she beat her way through thick underbrush. Rain sluiced down, blinding her. She could hear Grunt shouting at her.

"Come back here, you little fool!"

She ran on, praying that the thunder would cover the noise of her flight. Turning to look back, she plowed headlong into a tree. The impact threw her into a bush, and she lay on her back, stunned.

"Anne! Don't be foolish—you can't make it alone!"

Rolling to her side, she doubled up, holding her breath. Grunt's voice boomed above the downpour.

"Miss Ferry! Anne!"

Squeezing her eyes shut, she prayed. *Don't let him find me; please, please, don't let him find me.*

"You can't get away—don't try it!" His voice sounded nearer at times, then farther away.

"I can, if I escape you," she whispered.

The minutes crept by. Her legs began to ache, but she couldn't move. Any sound, even in the pouring rain, would alert him. She was chilled to the bone now. How long before he would give up and return to the cabin for help? By then, she would be so far down the road they'd never find her.

She lay for hours, listening for footfalls, terrified to move. Toward evening, the rain slowed to a cold drizzle. Teeth chattering, she listened to small animals moving around foraging for food. A raccoon crept close, and she shooed it away with her hand. Two more appeared, their beady eyes wide with curiosity.

Her voice was barely a whisper. "Hungry, fellows?" She didn't blame them. The thought of bacon and bread and rich, black coffee haunted her.

She scavenged beneath the bush and came up with a handful of acorns, then gently pitched them several feet away. The coons darted off, investigating.

She hadn't heard Grunt calling her name for some time. She'd made it. *Thank you, God, thank you, God, thank you, God—*

She yelped when she suddenly felt herself yanked to her feet and a large, warm hand clamped over her mouth.

"You are sorely testing my patience," a rough voice rasped in her ear.

Her heart was thumping a mile a minute as he whirled her around and steadied her on her feet, none too gently. She blinked, weak with relief when she saw it was Grunt, not Big Joe, Boris, or Frog. His face was a storm cloud. "Don't you have a lick of sense?"

She tried to break his hurtful hold. "Let me go! You're not like the others. You're intelligent; you have a quality the others don't have—" She wrenched free. "Don't do this!"

"If I let you go, you'll be dead by morning." He took her by the shoulders and gently shook her. To her surprise, she saw concern in his eyes. "Why did you disobey me?"

"Please—"

"No."

She clamped her teeth together. She was wrong about him. He was just as mean and ornery and bullheaded as Big

Joe, Frog, and Boris put together. Her heart sank. She was doomed. She had failed at her escape, and they would watch her closer than ever now.

"Come on. You're going to catch your death out here." Keeping her firmly in check, he turned her in the direction of the cabin. Stopping at the shelter, he picked up his rifle and the squirrels, then continued forcing her ahead of him.

Despair enveloped her. She was going to die here in these awful woods. No one would know where she was or what had happened to her. If Grunt didn't strangle her, the others would.

"Please let me go," she chattered between breaths.

"You're staying with me." He latched onto her ear and marched her toward the cabin.

"Ouch . . . you're hurting me!"

"Just walk, Miss Ferry."

She was sopping wet, and her teeth were knocking together so hard she couldn't argue. It seemed like hours later when he finally shoved her inside the cabin. "Ouch, ouch, ouch!" Wrestling out of Grunt's grip, she stood in the middle of the floor, thick mud caked on her thin shoes, the hem of her dress dripping a stream.

Big Joe sprang up from the table, overturning a chair. His features were tight. "Where have you been!"

Lifting her chin, she crossed her arms.

She stumbled when Grunt pushed her closer to the fire. "Had a bear tracking us. Fired off a couple of rounds, but he dogged us most of the day. Had to hole up until we could shake him."

Hope gravitated toward the fire, seeking its warmth. His excuse barely registered with her. She needed blankets, hot coffee.

"A bear?" Boris sat up from his bedroll. "Did you git 'im?"

Grunt motioned toward Hope. "She needs dry clothes and something to eat. Now."

Boris grumbled but rolled to his feet and stoked the fire. Big Joe opened the suitcase and pushed it across the floor to her. She fished around for a clean dress and underclothing.

The men busied themselves with the squirrels. Grunt rigged a rope and draped a blanket over it, then heated water on the stove. Stepping behind the makeshift curtain, Hope removed her wet clothing, shaking so hard her hands refused to cooperate.

"Wrap a blanket around yourself." She froze when she heard Grunt's deep baritone on the other side of the blanket.

"What?"

"Wrap a blanket around yourself. I have a hot bath drawn."

Hope closed her eyes, so grateful she wanted to cry. Hot water. She picked up a second blanket and secured it tightly around her. A wooden tub slid behind the curtain.

She heard the front door close as the men stepped outside to allow her privacy. Climbing into the water, she sank down, allowing the steaming vapors to envelop her. Her body cried out with relief and she sighed, sliding deeper into the comforting warmth.

It occurred to her that Grunt had been out in the cold rain all day searching for her. He must be every bit as chilled as she was.

Soon heavenly smells filled the cabin. Rain pattered on the windowpane as Hope brushed her hair dry before the fire. Grunt was cutting up the squirrels and dipping them in flour. The meat sizzled when he laid the pieces in a skillet of hot grease. Boris mixed cornmeal and water—bannock, she heard him say—cakes of Indian meal fried in lard.

She listened as the men talked among themselves. Big Joe questioned Grunt about the bear. She thought she detected a hint of skepticism in his voice, but Grunt was adept at holding to the story. He was protecting her, but why?

As the mouthwatering smells permeated the room, Hope grew a little light-headed. She was so tired and so very hungry. And so grateful to Grunt for rescuing her. She might well have perished out there alone.

She stood up and walked to the table.

Grunt glanced up, continuing to dish up plates of hot food. The cabin looked spotless. The curtains had been washed, the floors scrubbed. "Sit down, Miss Ferry. Supper's ready."

Big Joe, Boris, and Frog scraped their chairs to the table and lit into the fried squirrel and johnnycakes like a pack of wild animals. Stunned, Hope watched them strip meat off the bones with their teeth, wipe their mouths on their sleeves, and belch between bites.

She had yet to pick up her fork.

When they noticed that she was staring, Big Joe glanced up, utensil paused in midair. "What?"

Her eyes silently condemned their atrocious table manners.

Boris lowered the squirrel leg he was gnawing on. "What's wrong now, Miss Snootypants?"

"Must you eat like mules?"

"Hum?" Frog asked, his mouth full.

"Your manners—they're disgraceful."

The men exchanged quizzical glances. "What's she yakkin' about now?" Boris complained, a piece of meat falling from his mouth as he talked.

"Somethin' 'bout manners. Cain't please her."

Picking up her fork, Hope looked at each of them. "It seems to me you would be interested in improving yourselves."

They gawked at her, mouths slack. Grunt moved to the stove and poured a cup of coffee.

Hope took a small bite of her meat. "Chew with your mouth closed, and if you take small bites you'll enjoy the food more. Besides, swallowing it all in one gob will give you indigestion."

Big Joe frowned. "Indi-what?"

"A sour stomach," Grunt said, sitting down at the table.

Boris swore under his breath.

"And please watch your language." Hope picked up the plate of johnnycakes. "It isn't necessary to curse in order to properly express yourself." She selected two nice brown cakes and arranged them neatly on her plate. "Papa says only a fool opens his mouth and proves it."

Forks and knifes clanked as the men returned to their meals. Hope quietly laid her fork aside and folded her hands next to her plate. A minute later, Big Joe glanced up, frowning when he saw her staring. His bushy brows lifted.

"Grace," she said.

"Who?"

"Grace. We haven't said grace."

Boris let out a blue curse, and Big Joe kicked him under the table, hard. Boris pinned Big Joe with a sour look; then, fork standing at sentinel, he bowed his head.

Hope began, "Oh, Lord, we are so grateful for the food you've provided, though we are so unworthy."

Frog snickered.

Hope's voice rose an octave. "We know your mercy is endless, Father, and I ask that that unbiased mercy be extended to these poor heathen souls—Big Joe, Boris, and Frog—" she glanced up to meet Grunt's eyes and hurriedly added—"and Grunt, who knows no better. Amen."

Opening her right eye, Hope studied Big Joe, who seemed to be trying to decide if he'd just been insulted.

Raising his coffee, Grunt quietly ended the prayer. "Amen."

When the meal was over, Big Joe pushed back from the table and walked over to his saddlebags. Hope felt as if she'd eaten with a pack of buzzards. All except Grunt. His table manners were flawless. Joe lumbered back to the table, looming above Hope with pencil and paper in hand as she savored the last bite of meat, allowing the tasty morsel to slide down her throat.

"Now write that note, girlie. We've waited long enough. We want five thousand dollars from Ferry by the fifth of next month."

"Fifth of next month! That's only two weeks away!" Hope protested. She set her fork on the table. "There isn't time—"

"Write the note."

Hope glanced at Grunt expectantly. He shrugged, draining the last of his coffee. "Write the note, Miss Ferry."

Well. He was no help. Did she dare to hope that was compassion she had seen in his traitorous eyes? Of course not. He wanted money, just like the others. What she saw was desire—the urge to be rid of her, no matter who she was.

Grasping the piece of paper, she smoothed it against the table. She held her hand up for the pencil.

Big Joe slapped one into her open palm.

Venturing a last withering glance at Grunt, she prayed that he'd intervene, stop this nonsense. He didn't. Instead, he got up for more coffee.

Sighing, she positioned the pencil. *God forgive me, but I fear even your power isn't enough right now.*

Biting her lower lip, she wrote: "Dear Daddy . . ."

Chapter Four

Senator, sir, your morning mail."

The butler set the silver tray on the corner of the desk. Thomas Ferry reached for his coffee cup, eyes glued to the newspaper article he was reading. A moment later he laid his paper aside and glanced at the three letters on the tray.

"An unusually small offering this morning."

"Yes, sir. Would there be anything else, sir?"

"No, thank you. Send Miss Finch in, will you?"

Thomas was a creature of habit. Rising early, he bathed, shaved, ate breakfast, and then finished reading the morning news in his office over a third cup of coffee. While reading the morning mail, he dictated responses as necessary, thus saving his secretary and himself valuable time.

Mardell Finch kept her employer on time. She was respected throughout the Ferry camp as efficient, loyal, and hardworking. A spinster of some forty-plus years, she was dedicated not only to Thomas but also to the office itself. Miss Finch was no slacker.

As Miss Finch entered the study, notebook in hand, Thomas opened the first letter. After ten minutes of dictation, he reached for the second envelope. Examining the missive, he frowned.

"Crude paper, but the writing is quite delicate. Hmmm, no return address."

He slit open the envelope and removed the creased paper. Then he blinked.

"Great day in the morning! Listen to this, Mardell: 'Some very dangerous men are holding me captive. They demand a ransom of five thousand dollars, payable in paper money within ten days once you receive this note. The money should be placed in plain wrapping and addressed to Joe Smith in care of Louisville, Kentucky, Post Office. When the money has been received, I will be released unharmed. At that time I will travel back to you. Love, Anne.'"

Thomas glanced at Miss Finch. "What do you make of that?"

"It must be a joke," Miss Finch responded.

"Bernard!"

The double study doors opened immediately. "You called, sir?"

"Go upstairs and make sure Anne is in her room."

The elderly white-haired gentleman frowned. "In her room, sir? The doctor left not fifteen minutes ago—I'm quite sure she's still abed with the sniffles."

"Check on her anyway, Bernard. I want to be certain of my daughter's whereabouts."

"Yes, sir." The door closed. Bernard's footsteps could be heard receding down the hall.

Thomas drummed his fingers on the desk, checking his watch fob every few minutes. Snapping the face closed, he got up to pace.

Miss Finch shut her notebook, primly crossing her hands in her lap. "I'm sure it's just someone's idea of a cruel joke, Mr. Ferry."

Footsteps once again sounded outside the door, and Bernard reappeared. "Miss Anne is resting comfortably, sir. She took some tea and toast a short while ago and said to tell you she plans to nap the morning away."

Thomas Ferry's face sagged with relief. "Thank God." He tossed the note into the wastepaper basket. "That will be all, Bernard. Now—" he turned back to address Miss Finch— "where were we?"

Hope pointed to a corner. "You missed a cobweb."

Boris picked up the broom, his beady eyes trying to pinpoint the offender. He swung the broom in the general direction of her finger. "Satisfied?"

She shrugged, smothering a cough. These pesky sniffles were getting worse. And her throat was scratchy this morning. It was this infernal drafty cabin. She'd be deathly ill if she didn't get warm soon. Her feet were like two blocks of ice. "It's still there."

"I can't git this stupid broom into corners," Boris groused.

"You can if you gently push, instead of jam," Hope explained for the third time that morning.

Boris rammed the head of the broom in the cracks, trying to dig the dirt out. "What do you think this is, some ladies seminary or somethin'?"

"No. I think this is a miserable excuse for a living establishment!" Hope snapped, then immediately repented. If the Lord could love Boris, surely she could put up with him awhile longer. "Though it is a great deal better than it was."

Which wasn't saying much.

One month. Had it been only a month since this unending nightmare had begun? It seemed like years. The men had kept their distance well enough. Grunt had seen to that, but she wanted out. She tried hard to keep up her spirits. Papa would say that everything that happened to a person was meant for a reason—though she couldn't imagine what good would come of her mistaken abduction.

Grunt continued to puzzle her with his soft-spoken commands and almost protective attitude toward her. Was he only looking after his interest? It was increasingly hard to maintain the belief that he was a ruthless outlaw when at times he seemed the exact opposite. Just last night he'd made sure she had the biggest piece of venison. That was nice—even if she did hate venison.

"Well, this ain't no boardinghouse, and I'm tired of washin' dishes, and I ain't sweepin' no more floors. And if I have to take another bath in that creek, I'm gonna prune up permanent-like."

Hope looked up as Grunt came in the front door. His dark eyes took in the confrontation. "If you're tired of keeping house, Boris, why don't you take these rabbits and dress them for supper?"

"Fine. Anything to get away from Miss Bossy." Boris grabbed the rabbits and stomped out the door.

Big Joe sat up on the cot, scratching his belly. "What'd you find out in Louisville?"

"Nothing at the post office." Grunt moved to the sink to wash up.

Big Joe frowned. "Nothin'." His eyes pivoted to Hope. "It's takin' too long—don't yore daddy care what happens to you?"

Her daddy had indeed cared for her. Unfortunately, Thomas Ferry didn't.

"Perhaps the ransom's been lost. That happens to mail, you know. Maybe—"

"Maybe you should just keep quiet."

"Well, maybe you shouldn't ask so many questions and make me have to talk."

"Well, maybe I like to ask questions!"

"Well, maybe I don't want to answer them."

"Maybe both of you should find something more productive to do with your time," Grunt snapped.

Hope rinsed the dress she was washing, then squeezed the water out. She flicked a few drops at Frog. He stiffened, shooting her a lethal look. Stepping around him, she announced, "I'm going to hang my wash."

"Good," Joe mumbled and dropped his head back to the pillow. "With any luck you'll hang yoreself."

Or you, Hope thought. He was just sore. She'd made him wash his filthy shirt yesterday, and Joe didn't take kindly to soap and water. He'd griped for hours afterward, complaining that he smelled like a girl. She relented and rewarded him by washing dishes last night.

As she hung the dress on the line, she heard the men talking among themselves.

"Boris, maybe you ought to ride back to Louisville and git a paper—see if there's anything in there about Ferry's daughter being held for ransom."

"Why me? Grunt was jest there."

"'Cause Grunt didn't git no paper. Cain't you take orders no more?"

"What makes you think there'd be anything in the Louisville paper?" Grunt's voice drifted through the open doorway.

"News that the senator's daughter's been kidnapped will be in every paper!"

"Maybe Ferry's kept the news quiet."

"No way! He'll have every Tom, Dick, and Harry in the county lookin' for her."

After all the arguing, Boris was elected to ride back to Louisville the following morning. They waited for him to return with news of Ferry's distress.

On the third morning, Hope awoke with a splitting headache, a hammer pounding between her temples. She emerged from behind the blanket that afforded her privacy. She was aware of Grunt's eyes on her as he put sausage in the skillet to fry. Concern tinged his features. "Are you ill, Miss Ferry?"

"I have a small headache." Hope sat down at the table, feeling a little light-headed. The scratchy irritation had turned into a ferocious sore throat, and she felt hot all over. She got up to put plates on the table.

Big Joe and Frog were stirring by then, grumbling about all the racket. Five adults in one cramped room wasn't the most pleasant way to spend a life. They were getting on each other's nerves.

By the time breakfast was over, Hope was feeling decidedly worse.

Aware that Grunt was still watching her, she got up from the table, leaving her plate of food virtually untouched. She couldn't let them know she was ill. She had her bluff in on Big Joe, and she intended to keep it that way.

"I'll wash the dishes," she volunteered, forcing herself to sound perkier than she felt.

"Sit down," Grunt ordered.

"I want to wash—"

The outlaw sat her down in a chair, then touched his large hand to her forehead. "She's got a fever."

Big Joe turned from the mantel. "Sick? She's sick!"

"I'm not sick. . . . I'm only feeling slightly unpleasant." Sick as a dog, actually, but she couldn't, just couldn't, give in to whatever had her feeling so bad.

They turned as the door opened and Boris stomped in. Giving Hope a dark glance, he strode into the room, shrugging out of his coat.

Big Joe frowned. "Well?"

"She ain't Ferry's daughter!" he declared hotly, throwing his hat onto the table. Hope shrank back as he glared at her.

"What?" Big Joe's head snapped up. "What d'you mean, 'She ain't Ferry's daughter'?"

"She ain't his daughter!" Boris repeated.

"Who told you that?"

"This." Boris tossed a copy of the *Louisville Courier-Journal* onto the table.

Big Joe glanced at the paper, then colored a bright crimson. "You know I ain't got no learnin'. What's it say?"

Grunt picked up the paper, his eyes scanning the headlines. He read, "Distinguished Kentuckian Honored by Michigan Senator.

"William Campbell Preston Breckinridge, distinguished Kentucky lawyer, editor, soldier, was a special guest in the home of Michigan's Senator Thomas White Ferry. Mr. Breckinridge was the honored guest at the annual Spring Ball held last week, where he was accompanied by Miss Anne Ferry, the senator's daughter—"

The outlaws turned to look at her.

Hope slid out of the chair in a dead faint.

Angry voices tried to penetrate her thick fog. Hope struggled to consciousness, wondering what those awful men were squabbling about this time. She felt as hot as a firecracker, and her head threatened to split in half. If only the voices would go away. They were angry, full of rage.

"No arguin'. We gotta get rid of her!" Boris declared.

"Who is she?" Frog asked. "If she ain't Anne Ferry, who in the blue blazes have we had to cotton to for the past month?"

"She must be that Hope . . . what'd she say her name was?"

"Who cares who she is?" Big Joe said. "Boris is right. We gotta git rid of her."

Grunt? Where was Grunt? Did he want to get rid of her, too? Hope coughed, a racking hack that brought all conversation to a halt.

"She's gettin' sicker. Maybe we won't hafta do away with her. Maybe she'll just croak on her own."

"She's too mean to croak on her own." Big Joe's voice filtered through the deep fog.

"What's wrong with her?" Frog asked.

"How should I know?" Big Joe shot back. "I ain't no lady's maid."

Cool fingers touched her forehead. Her eyes refused to open, but she sensed it was Grunt. The touch was infinitely gentle.

"Her fever's rising. We've got to get it down."

She heard Boris back away. "She got somethin' I'm likely to catch? I git the ague real easy—"

"Shut up, Boris."

Hope whimpered when she felt a cold cloth pressed to her forehead.

"She's caught cold. Frog, get some more blankets."

Hope moaned. She didn't want those dirty old blankets on her. They weren't fit for an animal, let alone a lady. She pushed at the gentle hands that now securely held her captive.

"Don't waste time with blankets. Put her outside and let's be done with it. She'll be dead by mornin'."

"Boris is right," Frog said. "Put her outside and lock the door. Good riddance."

"No one come near her," Grunt warned. "We're not going to let her die."

"She ain't Ferry's daughter, what do you care?"

Grunt's voice firmed. "No one lays a hand on her." She heard him do something. Cracking an eye open, Hope saw Grunt reach for his gun belt and strap it on.

With a sour look Big Joe returned to the fire.

"I still say we get rid of her," Boris growled. "She ain't no use to us! Jest a millstone around our necks."

The outlaws' voices faded as Hope slipped back into unconsciousness.

She was running now from something dark and sinister. Glancing back over her shoulder, she stumbled over rough ground, trying to make out the shadowy form that was chasing her. She opened her mouth to scream, but no sound came out. Just incredible heat, a furnace filling her whole body. She didn't know where she was; everything was so black and closing in. Hot. She was so hot! Water. She needed water . . . cool water. The murkiness drew her deeper, covering her mouth. She was choking, clawing at this thing. . . .

Suddenly her fear was reality. The darkness was real, and there was something hard and persistent across her mouth. She clawed at the thing, trying to rip it away. She heard a grunt as she was tossed over a man's shoulder like a sack of flour. Awake now and terrified, she kicked and lashed out, trying to free herself. The darkness she'd desperately tried to escape was real, and someone was carrying her off into the night. Hope's worst fears were coming true. The outlaws were going kill her.

Bile rose to the back of her throat, and she struggled with all her might. The man was large and strong, his shoulder pressing into her middle. She was going to die, and no one would know. Murdered somewhere in the Kentucky wilderness. Was she still in Kentucky? She couldn't be sure . . . she didn't even know! Mr. Jacobs would think she had abandoned him, changed her mind about marriage. Her sisters wouldn't know what had happened to her. Aunt Thalia would take to her bed when she learned that Hope had disappeared and never been heard from again.

This isn't fair; it isn't fair, Lord! I never asked for anything more than a husband so I wouldn't be a burden to Aunt Thalia. And now she was going to die at the hands of ruthless outlaws, and not even her family would know what had happened to her. *Why, God, why did you let this happen to me? God isn't there. He truly isn't there!*

Her captor laid her across a saddle, then climbed on the horse behind her. The moonless night was so black it was impossible to identify her abductor. Was it Frog? No, Frog smelled like rotting garbage.

She was chilling now, her teeth chattering in the night air. It felt like there was an anchor sitting on her chest. The man kicked the horse into a gallop, and then they were riding headlong down a long lane. She drifted in and out of consciousness, aware only of the jarring motion. Whoever he was, he was taking her deeper into the wilderness. Boris? Big Joe? A shudder escaped her, and she felt the man's hand on her back, soothing her. Not, not Boris. He was never gentle. Her fear began to ease. Grunt. Why was Grunt taking her away?

It seemed hours before the horse slowed. Hope mumbled incoherently as she was lifted off the saddle and gently eased onto a pallet.

"Cold," she murmured. "Please, I'm so cold. . . ."

The sweet scent of rain teased the air. Then it was raining hard . . . rain falling in blinding sheets.

A blanket settled around her, then another. She groaned and sought its warmth.

"Thank you . . . thank you . . ."

Throughout the long night, Hope was aware of kind hands alternately holding her head and forcing her to swallow something warm and salty, and bathing her face and neck with cool water.

She was only vaguely aware when a new day dawned. Outside, the storm raged. Hope drifted in and out of consciousness, her fever soaring. Tender hands ministered to her needs, hands that she occasionally associated with Grunt. But he'd wanted to harm her, not help her. . . . She didn't understand.

On the third morning Hope slowly opened her eyes. She lay for a moment, trying to orient herself. She was in some sort of shelter . . . a cave? Was it a cave? She heard the fire pop, and she turned to see her captor's eyes fixed on her. She groaned, bringing her hand to her fevered forehead. "Grunt?" she murmured.

Dan closed his eyes. "I thought you were . . ."

She struggled to sit up. "Where am I? . . . Where are the others?"

He was by her side, pressing her back to the pallet. "Lie still. You've been sick."

"Where—where are we?" She ran her tongue over her dry lips, surprised they were cracked and swollen. "I'm so thirsty."

"Drink this."

Tilting her head, he held a cup of water to her mouth. She drank deeply.

"So good," she whispered, then lay weakly back on the pallet. Her eyes scanned the dim interior. "Where are we?"

"I'm not sure—somewhere near the Kentucky line."

A frown creased her brow. "It was you . . . you were the one—" She coughed, pain distorting her features. "You took me away during the night."

"I felt it necessary to remove you from the situation."

"Yes . . . I remember now. Boris found out I'm not Thomas Ferry's daughter."

"Yes."

"So you . . . kidnapped me again?"

"I moved you to safety."

"But why?" Nothing made sense to her. Grunt was one of the outlaws. Why was he being so kind to her?

Settling her head in the crook of his arm, he said quietly, "Listen to me, Hope." He took a cool cloth and bathed her forehead. "I'm not a part of Joe's gang."

She stared at him blankly for a moment. "I didn't think so—you're different."

"I work for the government."

"But why—"

"I'm on assignment. I've been riding with Joe, Frog, and Boris, trying to learn how they've successfully captured a number of army payrolls."

"Joe and Frog? Those imbeciles have actually done something right?"

"It's hard to believe, but yes. Actually, they've stolen a good deal of money."

"With your help," she reminded him. He'd been there the day they took her off the stage and stole the strongbox.

"Not really. I just don't do anything to stop them. My job is to find out who's filtering information to them on the payroll shipments."

She struggled to sit up. The fever must be making her delirious. "I don't believe you." But oh, how she wanted to believe him. Though he'd spoken sharply to her at times, she'd sensed it was for her welfare. She tried to focus on him, but his large form was wavy, fading in and out. "You're not an outlaw?"

He shook his head. He looked very tired, she realized. A dark beard coated his handsome face, making him seem more dangerously appealing. "I don't expect you to take my word for it, but I'm not."

No, he wasn't, she realized with a start. She'd known that in her heart from the moment they met. He wasn't like the others.

"I'm not an outlaw. A rebel at times, but not on the wrong side of the law." He smiled, and Hope was reminded how sorely tempted she was to like him.

Closing her eyes, she thanked God for placing her in Grunt's hands. "I'm glad. I knew you were different."

A smile touched his eyes. "How could you tell? I've treated you badly. I hope you understand—"

"It's all right," she whispered. "You were trying to protect me."

"Speaking of which—exactly whom am I protecting?"

"My name is Hope Kallahan. I was traveling to Medford to meet my husband-to-be, John Jacobs, when the stage was attacked. Mr. Jacobs and I are to be married soon."

"You're promised to this man?"

Was there disappointment in his voice? Her heart soared, then plunged. Or did she only want to hear it? Nodding, she motioned toward the cup. He brought the water back to her lips, and she drank thirstily. She pushed the tin aside and met his gaze. "What do we do now?"

"We wait here until you're stronger, then we'll move out under cover of darkness."

"And then?"

"Then I'll escort you to your fiancé in Medford, and I'll return to Washington. My cover is blown; there's nothing more I can do here. Until you're better, I'll sleep just outside the doorway. You'll be safe, for now."

"I can't ask you to bother with me." He'd protected her these past weeks, kept her from certain harm. She couldn't impose on his generosity any longer. "I've inconvenienced you quite enough. If you'll be so kind as to see me to the next town, I'll catch a stage."

"No. No stage."

"Why not?"

"Because it isn't safe. Big Joe is still in the area. He'll be bent on taking you hostage again."

"But why? I'm worth nothing to him. I'm not Anne Ferry; they'll get no ransom for me."

"You're still of great benefit to these men, Hope. Trust me."

She pulled the blanket tighter around her. At the moment she had no choice but to trust him with her very life. "They'll be after you too," she murmured sleepily, feeling her strength drain. "And they'll be angry that you took me away from them—furious, should they learn that you're working for the government."

He shrugged. "Their anger doesn't concern me as much

as getting you safely to Medford. As far as I can tell, Medford's still a good fifty miles away. A lot can happen in fifty miles."

Hope closed her eyes; fatigue was beginning to overtake her. Her mind refused to absorb what he was saying. An incredible peace came over her. Grunt was here, offering to help her. Could she trust him? Was he actually a government official, or was this just another cruel hoax? She sighed. Whether she believed him or not made little difference. God had seen fit to place her earthly life in this man's hands. They were both in danger from Big Joe, Frog, and Boris. If only she could believe that God would deliver her . . .

The absurd situation suddenly struck her funny, and she burst into laughter.

Grunt glanced at her, frowning. "I'm glad to see that you still have your sense of humor—but what's funny about our situation?"

"You don't know?"

"No, I'm afraid I don't."

"I've spent a month in your company, my life is in your hands at the moment, and I don't know your name."

"It's Grunt."

Her merriment increased, causing her to break into another fit of coughing. Dan gently lifted her to a sitting position.

When the spasm subsided, she lay weakly back against his chest. "I'm reasonably sure your name isn't Grunt. I doubt any mother would do that to her poor, helpless newborn."

"No?" He grinned. "You don't like the name Grunt?"

She shook her head. "It's truly inappropriate."

He carefully settled her back on the pallet, and she sighed. His blanket smelled of wood smoke and lye soap. "My name is Dan Sullivan."

"Dan." She closed her eyes, testing the feel of his name on her tongue. "Daniel?"

"Daniel."

It was a good, strong biblical name. And they'd surely both been in the lions' den.

"How did you know I wasn't Anne Ferry?"

He reached for a stick of wood and laid it on the fire. "I met Anne Ferry at a Christmas soirée a few years back. Thomas Ferry is a personal friend of my commander." He moved back to the pallet and knelt beside her, gently smoothing hair back from her face with the cloth. "I knew the moment I saw you that you weren't Thomas's daughter. You're prettier than Anne."

Prettier than Anne. She felt a pang of envy for Anne, who had probably danced with this handsome man, been held in his arms. She wanted to hold his words close to her heart, but she was so weary she couldn't think at all. She couldn't imagine why Dan Sullivan's flattery meant so much to her. She was betrothed to John Jacobs, and Mr. Jacobs must be worried sick about her whereabouts.

Dan's voice was solemn now. "Hope, what were you doing with Anne's bags and her personal effects?"

When she heard uneasiness in his voice, she smiled. "Anne and her companion, Della DeMarco, had been traveling with me earlier. Miss DeMarco took ill, and Anne returned home in order for Miss Della to have the proper care. They left so suddenly that Anne forgot to get her things."

Hope smiled when she heard him exhale with relief. A moment later, she drifted off, his words tucked neatly inside her heart: *You're prettier than Anne.*

She awoke later, aware that she was alone now. Dan? Had he left? *Please, Dan . . . no . . . stay with me.* If he left her, there would be nothing she could do. She had no idea where she was nor one single way to care for herself. He'd surely take the horse.

She lay in the light of the flickering fire, waiting, listening, and praying that he wouldn't abandon her. He was, after all, a government agent . . . now she was part of that job.

Hot tears slipped from the corners of her eyes and rolled down her cheeks. Her thoughts—about God, about Dan Sullivan—were confused and jumbled. *Lord, please help me trust you like Papa did. Help me to believe—*

A sound caught her attention, and she opened her eyes. For one brief, elated moment, she saw Dan standing at the cave's entrance with two fat rabbits in his hand.

"You're back."

"Sorry it took so long. Game's scarce."

"It's OK." Giving him a smile, she closed her eyes again. Dan hadn't left her. Perhaps God was still watching out for her after all.

"Dan?"

"Yes, Hope?" His voice seemed to come from a long way off.

"Do you honestly think I'm prettier than Anne?"

The soft, masculine chuckle made her blush. "Well, Miss Kallahan, if I were to say who's the prettiest . . ."

She drifted off without ever hearing him finish the sentence.

Chapter Five

John Jacobs teetered on a wooden ladder propped against the wall case of the Jacobs Mercantile, straining to reach the top shelves with the feather duster. No one could ever say they'd purchased a single item from Jacobs Mercantile that was the least bit neglected.

No sir. When one bought from Jacobs, one got quality product, down to the last needle and spool of thread. He paused on his perch to glance around the store, mentally cataloging each aisle of merchandise. Fresh goods and perishables were toward the front where people could see for themselves that Jacobs had nothing but the freshest. Of course, part of his strategy was moving the stock around a bit each day, but that never detracted from quality.

Canned goods were centered on the right; material, spools of thread, cards of ribbons and the finest laces neatly piled on tables—center aisle. Ready-made dresses to the left. Hand tools, men's pants and shirts were at the back, near the stove where men were prone to gather while their wives shopped.

Stepping off the ladder, John nodded absently to himself. Yes, he ran a tight ship. He was proud of his accomplishments, and rightfully so. It was a solid start for his soon-to-be family. The family he hoped to build with Hope Kallahan.

Hope. How often he thought about his mail-order bride. Concerns whether she'd like him or could ever care deeply for him were never far from his mind. Betrothal to a man she'd never seen, had only seen a poor likeness of, must be a matter of discomfiture. Nevertheless—and the fact was of no small satisfaction to him—she had answered his ad.

The ad.

Wonder filled him anew. Placing that want ad in the Heart-and-Hand column of the *Kentucky Monthly*—then having that journal miraculously make its way to Michigan and into Miss Kallahan's possession. . . . He drew a deep, shuddering breath. Well, it was just a miracle, that's what it was. Just one more of God's abundant blessings, and there had been many of those in John Jacobs's life.

The moment he'd placed the ad, he'd been assailed with doubt. What madness had driven him to do so? He was reasonably happy with his life, though admittedly lonely since Mother had passed on two years ago. But life had settled into a comfortable routine. He went to work each morning.

Then at night, with his trusty hound, Oliver, he climbed the stairway to his apartment above the store.

He'd told no one about the ad. In fact, he'd been so abashed about having put his private life in the public eye that he'd tried to forget about his impetuosity. But then Hope's letter arrived.

John shook his head in wonder. He'd been so taken aback by the letter, by the delicate spidery script on the envelope, that he'd waited a whole day and a half to open it. Hope had introduced herself, telling him about her Aunt Thalia and about her sisters embarking upon their own mail-order-bride adventures. John had felt encouraged. It took him another two days to compose a letter in return. With mail service between Michigan and Kentucky so slow, it took forever, or so it seemed, to receive her reply to his letter.

If Hope were nearly as beautiful as the picture that had accompanied her third letter, then he was the most fortunate man on earth! That is, unless she took one look at him and got back on the stage.

The picture he'd sent to her had been a poor image, but he wasn't a handsome man. He was a loyal man, moral, read the Good Book and did his best to live by it. But by no stretch of the imagination was he a handsome swain.

Oh, he knew full well the gamble he was taking, hoping that a woman of Miss Kallahan's exceptional beauty would agree to travel all the way to Medford to form a union with him, John Jacobs.

John stepped to the front window of the store, trying to

see the town as Hope might perceive it. Medford had fared well during the war, with minimal damage from marauders. Like most towns of its size, Medford had a main street with two crossroads. The Basin River ran the length of the community. During heavy rains, it overflowed its banks and caused more than its share of headaches for the townspeople. Most, if not all, of the shop owners in town lived above their businesses. A spattering of town residents, generally the elderly or widowed, resided in small two- or three-room dwellings interspersed between storefronts. The larger portion of the population lived on the outskirts and ventured into town once a month for supplies.

Would Hope find Medford too . . . dull? too confining? There wasn't much here. Besides the Mercantile there were Pierson's Hotel, Hattie's Millinery and Sewing, Porter's Feed and Grain, Grant's Smithy, the livery where he boarded his own team and buggy, the church, and, of course, the school. Townsfolk took great pride that the school went to the eighth grade.

It was a simple, unassuming, friendly town. He was a simple, unassuming, friendly man. Would Hope find it in her heart to make her home here with him? *Father, I pray you will send a woman whom I can make happy, for indeed I will do my best to be a good husband.*

With both hope and trepidation, John stored the duster under the counter, then bent to retrieve a new roll of wrapping paper from the bottom shelf. About to heave it onto the countertop, he spied Veda Fletcher crossing the street, scurrying toward the Mercantile. Tucked beneath her arm was a familiar package. Even from this distance, he knew it was a towel-wrapped, glass casserole dish. He'd seen that particular sight many times.

"Oh, no," he muttered, quickly ducking down behind the counter. He dropped to his knees, lifting his head for an occasional peek over the countertop. Veda was still on target, her plump, rouged cheeks puffing with exertion.

The spunky, rotund widow had lost her husband some years back, and she now spent most of her time officiating as town matchmaker. Veda was just one of a whole list of town "mothers" who tried to initiate a match between John and their daughters or, in Veda's case, her spinster niece.

Attending town social functions had become more of a burden than a joy, what with mothers plying him with food while parading eligible daughters in front of him like prize mares. Why, at the church picnic, he'd ended up with no less than nine pieces of dried-apple pie after Mrs. Baker discovered it was his favorite. He'd taken to eluding any community gathering whenever he could to avoid being up all night, gulping down soda water for indigestion.

For the past couple of years, Veda had been fixated on John carrying on a long-distance courtship with that niece of hers. Fortunately, Ginger lived in San Antonio. Unfortunately, Veda lived at the edge of town.

Being a social swan herself, Veda made her way to the store at least twice a week, each time managing to drag Ginger's name into the conversation. John had explained no less than a hundred times in the last few weeks that he was betrothed, but Veda didn't listen.

It was his fervent prayer that with Hope due to arrive any moment, the campaign—no, outright war—waged by the mothers of Medford to get him married off could end. True, Hope was a month overdue, but surely she was en route. He clung to the hope much like a drowning victim clings to driftwood.

Attempting to avoid another "visit" with Veda, John crept on his hands and knees toward the front door, pushing a sleeping Oliver out of the way. He didn't want to hurt the woman's feelings, but he just couldn't face her again. Not today.

Just as John peeked from his hiding place, Veda put on the brakes and stopped to peer in the window of Hattie's shop. Seizing his chance, he bounded to his feet and slipped the lock on the front door, then hurriedly crept back behind the counter.

Shortly, he heard the doorknob turn and the door rattle. A moment later someone pecked on the front window. John wished she'd just go away. But not Veda. She knocked, rapped, and jiggled the knob loudly. John peeked around the edge of the counter, only to glimpse her cupping her hands on the glass to peer inside, her parcel tucked securely beneath her elbow.

John held his breath. *Go away, Veda.*

"John? The door is locked!" She tapped again. "John?"

He heard her mutter something; then it was quiet. When

he thought it was safe, he again peered around the edge of the counter.

Veda was gone.

Thank you, God.

He rose a fraction—not much—just enough to glance out the front window and see her plump backside hurrying down the street, apparently heading for home.

Releasing a sigh of relief, he sat down flat on the floor. He liked Veda. He really did. But he just couldn't force down another forkful of chicken casserole. At least, not the way Veda fixed it with all that stuff in it. It had been a sad day indeed when Veda accidentally overheard John telling old Mrs. Brandstetter that his favorite dish was chicken casserole. Unfortunately, Mrs. Brandstetter died the next year, and when they buried her, they also buried the only recipe for a decent chicken casserole in the whole town.

He thought about Mae Brandstetter's casserole, and his mouth watered. Though he was quite adept at keeping his living quarters tidy, he'd never mastered the kitchen. His meals were quite inedible—suicide on a plate, his friends were wont to remind him. In order to keep from poisoning himself, he took most of his meals at the Pierson Hotel. Unfortunately, doing so exposed him to the cunning devices of the mothers of Medford. So much so that he'd taken to eating at odd hours. As a matter of fact, he'd missed lunch today.

A noise at the back door caught his attention. Straightening, his heart sank when he saw the door open and Veda Fletcher elbow her way inside.

"John, did you know your front door is locked?"

"Mrs. Fletcher—" His eyes focused on the casserole dish in her hand. Dear God. He would be up half the night. "Door locked? Now how did that happen?"

"Who knows—it's fortunate I came along." She set the bowl on the counter, eyeing him slyly. "Now let me guess: You missed lunch."

"I had a large breakfast—"

"Breakfast! That was hours ago." Beaming, she whisked the lid off the bowl. "Look, John. I brought you one of my chicken casseroles."

She looked so proud of herself, he couldn't think of hurting her feelings.

"Why, that's very nice of you, Mrs. Fletcher."

"No trouble at all. I enjoy doing for people. It's a family trait, you know. The Fletchers are all nurturing people. Why, you remember my niece, Ginger? She's exactly like me—chip off the old block. Just doing for someone all the time. Everyone who knows Ginger says—"

John reached for the dish. "You're right, I did miss lunch." He lifted the lid and sniffed, rolling his eyes with feigned pleasure. "This will certainly hit the spot."

Veda's smile was so genuine, John's guilt lessened at his insincere show of appreciation. If something this simple gave Veda so much pleasure, who was he to complain?

"Thank you again, Mrs. Fletcher."

"Veda. Everyone calls me Veda, John, and you've known me since before your mother died. Why, I feel like you're part of the family." She giggled like a small girl. "And maybe one day you will be. Well, I'll run along now and let you eat. Laundry waiting on the line."

If nothing else, John knew Veda Fletcher was a good housekeeper. Like clockwork, her laundry was on the line by nine o'clock every Monday. She was proud to remind her friends and neighbors that she ironed on Tuesdays, baked on Saturdays, and sat third row from the front at church on Sundays. Likely as not, she would invite Pastor Elrod and his family home for dinner and generally add another family or two as well. Generous to a fault—that was Veda. He couldn't help liking her, even if she did drive him to distraction with her tasteless chicken casseroles and constant hints about her niece, Ginger.

"Oh, I almost forgot. I just received a letter from Ginger." She turned back toward John and wiggled her brows. "She's been planning a visit for some time, you know, and she'll be here any day now. Isn't that wonderful? I can hardly wait for you to meet her. I just know you two will have so much in common."

"Mrs. Fletcher, you know my fiancée is expected any day now. We plan to be married—"

"Oh, I know that's what you plan, but would it hurt for you to just meet my niece? My goodness, John. I'm not exactly asking you to marry Ginger. Well, look. The dear girl has sent a picture in her last letter. Just look at her. Isn't she the prettiest thing you've ever laid eyes on?"

John took the tintype Veda thrust at him. He could tell absolutely nothing about the girl from the blurry image. He wasn't even sure it was a girl.

"She's lovely." He handed the picture back.

Veda cradled the photo in her hands. "She is, isn't she? Such a charming girl. Looks exactly like my sister Prunella looked when she was Ginger's age."

And Jake Pearson's granddaughter was outrageously charming, and Greta George's daughter, and Marly Jenkins's sister. In fact, Freeman Hide's granddaughter was also coming for a visit soon, and John wasn't looking forward to meeting her, either!

"I was talking to poor Ben Grant the other day, and you know his wife isn't getting any better." Veda shook her head sadly. "He can't take care of her and run the blacksmith shop too. He's going to have to find someone to take care of Mary while he's working. I was thinking Ginger could do that. That way, she could stay here in Medford. Wouldn't that be wonderful?"

Simply ducky. Somehow, in her own seemingly innocent way, Veda was always first to know what was going on in Medford—often before the involved parties did. Granted, everyone knew Veda had a good heart, so her questions were never considered prying, and she was always the first to be at the door if there was a need. There was absolutely no question that Veda Fletcher was a loving, caring woman who, after her husband's death, had devoted herself to serving the town and its citizens. And wasn't that, after all, what people were supposed to do? Take care of one another?

Unfortunately, John was her one blind spot. He and that niece of hers. Veda was determined to get them both to the altar. Together. And soon.

"It would help Ben, I'm sure."

"It would. And Mary is such a dear soul. I'm sure Ginger would be such a blessing. And—" she smiled guilelessly—"her being here for an extended length of time will give you two time to get to know each other." She clapped her birdlike hands together. "I'm so pleased this is working out so well."

"I'm sure you'll enjoy your niece's visit." Should he suggest an earpiece? He was already engaged to another.

Tucking the photo of Ginger into her pocket, she smiled. "I'll introduce you the moment she arrives; you know how unpredictable the stages are. Why, out of the last scheduled four, three haven't come in at all."

John knew that quite well. In fact, Miss Kallahan had been due for the past four weeks and she wasn't here yet. What with the spring rains and muddy roads, there was no telling when the stage could get through.

But Miss Kallahan would come. Her letters had shown her to be a woman of integrity and honesty. He could hardly wait for her arrival so this constant parade of eligible women would cease.

"I'm sure your niece will arrive in good time, Veda. And I'm sure you'll enjoy her visit. If she can help Mary and Ben, then that's wonderful. Now, I have work to do—"

"Eat your lunch," Veda advised with a pat on his arm. "Young men need to keep up their strength."

"Thank you, I will."

"Enjoy."

"Thank you again," John called as Veda headed for the front door.

"Have a good day, John."

"Same to you, Veda."

He waved as he shut the door behind her, then snapped the lock back into place.

Turning, he took a deep breath and faced the chicken casserole.

Chapter Six

Under the cover of darkness, two figures silently emerged from the cave and crept toward a waiting horse. A moment later hoofbeats broke the quiet of the night.

Hope held tightly to Dan's waist, praying that the Lord would guide his efforts. She was still weak from the illness and incredibly tired. She longed for a bath, clean clothing, and a soft bed. Though Dan was most considerate of her needs, there was nothing he could do about clothes and hot water. The best he'd been able to provide was a "spit" bath from rainwater he'd caught in their one cooking pot.

Resting her head against his broad back, she clung to him, dreaming of a steaming tub, pots and pots of hot water, and sweet-smelling lavender soap.

The night seemed endless. Dan promised they would ride

down dark lanes, keeping to the side of the road in case they encountered other nocturnal travelers. Hope visualized Big Joe and the others hiding behind every rock and bush, ready to pounce and seize them captive, only this time Dan would be a victim, too. Big Joe would make sure neither she nor Dan got away again. Her hold tightened around Dan's waist.

Her knight in shining armor glanced over his shoulder, the pale moonlight throwing his handsome profile into shadow.

"I know you're getting tired, but if your strength holds up, I want to make as much time as we can."

"Ride as long as you need." He'd been so considerate, so attentive, during her infirmity, she'd be forever grateful. He'd fetched water, kept her fever to a tolerable level, and rarely slept while watching over her. She'd heard him outside the cave tossing in his bedroll. Even in her misery, she was confident he had one ear attuned for danger.

When she'd stir, he was there to see to her every need. At night in the light of the campfire, he read to her from a small Bible he carried in his coat pocket. His responsibility for her weighed heavily on him. She could see it in his eyes and hear it in the timbre of his voice.

"The worst is behind us," she'd whisper, reaching out to take his hand. They had to keep their spirits up if they were to survive the ordeal.

"I pray you're right," he'd answer, and it was easy to tell he was worried.

The horse carried them through the dark night. They

passed no one on the road. The infrequent homesteads they encountered lay dark and unthreatening beneath the waning moon.

Hope thought it must be close to dawn. Shadows gradually lifted, and the eastern horizon grew light.

"I'd like to ride until sunup," Dan said over his shoulder.

Hope shivered, puzzled by the effect his calm, reassuring voice induced. Normally she'd be frightened half out of her wits, racing through the night with a man she trusted only by faith. But with Dan, she felt safe, protected, as if no further harm could touch her. "Don't worry about me; I'm fine."

She wasn't fine, but she wasn't going to fret about petty complaints. He didn't have to personally escort her to Medford; he was risking his life by doing so. He could easily put her on a stage and be done with his responsibility.

But Dan Sullivan wasn't one to shirk duty. He was a man of exceptional character. A man any woman would be proud to . . .

She checked her thoughts. The fever had addled her brain. Aunt Thalia would say, "Keep your mind on your business, young lady!" Unfortunately, her business wasn't Dan Sullivan. Her business waited for her in Medford, and she was now more than a month late.

For all she knew, Dan might very well have a lady in Washington awaiting his return. The idea didn't set well with her. In fact, it reminded her of one of Aunt Thalia's awful duck recipes that soured her stomach.

She checked her thoughts a second time. What was she

thinking? Riding around the countryside, depending on Dan to look out for her welfare. She'd never depended on anyone except family and God. In spite of the goodness she saw in Dan, she didn't know him—didn't know anything about him. What if he was deliberately misleading her—hoping to gain her confidence and—

What if he had other reasons for befriending her—sinister reasons? She shivered.

"Cold?"

"No, someone just walked over a grave."

"Pardon?"

"Someone just walked over a grave: Aunt Thalia says that's what causes shivers."

"Is that right?" Humor colored his tone.

"That's what my aunt says."

"Then it must be true."

Kidnapped, mistaken for someone else, held captive in a filthy cabin, fed vile food, been deplorably ill . . . and now, riding through the darkness with a man who makes me have thoughts I have no right to think.

I'm weak, Lord! I'm not able to do this!

"You're tired," Dan said, and she wondered if he'd read her thoughts. Heat crept up her neck and covered her cheeks. Oh, she hoped not! It was bad enough to think them!

"We'll stop for the day."

His kindness brought tears to her eyes. "Thank you," she whispered, wondering anew how he could be so attuned to her necessities.

He cut the horse into a thicket and a few moments later lifted Hope down from the saddle. She closed her eyes, trying to absorb his strength, wishing that she had a small portion of it. To the left was a low outcropping where she assumed they would rest for the day. Dan held her for a moment, decidedly a bit too long, then gently set her aside.

"We should be safe here for the day. I'll get a fire going. You're chilled." When he stepped away, she felt as if part of her left with him.

Tears stung her eyes and she swallowed, fighting to stem the rising tide. *Don't cry, Hope!* All he needed was a weepy woman to add to his troubles. Yet teardrops formed in her eyes, and she realized whatever earlier strength she'd boasted of having had vanished with the night. She felt weak and drained.

Dan returned momentarily. Removing the lid from the canteen, he handed it to her, his eyes gentle.

"Thanks." Did he understand what she was feeling? She couldn't meet his gaze for fear of bursting into unmanageable sobs. Right now, she was primed for a pretty good pity party he wouldn't want to attend.

A smile touched the corners of his eyes. "You don't have to be so polite. If you want to scream, tear your hair out, you've earned the right."

She gave him a lame smile, lifting the canteen to take a long swallow. She'd like nothing better than to scream and rail at the injustices she had endured, but no one except Dan would hear, and he certainly didn't deserve to be party to her hysteria.

"Hungry?"

She shook her head. She couldn't remember the last time food interested her.

"Well, no matter how bleak our situation looks right now, a person has to eat. John Jacobs won't take kindly to my depositing a skeleton on his doorstep." He wiped away the one tear that trickled down her cheek with this thumb. The intimate gesture was oddly comforting. "No matter how pretty she might be."

Hope searched somewhere deep within herself and managed to come up with something she hoped resembled a smile. At least he was still optimistic that they'd reach John Jacobs. She wasn't so sure.

"Sorry, I don't mean to be whiny—"

"You're not whiny, Miss Kallahan." He stripped the saddle off the horse and carried it to the outcrop. Her eyes focused on the ridge of impressive muscle that played across his back, shamefully aware that her thoughts should dwell on more fruitful ground. She followed him to the campsite.

"The kidnapping, Big Joe and the gang. It all seems like a bad dream."

"It will be over soon." He straightened, his gaze assessing her soiled appearance. She must look a sight. Her dress was disheveled and dirty, and she'd only half managed to twist her hair into a bun and secure it with the precious few pins she had left.

"Do you like fish?"

She nodded. "I like fish."

"Good, because I spotted a stream a short while back. With any luck, I'll catch our breakfast."

He settled her on a blanket and started a fire. Then he took off in search of the stream. Huddling close to the snapping fire, she watched his tall form disappear into the undergrowth. Goose bumps swelled, and she rubbed her arms, uneasy when he was gone.

Within the hour he returned, whistling and carrying his catch. She smiled at the sight of the large bass. Dan Sullivan's woman would never fear for her next meal.

"Breakfast," he announced with a cocky grin.

"Congratulations."

Squatting, he piled more brush on the fire and grinned up at her. "Dan, you incredible man, you. How did you get so good at catching fish with your hands? she asks."

She blushed at his teasing.

"Well, thank you, Miss Kallahan. I hoped you'd notice my exceptional sporting skills. I got good at catching fish with my hands during the war. Many nights our company would have gone hungry if we hadn't devised our own means of providing food."

"You fought in the war?"

"Yes, ma'am, for way too long." A mask dropped over his features, and she realized she'd touched on a painful subject.

They chatted while he cleaned then skewered the fish and hung it over the flames. They talked briefly about the War between the States and the terrible atrocities it brought upon the people. Kentucky had tried to remain neutral, Dan told her, but that wasn't possible.

"How do you know so much about Kentucky?"

"Had a good friend who lived here."

"Is he here now?"

"He's buried in Lexington."

"I'm sorry," she murmured. "Do you ever feel as if the world is spinning out of control?" She sensed his smile, though he had his back to her.

"Occasionally."

"I never had, until recently. I thought God would keep me safe from all harm."

Lately, God had challenged those thoughts. He never promised there'd be no trials, but somehow she'd just expected her life to be different. Adversity happened to others, not to her. Not until Papa died. Or until she and her sisters split up, and she didn't know when, if ever, she'd see them again. Or until Big Joe took her hostage.

"No one is protected from trouble, Hope. Not on this earth," he said quietly.

They shared the moist, tasty bass, and then Hope slept the day away. She was vaguely aware of Dan keeping watch as he dozed intermittently, but she was too tired to insist that he rest while she guarded their small sanctuary. Toward evening, they finished the last of the fish before Dan doused the fire and saddled the horse.

As twilight faded, they rode on, pausing the second night only long enough to rest the horse and drink from icy cold streams. By the time the sun came up the third morning, although Hope was still reeling with exhaustion, the healing rays were warm on her face, and she thanked God for a new day.

Dan's soft warning jarred her from her lethargic state. "Let me do the talking," he said quietly.

Half asleep, she started at the sound of his voice. "What—what is it?"

"There's a wagon coming."

Her heart raced. Would they be discovered? Why didn't he cut off the road? "Big Joe?"

"No, Joe wouldn't use a wagon. Probably a farmer on his way to town."

A team of sleek black horses came around the bend, and Hope spotted an old man and woman sitting on the spring seat of a short wagon. The woman's pale hair, shot with silver, had come loose from her bonnet. Her body was more square than angular. The old man looked exactly like her—*bookends,* Hope thought, except for the rim of snow white hair protruding wildly from beneath the battered hat he wore low over his lined face. The wagon pulled even with Dan and clattered to a halt.

Smiling, the old man showed a row of uneven, yellow teeth.

"Howdy. You folks are out purty early, ain't ya?"

Dan eased Hope down from the back of the horse. She straightened, working the kinks out of her back. She was grateful for the brief reprieve. The old couple looked harmless enough.

Stepping out of the saddle, Dan walked over to shake hands. "My sister hasn't been well lately. We started out before sunrise to find a doctor, but she's feeling poorly again."

Hope shot Dan a disbelieving look. Sister? Of course. They couldn't announce they were unmarried and traveling together. His returning gaze warned her to go along with the facade.

"We were about to rest a spell when we heard your wagon."

Hope would play along, but she didn't approve of fibs. She could still remember the sting of Papa's hickory switch on the backs of her legs when he'd caught her lying.

Removing his hat, the old man scratched his head. "Well, our place is up the road aways. You and yore sister are mighty welcome to stop in for a cup of Harriet's coffee."

Hope studied the old woman. Her face was flushed, and she looked as if she'd wallowed in a mudhole in her plain brown cotton dress.

"You shore are!" she invited. "We'd be right proud to have you join us for breakfast."

"Oh no. We couldn't," Hope protested. She shot Dan an anxious look.

"No." Dan smiled. "We don't want to impose—"

"Land sakes! Be no imposition! Got plenty of fresh eggs, and it won't take a minute to whip up a fresh batch of biscuits. Come on now, yore sister looks downright peaked."

Dan glanced back to Hope and she smiled. Lamely, she knew, but it was the best she could do. The thought of a hot meal did sound good.

"I guess we could stop for a minute. Much obliged." Dan

reached for the horse's reins. "If you don't mind, would it be all right if my sister rides with you? As I said, she's been feeling poorly. . . ."

"Why, she's welcome as rain. Name's Harriet Bennett. This here's my husband, Luther." She grinned, showing a front tooth chipped clear to the gum. "Just tie your horse on to the back, Mister, then hitch yoreself a ride on the tail."

She jerked a thumb toward the back of the wagon. "Just shove the pig out of the way. She ain't gonna give you no trouble."

"Yes, ma'am." Pig? Hope peered over the side of the wagon. An old sow was standing in the back of the wagon—a very large, very smelly old sow—taking up a full third of the bed. She glanced at Dan, frowning.

He lifted an amused brow. "You heard the woman, Sister—just push the pig out of the way."

Hope climbed aboard the wagon, keeping an eye on the sow.

It eyed her back, snorting.

If they thought she was going to push anything that size out of her way they had another think coming. Scooting to the far side of the bed, she settled back against the sideboard, drawing a deep breath. A pig! She was now riding with two strangers and a pig! She hoped Aunt Thalia never heard about this.

Lord, can it get much worse?

Securing the horse to the back of the wagon, Dan hopped

aboard. Luther slapped the reins, and the wagon lurched forward.

"You see ol' Doc Jimster?" Harriet turned to ask above the clattering wheels.

Dan glanced at Hope. "No—the one in Medford."

"Medford!" The old woman turned further in her seat to look at him. "Land sakes! That's a fur piece away." She looked at him as if he, not his sister, needed medical attention.

Dan smiled. "He's family—Sis won't let anyone but Doc—"

"Power," Hope finished. She grinned. "Good ol' Doc Power—worth his weight in gold. Wouldn't see anyone but . . . Doc."

"Well," Harriet frowned. "Ain't goin' nearly as far as Medford, but one more mile along the way is a help, I'd reckon."

Leaning back, Dan met Hope's worried gaze with his own. "Reckon it is, ma'am. We appreciate the ride."

Harriet again turned to look over her shoulder. "Dearie, you look real feverish. You doin' anything for what ails ya?"

Dan answered. "We've been doctoring it, ma'am."

She reached back to give Hope's leg a pat. "We'll have you in a nice warm kitchen afore too long, drinking one of my hot toddies."

The old man chuckled. "Harriet's hot toddies will either kill ya or cure ya."

"Oh . . ." Hope smiled, preferring the latter. "I'd like that. Without spirits, of course."

The old woman nodded enthusiastically. "'Course!"

The four looked up as the sound of fast-approaching horses caught their attention. Two men, leaning low over the necks of their animals, galloped full speed around the bend.

The old woman grasped her husband's arm. "Luther!"

About the same time Harriet yelled at her husband, a bullet whizzed past Dan's head. Bolting upright, Hope tried to see what the commotion was all about, but Dan pinned her back down with a hand.

Luther whipped his team of horses to a full run. A second bullet whistled overhead as Dan bent over Hope and pulled out his revolver.

"What's going on?" Hope shouted above the clacking wheels. The old buckboard threatened to break apart as it churned headlong down the road, hitting potholes and deep ruts.

"Stay down!" Dan shouted.

"Hang on!" Luther cracked the whip and the team strained, running harder. The horses barreled down the road, trying to outrun the two men on horseback who were now pursuing them with devilish fervor. "Hold on! We're headin' for th' barn!"

"What's he mean?" Hope grunted, clinging to the side of the wagon. "Heading for the barn—what's going on?"

The pig squealed in protest, rolling wildly about the

wagon bed on its fat sides. Hope moved her foot to keep it from being squashed, scooting more to the left.

The old man cackled with glee as he swung the whip over the team's backsides. "Hold on, kiddies!"

Pulling himself upright, Dan leaned close to Harriet's ear. "Who are those people?"

"It's just Lyndon," the old woman shouted. "Nothin' to concern your head about!"

Hope struggled to sit up, but Dan kept pushing her down. "Who are they? Robbers?" That's all she needed—to be taken hostage a second time. John Jacobs would never buy that story!

"It's Lyndon," Dan told Hope.

"Oh." She lay back, trying to hang on. *It's Lyndon.* . . . She frowned. *Who is Lyndon?*

The wagon wheeled around a corner and up a narrow lane. Hope's teeth chattered as the wagon bed bounced over the uneven terrain. Low-hanging branches slapped the wagon, keeping Hope off balance. The riders were closing in, close enough for Hope to get a good look at Lyndon—whichever one he might be.

"Run for th' house," Luther yelled as they shot through the open barn doorway. Sawing on the reins, he stopped the team. Harriet sprang from the wagon seat, motioning to Hope. "Come on!"

Dan lifted Hope from the wagon, and they dashed toward a building that Hope thought faintly resembled a cabin. The boards were nailed haphazardly together, and the roof was fashioned from various pieces of colored tin. Red, blue, yel-low—there seemed to be no pattern.

Chickens flapped and darted for cover as Hope's feet hit the porch. Luther followed close on her heels. She could hear him cackling as he shot looks over his shoulder at the pursuers. Hope flew through the front door ahead of Dan and Harriet. Luther waited until the pig cleared the door frame, then slammed the door shut. Leaning against the thick wood, he swiped his brow. "That was close."

Oinking, the pig calmly meandered to a corner and col-lapsed, obviously fatigued after her spirited trip across the yard.

A bullet chunked into the side of the cabin, sending splin-ters of wood flying. Luther grabbed a rifle and ducked behind the front window.

"That crazy Lyndon," he muttered. "The old fool's gonna git hisself shot."

Hope and Dan stood in the middle of the kitchen, look-ing at each other as Harriet hustled into the bedroom and came back toting a double-barreled shotgun. Kneeling on the opposite side of the window, she hefted the weapon to her shoulder.

A volley of bullets drilled into the front door. Dan and Hope dove for the floor. Crawling beneath the rough-hewn kitchen table, they stayed there.

"Luther?" Dan shouted. "Who is that out there?"

"Oh, it's jest my brother," Luther said, sighting through his rifle. "The thief."

"Thief?"

"Yeah. He stole half our chickens yesterday, the low-down, rotten—"

"Luther," Harriet cautioned, "we got guests."

"If he stole your chickens, why is he shooting at you?" Dan called.

Luther stood up, fired, then ducked down. "'Cause we got his pig."

"Yep," Harriet crowed. "We got his finest porker this mornin'."

Hope looked at Dan. "A family feud—we're in the middle of a family feud."

"How rotten can our luck get?" he muttered.

Luther poked the rifle out of the open window and fired. A return volley peeled bark off the front of the cabin. The staccato salvos shattered the front windowpane, throwing glass into the room.

"Whooeee, that was close!" Luther chortled, reloading. "That ol' coot! Thinks he's a good shot. Couldn't hit the broad side of a barn."

"Dan," Hope whispered, scooting closer to him. His arm came around her protectively. "Shouldn't we make a run for it?"

"No—it's too dangerous—" Dan ducked as another round of bullets showered the room. "Let's wait it out."

On her hands and knees Harriet crawled across the floor to the back window. "Jest hold on, young'uns. I'll put that pot of coffee on in a few minutes."

"Harriet?" Dan called.

The old woman glanced over her shoulder. "Yes?"

"How long has this been going on?"

The little woman paused, pondering the question. "Well, now—I reckon for forty year or so. That Lyndon's jest a real pain in the get-a-long. Always has caused trouble. He's had it in for Luther and me since the day he got it in that stubborn head of his that Luther took one of his calves. Wasn't Luther, 'course, but from that moment on, Lyndon jest plain went off his rocker. Started takin' things. So, we jest been takin' 'em back."

Shots rang out, and Harriet sprang to her feet and fired. Ducking, she grinned at Dan. "Me and Luther bested him this week. Yesterday Lyndon and his boys stole six of our ol' scrawny hens ready for the stewpot. This mornin' Luther and me got up real early and stole his best hog—the one he's plannin' to butcher this fall." She poked her head up and fired off another round. "Watch it, Luther. Mary Jane's out to the side. Sneakin' through the blackberry patch."

"Fire a shot over her head, Harriet. Let 'er know we see 'er."

Harriet fired a shot out the window, and the woman running along the back of the lot picked up her skirt tail and ran faster.

Harriet sank to the floor and shoved another round into the chamber. "Me and Luther's lived here nigh on to forty years—since the day we got hitched. I was fifteen and Luther here was eighteen. Lyndon and Mary Jane tied the knot the next year. They live 'bout three miles down the road. To the south. Real good neighbors 'till Lyndon gets riled."

Hope sent Dan a perplexed glance. If this wasn't a fine kettle of fish! How much time was this delay going to cost them?

Harriet sprang up and squeezed off another round. "Lyndon had an eye for me, you know. He's a couple years older than Luther and thought he might have first claim. Our place was just over the holler, and he'd come by every week or so. He was sweet on me, real sweet, but I didn't cotton to him." Harriet shrugged. "Only had eyes for my Luther."

Hope's gaze traveled to the old man crouched at the window. Love was an odd thing.

"And this feud has been going on ever since?" Dan called from beneath the table.

"Yep. It's jest a cryin' shame." Harriet popped up and blasted another round.

"I'll say," Hope murmured. "I feel like crying myself."

The impasse kept up all morning. Exhausted from traveling the night before and with nothing else to do anyway, Dan and Hope sprawled on the floor and rested while the old couple kept vigil. They awoke by late afternoon. Hope's legs were numb, and he was fit to be tied.

"We've got to do something," Dan muttered. He tried to get up and straighten his long legs. Just then a shot zinged against the house again. Dan dived under the table. Hope grinned, though she found the situation anything but humorous.

"What can we do?" She tried to rub feeling back into her legs. "This could go on all night."

Harriet turned from the window as if she'd just remembered she had guests. "Land sakes, Luther. These young'uns must be half starved. We never did git around to feedin' 'em breakfast."

"Could eat the south end outta a northbound critter myself, Harriet. It's gittin' dark. Lyndon and his bunch'll be headin' home directly." Luther straightened, his eyes narrowing. "Uh-oh."

"What?" Harriet asked from her stance at the back window.

"Mary Jane's got the horse."

"The young'un's horse?"

"Yep—she must think it's ours. She left the saddle though—right thoughtful of her."

"My horse?" Dan whacked his head against the top of the table, wincing. He crawled out, and Hope followed him.

"No need to fret, son. We'll get 'im back," Luther promised. "Boy, my lumbago's killin' me, Harriet. We got any of that salve?"

Harriet came over to stand beside Dan. "We'll get yore horse back—might take a day or two, but we'll get 'im back for you. Don't you worry none 'bout that."

"I'm worried about the saddle. It's a personal keepsake."

"But we can't stay here," Hope protested. John Jacobs was this minute probably worried sick about her whereabouts. Two days' delay here—then another two to three days' ride. They couldn't stay; Dan had to make that clear to Luther. They'd just wanted a cup of coffee and a fresh biscuit!

"Don't you fret yore pretty little head one minute, young'un." Harriet hung the rifle over a peg and stepped to the stove. Pitching in a stick of kindling, she slid the lid over the burner. "Got plenty of room—you ain't puttin' us out a'tall. Glad to have the company. You and your brother kin stay right here 'til we git yore animal back."

Hope's heart sank. "No . . . really, we can't."

"Why, shore you can." Harriet waved off the courtesy. "Just took fresh sheets off the line yesterday. Luther and yore brother can bunk down in here. Me and you can take th' bedroom."

Hope was about to protest again when Harriet called over her shoulder. "No arguin'. We insist. You don't look none too strong. No way yore gonna make it all the way to Medford feelin' sickly like you do. You jest rest up here a spell afore you move on. Lyndon don't usually keep us pinned down more'n a few days."

"A few days?" Hope mouthed. What happened to one or two?

Dan stepped away from the window. "Ma'am, we wouldn't think of putting Luther out of his bed. We'll stay the night and leave first light in the morning. Hope can sleep on a pallet near the fire, and I'll bunk down in the barn."

"Now that sounds fair, Harriet," Luther said. "These old bones can't hardly take this old floor anymore."

Harriet dragged a heavy skillet out of the oven of the

woodstove. "Whatever you say, but I wouldn't be countin' on leavin' in the mornin'." She turned, grinning. "Now, how does ham and redeye gravy sound to everyone?"

The old cabin filled with the smell of supper. Hope cut biscuits while Harriet fried thick slices of ham. Hope kept an eye on the sow, praying the meat wasn't one of its relatives.

"Uh-oh," Luther said when he lifted the curtain aside to look out. Darkness had fallen, and a full moon was rising.

Hope had come to dread the phrase "Uh-oh." It invariably meant trouble.

The old woman glanced up. "What's the matter?"

"Lyndon's boys are still here."

"Well, ma's boots—they're gonna make us miss supper." Harriet leaned to peer over her husband's shoulder. "Yes sir, there's little Jim, and John over by the barn. There's Teddie to the right, and Eddie straight out. I'd say the others are farther back in the trees, probably sneakin' around to the back."

Hope glanced up from setting plates on the table. "How many boys does Lyndon have?"

"Oh, eight or so. Then there's four or five of them girls." She tsked. "Real homely, those girls are—though jest as nice as they can be. Real mannerly. He finally got that one, Ethylene, married off last year, but he won't be so lucky with those others. Do you think, Luther?"

"Not likely, though little Merline won't be so bad once she gets a little meat on them bones."

"Luther!" a voice shouted from outside.

"Who is it?" Luther yelled back.

"Teddie."

"What do you want?"

"Our pig."

"What pig?"

"Th' pig you stole from Ma and Pa!"

"Don't know nothin' 'bout yore pig." Luther sat down at the table, his face a mask of determination.

Silence stretched. Luther looked at Harriet and winked.

"Do too."

"Do not! You know anything about them chickens Lyndon stole from me?"

Silence.

"No."

"Do too."

The war of words waged on. Hope poured four mugs of boiled coffee, then wiped her hands on the muslin cloth she'd tied about her waist. Big Joe was after them, and now Lyndon's boys were lying in wait outside. Seemed to her things had gotten worse.

There was a real pig making herself at home in the corner, and those were real bullets imbedded in the cabin wall, and she was so hungry she could eat the walls down. She didn't know about the others, but she was eating.

"Supper's ready!"

Harriet turned from the window. "Why, child, it smells lappin' good. Luther, that young'un's done got supper on the table. Ain't that somethin'?"

"Shore is—real hospitable of you, young'un."

The men washed up while Hope took a pan of biscuits out of the oven.

"Land sakes," Harriet fussed, "I wish you'd let me do that. You not feeling real good and all."

"I'm better, Harriet. Thank you." Hope put two fat biscuits on Dan's plate. He smiled his gratitude, and she longed to give him a hug and tell him it would be over soon. One way or another.

"Why have Luther and his brother fought so long over something so insignificant?" Hope asked as she took her seat.

"Ah, the Bennetts are a hardheaded lot," Harriet explained. "Pride runs real deep."

"But Lyndon is Luther's brother. How can he bear to be at such odds with him? I have two sisters, and we've never had an argument that lasted more than a day. Nothing ever seemed so important that we ceased to be family."

"Well, it ain't a real pleasant situation," Harriet agreed. Luther, Hope noticed, just hung his head at the subject.

Breaking two biscuits apart, Hope ladled gravy over them. "The Lord says don't be mean to your family, and try your best to love one another—"

Dan broke in quietly. "What Hope means to say is that the Lord instructs families to look past mistakes, forgive misunderstandings, and be slow to take offense and never hold grudges."

Hope pleated her makeshift apron between her fingers. So he knew his Scriptures. He didn't have to be so smart about it. "My Aunt Thalia says if you have family, you're rich. I wouldn't trade my sisters for anything."

Harriet hung her head. "Pride's a powerful enemy, all right. But once ill feelings get started there's no stoppin' them—leastwise not in the Bennett family. Too much water over the dam—too many hurt feelin's."

Luther spread a biscuit with fresh cream butter, his features tight with emotion. "Harriet's right. Lyndon can't be reasoned with. Never could be. Once he's got somethin' in his craw there's no gettin' it out."

They ate the remainder of the meal in silence. When Harriet got up to help with the dishes, Hope motioned her to remain seated.

Pouring Dan another cup of coffee, Hope met his gaze.

"Thanks," he said softly.

"You're welcome."

She liked it when he smiled at her; actually, she liked everything about him.

The pig in the corner grunted and rolled over.

The pig she didn't like.

Luther got up from the table and returned to the window. "Looks like the boys have bedded down for the night."

"Is it safe to sleep with them camped so close by?" Hope scraped leftovers into the dog's bowl.

"Oh sure. Those boys like their sleep. But come daylight, they'll be back at it." Harriet stifled a yawn. "I'll get some extra quilts. The old cabin gets chilly at night."

Harriet returned with an armload of bedding and laid it

on the table. "Take what you need for warmth, then use the rest for padding."

"Thank you." Hope smiled. "We'll be comfortable."

Harriet and Luther retired to their room, leaving Dan and Hope to stare at the stack of quilts.

Hope sighed. "Now what?" It wasn't proper for an unmarried couple to sleep in the same room.

"Let's see what morning brings. I don't want to endanger our lives if we don't have to." He handed her a folded quilt.

Hope closed her eyes, weariness overtaking her. "What about the sleeping arrangements? You can't go out to the barn."

"Harriet and Luther are in the next room—we have chaperones. You can sleep on one side of the stove; I'll sleep on the other. We won't be able to see each other."

Hope was too tired to argue. "I don't know why this is happening to us."

"Who would you like it to happen to?"

She could think of several right now. Big Joe at the top of the list. She looked up when Dan took her hands.

When he looked at her like this, all polite and gentle-manly, it was hard to remember that she was trying to reach John Jacobs—the man she was about to marry.

"I know you're worried, but now's the time to put your faith to the test, Hope. I'll get us out of here, but I'm not going to do anything foolish."

She sighed. "Papa said we were to never lose faith, no matter how hopeless the situation seemed—but this seems pretty hopeless. Lyndon's sons are out there just waiting for us to step outside. Harriet and Luther may consider this just harmless fun, but those were real bullets they were firing at us. For all we know, Big Joe, Frog, and Boris have heard the commotion and have come to investigate—" She blinked back sudden tears. "And Harriet and Luther think we're brother and sister."

She felt anything but "sisterly" toward him.

"Don't you believe God can and will take care of us?"

"I don't know," she said, closing her eyes. She felt like doubting Thomas, but right now her faith was pretty weak. "He can, but—"

Of course she believed God was able; she just wasn't sure she was capable of trusting her life so completely to his care.

Dan blew out the lamp, and Hope lay on her pallet listening to him settle on the other side of the stove. He seemed so confident—so comfortable in his belief. He made her feel so ashamed of her doubts.

Hands tucked beneath her cheek, she lay in the dark, thinking about her life. The old sow snored, its fat sides heaving in and out with exertion.

Exactly what did she believe? Before she could decide, weariness claimed her.

Just before dawn, Dan gently shook her awake.

"The old couple are stirring."

It took Hope a moment to clear the cobwebs from her head. When she did, she got up and quickly folded her quilts. Running her fingers through her hair, she despaired of ever getting the tangles out. They had left the outlaws' cabin so abruptly that Dan failed to bring Anne's valise.

Hope fashioned a careless braid and coiled it at the nape of her neck and secured it. Shaking her skirts in a futile attempt at neatness, she started to the stove to stoke up the fire.

She ducked as a bullet whizzed by her head.

"Luther, they're gonna break every window in the house," Harriet complained, coming out of the bedroom with her gray hair streaming down her back.

"Howdy, young'uns!" Luther greeted as he ducked to one side of the window.

"Howdy." Hope concentrated on dipping water from the stove reservoir for coffee.

They wouldn't be leaving today.

Chapter Seven

The pig was restless. And Hope had had her fill of dealing with it. Three endless days and she'd had her fill of this senseless feud.

She had used water sparingly, but it was getting dangerously low, and the monotony of the meals was beginning to dim everyone's appetite.

"Can't we leave?" she asked Dan the third morning. She glanced toward Luther and Harriet's closed door. She wouldn't hurt the old couple's feelings for the world, but this was their fight, not hers and Dan's. The Lord knew they had enough problems without taking on more. "I can't stand being cooped up in this tiny room any longer. And if I have to clean up after that pig one more time, we're having pork for supper."

Dan pulled on his boots, his face lined with concern.

"This has gone on long enough. Watch for my signal today. Be ready. When I think it's safe to make a run for it, we'll go."

"Thank goodness." She lifted the curtain to peek out the window. "There's not a soul out there this morning."

"We need a horse."

Hope stepped back to stir a pan of gravy bubbling on the stove. Sunlight streamed through the small window above the cookstove. This morning had been eerily quiet. The usual "I'm here" shots had yet to be fired. Yesterday the only real activity had come from the line of cottonwoods running parallel to the house and then only when Dan had recovered his saddle and put it in the barn. He seemed protective of the saddle, and she remembered that it held special significance for him.

She focused on the gurgling creek running alongside the cabin. If her eyes didn't deceive her, that was watercress growing along the bank. She'd bet Aunt Thalia's best broach that tender mushrooms grew in the shaded areas to the east of the stream and perhaps some poke greens at the edge of the clearing. Her mouth watered at the possibilities. For the past two days they'd eaten nothing but meat and potatoes.

Fresh greens sounded so tempting. The pig oinked and shifted. She turned to give it a sour look. Fresh greens with ham hocks.

Luther emerged from the bedroom and sat down at the table with Dan. Hope could hear Harriet moving around in the other room, pulling the quilt up over the sheets.

She had to get out of the cabin. Just for a moment—one blissful moment—when she could breathe fresh air. She was suffocating from all the closeness.

The men were up at the stove now, pouring themselves coffee. Taking a deep breath, Hope edged toward the back door.

The pig lumbered to its feet and nosed after her. She tried to nudge it away with the tip of her shoe, but the old sow was just as eager for freedom as she was.

Dan turned when he heard the door open.

She smiled. "Just stepping out for a moment."

"Hope—don't be foolish—"

Her words came in a rush. "I'll only be gone a moment. There isn't anyone out back right now—not one shot has been fired this morning."

"You can't be sure there's no one around. I'll go with you—"

"One shot, and I'm back in the house, I promise." She quickly closed the door before he had time to argue.

Bounding off the porch, she glanced both ways for any sign of the other Bennetts. Songbirds chirped overhead, and fat robins hopped around pulling worms from the rocky soil. The pig, obviously with no consideration for her future, shot past and waddled straight for a sturdy-looking pen with a beckoning mudhole. Hope hurried ahead to unlatch the gate.

"Try to clean up a little," she muttered.

Grunting, the old sow settled herself into the mire as

Hope quickly swung the gate closed and fastened it with a loop of wire.

Hurrying to the edge of the trees, she quickly gathered greens, keeping one eye on the cabin. Dan would come after her if she stayed out too long, but the idea of fresh greens was just too tempting to pass up.

Using her apron to cradle the tender shoots, Hope poked around in the damp shadows, hoping to find some small, tender morels. She'd barely gathered a handful when she heard a twig snap to her left. She froze, her blood curdling in her chest. *How foolish of me to risk my life for some old greens,* she thought. *Now I've gotten myself into a pickle, and Dan will be upset with me.* He'd have every right to give her a tongue-lashing.

Crouching low in the shadows, she searched the undergrowth for some clue to the stealthy movements that continued a short distance in front of her. Holding her breath, she prayed that an innocent woodland creature was causing the soft rustlings. She'd even welcome a skunk. That would be preferable to a Bennett boy with a shotgun in his hand.

The sounds stopped, and Hope's heart thrummed. A face materialized, not five feet from where she stooped. She strained to make out its features. Blood pounded in her ears. Was it a bear? No, it wasn't an animal, nor was it one of the Bennett boys—it was a girl.

Caught by surprise, the two women stared at each other. It took a moment for Hope to summon the courage to speak. Then her voice came out in a minuscule squeak.

"Hello . . . I'm Hope. Who are you?"

The startled girl didn't answer; she simply stared like a doe caught in a rifle sight. Her elfin features were white with fright, her black dress dirty and unkempt.

"Don't be frightened—I won't hurt you."

The girl's eyes were the color of green grass.

Smiling, Hope extended her hand. "Can you tell me your name?"

"Fawn. Fawn Bennett."

One of Lyndon's children. Luther's niece.

"Lyndon Bennett's daughter?"

"Yes'um." She glanced toward the stand of trees. "I'm the baby—only I ain't no baby no more. I turned thirteen last month—I'm a woman now."

"What are you doing out here, Fawn?"

Her face turned defensive. "Brought my brothers some biscuits and bacon from home. They sent me around back to watch the house whilst they et."

Hope turned to look toward the cabin. No sign of Dan yet. "Your brothers are still out here?"

The girl flashed a quick grin. "Yes'um. My brothers ain't too bright, but they hide real good." She darted a quick look toward the trees, then back to Hope. "You'd better go. They might shoot you."

Startled, Hope started back toward the house, then paused and turned around. "Do you think they'd honestly shoot me?"

The girl thought about it. "Naw. They jest want to skeer you, liken they do Uncle Luther and Aunt Harriet. I best be goin'. They wouldn't want me a jawin' with ya." The young girl turned to leave.

"Wait," Hope whispered. "Can we talk a minute?"

The girl looked doubtful, then gestured for Hope to follow her. A moment later Hope entered a small clearing to the east of the cabin. An abundance of mushrooms grew in the shadows of a fallen tree. She quickly gathered an apron full.

"It's lovely here."

Fawn shrugged. "I like it. Makes me feel close to the Almighty when I'm here."

"Tell me about the feud." Hope set the apron containing mushrooms and greens on the ground, then settled on a rock.

Fawn paced the clearing, apparently uneasy with the arrangement. Her eyes darted back and forth as if she expected her brothers to burst out of the brush any minute. "What about it?"

"Don't you think it's silly? It's senseless for families to be shooting at each other."

The girl turned to look at her. "It's always been this way. Since before any of us young'uns was born."

"How sad. I'm sure it must be hard to live with such hostility."

The girl's shoulders lifted with acceptance. "Every few weeks or so, Pa'll swipe something from Uncle Luther, and Uncle Luther will steal somethin' back. It ain't real pleasant."

"How long does this go on?"

"Until they get back whatever the other took."

Hope couldn't imagine such a dreary existence. "Hasn't anyone thought to settle the problem?" Seemed easy enough to sit down and talk it through, pray for forgiveness—try to respect the other's rights.

Fawn's smile was fleeting. "I'd think so, but Pa won't hear of it. Ma'd like to be friends with Aunt Harriet. She gits real lonely. This fightin' seems ta be the only way they kin talk to one another."

What an interesting thought. "That's too bad."

"Yes'um. Shore nuff is."

"So, you would like to see this end?" Hope said softly.

"Yes'um—real bad. But it don't never seem likely."

Hope was drawn to the girl. For one thing, she seemed the only person in the Bennett family with common sense. For another, she was a lovely waif who seemed at odds with her destiny.

"Then perhaps we can do something about it."

The girl stared at her as if Hope had suddenly grown two heads.

"What kin we do?"

"Does your family believe in God?"

The girl's head bobbed enthusiastically. "Ain't got no church round here, but a preacher comes round once a month and holds a meetin' at somebody's house."

"Well, my papa was a great one for reading the Bible. He had Scripture for every problem."

Fawn's lips curved in a near smile. "Think he'd have one for this?"

Hope nodded. "Most assuredly, if he were alive. He died a few months back."

Fawn paced the clearing, in thought now. The sun ducked behind a cloud, and the wind had a chill that reminded one it was still early spring. "It'd shore be nice not to hafta be afraid all the time, to have the two families git along."

Hope longed to give Fawn a reassuring hug, but she didn't want to frighten her. "Can you read?"

The girl lit with excitement. "Yes'um, I can read real good-like. Learnt how last year. Mrs. Yodler taught me."

"Do you think you could talk to your family? Read the Ten Commandments out loud to them. Be sure both your brothers and parents understand the commandment 'Thou shalt not steal.' Can you do that?"

She frowned. "I kin try. Where is those commandments in the Bible?"

"In Exodus." Hope wracked her brain. What chapter was that? Ten? Eighteen? Twenty! "Chapter 20! Do you have a Bible?"

"Part of one."

Hope hoped it was the Old Testament part. "Good. And I'll try to reason with your Aunt Harriet and Uncle Luther. Perhaps together we can reunite your families."

The young girl's features sobered. "Oh no, ma'am. I cain't light my family. I wouldn't burn 'em or hurt 'em—"

"No, not 'light' them—reunite them—bring them together."

Fawn brightened. "Oh, well now, that'd be real nice."

The girls turned when they heard Dan's voice shouting for Hope.

Hope jumped up from the rock. "I have to go."

"Yes'um—me too." Fawn hurriedly helped her gather the greens and mushrooms back into the apron, cringing as Dan's worried shout filled the small clearing. "HOPE!"

"Better hurry now. Yore mister sounds a mite put out."

Patting Fawn's arm, Hope started off. "I'll pray we both have success in making the family see the error of their ways."

"Yes'um—Mrs. Yodler—she's that nice woman who learnt me how to read? She says the Almighty is powerful 'nough to move whole mountains. Is that right?"

Hope nodded. "That's what the Good Book says."

"Then he ought not to have any trouble gettin' Pa and Uncle Luther to stop stealin' each other's chickens and hogs."

Dan's voice again shattered the tranquil morning. "Hope!"

Hope ran from the clearing, carefully cradling the greens and mushrooms in her makeshift sling.

Dan was standing at the doorway with a rifle in his hand. When she bounded onto the porch, his face drained with relief. "Have you lost your mind?"

"No," she said, brushing past him. She dumped the greens and mushrooms on the table.

"You could have been killed!"

"Yes, but I wasn't."

He didn't have to remind her that what she'd done was

foolish, but if Fawn could make her family see how silly this feud was, it was worth the risk.

Luther bolted to the door, his eyes scouting the backyard. "Where's the pig?"

"In the pen—"

The old man shot out the back door and returned a few minutes later dragging the reluctant porker by a rope.

Dan slammed the door behind the muddy entourage and locked it. When his eyes pinned Hope, she got the message. She wasn't to go out again until he gave the signal for escape.

"Luther, for heaven's sake. You're muddying up the kitchen!" Harriet complained.

"Cain't let nothing happen to this hog, Harriet. Lyndon would never forgive me."

Hope ventured a glance at Dan and winced when she saw his stormy features. "I didn't mean to stay so long. I saw these wonderful greens and mushrooms and—"

"Don't leave this cabin again unless I tell you to." He hung the rifle back over the fireplace. "Understand?"

Eyes narrowed, she snapped to attention, saluting him. "Yes, sir, General Sullivan. At your service, sir!"

He turned; he was not amused. "Grow up, Hope. You could have been shot out there."

Grow up? Well! How dare he talk to her like that! Perhaps she had been careless, but nothing had happened.

Harriet resumed her vigil beside Luther at the window, and Hope dumped the mix of greens and mushrooms in the sink and poured a little water into the basin. "You know,

Luther, I think this feud would be over if you would stop retaliating. It won't be easy, but if you'll take the first step—apologize to your brother for stealing his pig—then maybe he'll reciprocate and you can put this feud behind you."

"Lyndon steals from me."

"Two wrongs don't make a right." She picked up the cleaned greens and carried them to the stove.

"Hope." Dan's eyes sent her a silent warning. "Luther and Harriet should settle their own problems."

They should, she agreed silently. But obviously they hadn't.

Harriet spent the afternoon sitting next to Luther, knitting. Dan paced the small cabin, occasionally stepping to the back door to look out. Hope held her breath. She could see he was contemplating leaving, and it couldn't come soon enough for her.

Luther praised the tasty greens during supper, and Hope shot a smug look at Dan. The old couple excused themselves right after the dishes were washed, saying the events of the past few days had plain tuckered them out.

Soon they heard snores coming from the old couple's room. Hope sat cross-legged on her bed pallet, brushing her hair. Harriet had come up with an extra brush for her; at least she could groom her hair now. Once she would have been preoccupied with her looks, but lately she praised God for a comb.

"You're used to dealing with men like Lyndon's sons, aren't you?"

Dan sat at the table sharpening his knife. "I've met a few like them in my time. Hotheaded, single-minded."

"Is that why we haven't tried to get away before now?"

"No, I just don't see any purpose in risking our lives until it's necessary."

"We could have gotten away this morning when the Bennetts were eating breakfast."

"We could have, but that's what they expect us to do. We'll leave soon."

Dan wasn't inclined to open up to her, and that bothered her at times. Sometimes she wondered if he even liked her anymore. He seldom addressed her personally, yet she caught him staring at her when he thought she wasn't watching.

"You've done this a lot, then?"

"Been stranded in a cabin with an old couple, a pig, and a chatterbox?"

She threw the brush at him. "Joined gangs, pretended to be someone you're not, escorted women to fiancés."

He dodged the weapon, smiling at her. "Occasionally."

Occasionally, she silently mimicked. That was his standard answer when he didn't want to address her questions.

"How can you do that? Pretend you're someone else for months at a time?"

"That's one of the reasons I'm retiring. I'm tired of violating my conscience."

"Apparently you've been successful at your work. Can you leave the service so easily?"

"As easily as you can marry a man you've never met."

His mild accusation surprised her. Is that what he thought her marriage to John Jacobs would be—a loveless union between two strangers? It didn't have to be that way . . . she hoped.

"It isn't the same thing."

"Really."

"No—it isn't uncommon for a man, a lonely man, to send for a wife. My sisters are each marrying a fine man: Nicholas Shepherd is a rancher; Eli Messenger, a preacher." She paused, gathering her confidence. "Are you married?"

He shook his head.

"Someone special waiting for you to come home?"

"My dear Miss Kallahan, has anyone ever told you that you talk too much?"

"No, the only thing they've said is 'Grow up, Hope.'"

He glanced up, and she made a face at him.

Returning to his task, he said quietly, "When I leave the service, I'm going to buy a few acres of land in Virginia and farm it. No woman, no prior commitments, no prospects in sight."

"By chance?"

"Nope, by choice."

"You sound as if you don't want commitments. Or a wife."

"I don't, at least not right now. Maybe never."

She got up and put a pan of oil on the stove. "Ever been

in love, Dan Sullivan? Really, hopelessly, out-of-your-mind in love?"

"Not in a long time."

Hope didn't know why his admission pleased her—almost made her giddy with relief. Just because he wasn't spoken for didn't mean she could have him. He'd just said he wasn't in the market for a wife.

"But you were once." Hope wasn't going to like this part because she knew the answer before he said it.

"Once. A long time ago."

Dumping kernels of dried corn into the pan, she added a handful of salt and put the lid on the pot. The smell of popped corn promptly scented the air.

"Want to talk about her?"

"No."

"But let's do because we're searching for something in common."

"You might be." He motioned to the sow. "Me and the sow aren't."

He seemed to enjoy teasing her, but she desperately wanted a serious conversation with him. She removed the pan from the burner, drizzled butter over the hot corn, and dumped it into a bowl. Carrying it to the table, she sat down and scooped up a handful. "What's her name?"

For a moment, she thought he wasn't going to answer her. Absently reaching his hand into the bowl, he met her eyes.

"Katie Morris."

"And?"

"And, nothing."

"Oh, no. There was something." She scooted her chair closer. "You loved her madly—out-of-your mind loved her."

"I thought so, at the time."

"But she didn't love you back?" Hope couldn't imagine a woman failing to return his affection. Why, if he loved her—it wouldn't take any effort at all to love him back.

"Katie wasn't ready for marriage or family life. She went off to an eastern women's college. We agreed to write—keep in touch—but after a few months I never heard from her again. Years later I heard that she married a professor."

Hope's handful of popcorn paused at her mouth. "That must have hurt."

He shrugged. "Life hurts sometimes, Hope. You get used to it."

His answers were so simple, so to the point. If only life were that easy.

"I hope to find love with John," she admitted softly.

Laying the knife aside, Dan's eyes met hers over the flickering candle. Goose bumps rose on her arms, and she told herself it was the sound of the wind making her insides feel jittery.

"What about you? Have you ever been in love?"

"Oh . . . no. Maybe puppy love, once. A boy in our church—Milo Evans. Milo was nice and cute, but he married Ellie Thompson last year. They have twins already."

The old clock on the mantel chimed nine. Outside, the

wind battered the shutters, but inside, in her heart, sitting with him in this room, snug and warm, the smell of popped corn pleasant in the air, she felt . . . happy. Content.

"My sisters and I didn't want to burden our elderly aunt after our father died," she said, hoping to make him understand why she'd agreed to a mail-order husband. "We prayed a lot over the decision and felt that God was leading us. We did what we felt we had to do."

Of course, she wished she could have met a man and fallen in love, married in the normal manner. But she hadn't. What had Dan just said? Sometimes life hurts?

"There were no men in Michigan?" he asked gently.

"Not where we lived—not suitable men. Dan . . . I'm sure Mr. Jacobs is a good man." If that's what he was concerned about, she could read him all of Mr. Jacobs's letters—put his mind at ease.

His thoughts, if he had any in particular, didn't register on his face. Pushing the knife back into its sheath, he moved back from the table. "It's late. Time we turned in."

"I guess so." For some reason, she wanted to sit up and talk all night. About nothing, or about everything. The subject wouldn't matter; being with him did.

Reaching for the old Bible in the middle of the table, she opened it to Genesis. "I'm not sleepy yet. You're right. I have been too lax with my studies. I'll get started on memorizing a few verses tonight."

"You're going to start with Genesis?" Dan asked. He glanced at the clock.

She excused the incredulous note in his voice. She didn't intend to memorize the whole thing tonight.

"I'll just read a few chapters—then go back and memorize those three verses a day you advocate."

"Genesis?" he repeated. "Couldn't you start with something simpler—maybe the Beatitudes?"

She thumbed to Genesis 1. "Oh . . . that's all that 'Blessed are' stuff, isn't it?"

"Yes—"

"I think I'll just start with Genesis and work my way right up to that worrisome stuff."

"Revelation?"

She nodded, smoothing the Bible's worn, yellow pages into place. She read to chapter 5, her eyes widening. "My . . . there're an awful lot of 'begets' in here, aren't there?" She glanced at the clock.

When Dan rolled up in his blanket, she was sitting at the table trying to memorize Genesis 1:1-3. Muttering under her breath, she squeezed her eyes shut, whispering, "'In the beginning God created the heaven and the earth.' Verse 2: 'And the earth . . .'"

Pause.

"Verse 1: 'In the beginning God created the heaven and the earth.' Verse 2: 'And the earth . . .'"

Pause.

"'Was without form, and void; and darkness was upon the face of the deep,'" Dan muttered sleepily from the other side of the stove. He pulled his pillow over his head.

"Thank you. 'And the earth . . .'"

Pause.

"Verse 1: 'In the beginning God created the heaven and the earth. . . .'"

"Hope, you have company."

Hope looked up at Dan's soft announcement. It was still so early that the sun was barely visible through the broken windowpane. Luther's intermittent snores resonated from behind his and Harriet's closed door. "Me?"

Parting the curtain a fraction more, Dan said softly. "It's a young girl."

"It must be Fawn, the youngest Bennett girl. I spoke with her yesterday. Maybe she's talked to her parents." Quickly brushing her hair, Hope slipped into one of Harriet's over-sized coats and headed for the door.

Dan was waiting for her, arms crossed. Wearing his coat now, he blocked her path. "You're not going out there."

"But she wants to talk to me—she isn't a threat."

"You're not going out there alone."

Hope opened the door a fraction, and the pig squeezed around her. Dan lunged for the animal, but its fat backside was already waddling toward the open pen.

Hurriedly stepping outside, Hope watched the old porker settle into the mudhole with a satisfied grunt. Dan trailed her onto the porch.

"She won't talk with you here," Hope protested. "You'll only intimidate her. Stay here."

Grasping her shoulders, he turned her toward the stand of cottonwoods. "What do you see over there?"

"The Bennett boys."

"Holding what?"

Hope squinted. "Rifles."

She turned to look at Fawn. The girl must have talked to her parents; otherwise she wouldn't present herself so openly.

Fawn waved, friendly-like. "It's all right, ma'am! My brothers ain't gonna shoot!"

"What do you think?" Hope whispered. She followed Dan's eyes back to the stand of trees. Four of Luther's off-spring stood leaning on their rifles, keeping an eye on the exchange.

Dan's voice brooked no nonsense. "I don't trust them. Come back into the house."

Hope continued to study the situation. She didn't trust them, either, but someone had to show a little faith, or the standoff would go on forever.

"I'm going out there."

"Hope," he warned, "you're not to go out there."

Now the Bible says, "Wives, obey your husbands." It doesn't say a thing about women obeying government agents—leastwise not flat out. "Keep an eye on that pig," she murmured. "If anything happens to her, we're sunk."

Right now that old sow was the only thing standing between Luther and Lyndon and all-out war.

Taking a deep breath, Hope walked to the edge of the

yard where Fawn was huddled deep in a bedraggled jacket that might once have been red. "Hi."

"Hi," Fawn said as Hope approached. "Need to do some serious jawin'."

"All right." Hope waited for the girl to put her thoughts in order.

"Pa's a knucklehead."

Hope felt a twinge of compassion. "You tried to talk to him about the feud?"

"Yes'um. But he's shore nuff a knucklehead." Fawn shoved her hands deeper into the coat pockets. "He won't listen to nary a word about a truce. Keeps jawin' 'bout 'an eye for an eye' or somethin' like that."

"He won't even talk to his brother?"

"No, ma'am. Says Uncle Luther's an even bigger knucklehead than he is, and he don't want nothin' to do with that Nut Muffin."

"Oh, dear."

The girl brightened. "Did you have any better luck with Uncle Luther?"

"No, your uncle's an even bigger Nut Muffin—won't even hear of a cease-fire." She planned to broach the subject again at breakfast, but her expectation was slim that Luther had changed his mind overnight. "We'll just have to pray about it. Papa always said God would supply our needs."

Fawn stood in the early morning light, tracing irregular patterns in the dew-covered grass with the tip of her scuffed boot. "Got me a plan."

"You do?"

"Yes'um—iffin you'll say it's all right for me to try it."

It wasn't Hope's place to grant her permission to try anything, but she certainly wouldn't stand in the way of progress.

"I'm for peace at almost any cost."

Fawn broke into a wide grin. "Thank ya, ma'am! My plan ort to work—but iffin it shouldn't, I want you to 'splain to the Lord that I done my best."

Smiling, Hope nodded. "I'll tell him. What is this plan?" Would Fawn propose they trick the feuding brothers into meeting—make them sit down and talk about the situation like rational adults? Luther could be stubborn—and Lyndon . . . Her eyes shot to Fawn, who suddenly broke away and was now dashing headlong toward the pigpen. Lightning quick, the young girl released the wire hook and threw open the gate. Waving her arms and yelling at the top of her lungs, she charged the sow. "Soooooeeeee!"

Startled, the old porker shot to its feet, making a beeline for the exit. Out of the pen it streaked, running faster than Hope thought her four squat legs could carry her.

When the girl and the pig were halfway down the road, Fawn turned to yell over her shoulder. "Don't be mad, ma'am! Now that Pa's got his pig back, there ain't no argument!"

Hope's jaw dropped when she realized that Fawn had outsmarted her!

Bounding off the porch, Dan started after the pig. Shots

sounded, and he turned in the middle of the yard and lunged toward Hope.

Speechless, Hope watched the devious girl and the pig hightailing it toward home. Pig snorts gradually faded in the far distance; silence surrounded the barn lot.

"Watch the pig, Dan," Dan mimicked as he came to a skidding halt beside her.

Hope slowly turned around to see the Bennett boys casually lift their rifles again and take aim.

"Ohhh . . . ," she murmured, "we are in so much trouble."

Chapter Eight

John Jacobs glanced out the front window and groaned. There was that nosy Veda crossing the street toward the Mercantile, carrying that infernal casserole basket. He set his jaw. This time, he was going to tell that woman to mind her own business. Whom he chose to marry was his doings, not the town's, and certainly not Veda Fletcher's.

Why, the reason he'd placed that ad in the journal in the first place was so he could court a woman without the whole town knowing about it. As it was, he had had to woo Miss Kallahan by mail, and Megaline Harris, the postmistress, had told everyone in town that he was exchanging letters with some woman in Michigan.

Some woman in Michigan. The very idea of referring to Miss Kallahan as "some woman."

Shouldering her way into the store, Veda set the basket on the counter. No doubt another gastric delight. John mentally cringed at the renewed determination in Veda's eyes.

"Afternoon, John."

"Afternoon, Veda."

"Looks like snow."

"Let's think spring, Veda."

"Think it if you like, but we still get snow this late in the year. I've pulled tender young green onions out of snow many a time. Never took my stove down until first of June—ever."

Lord, forgive me for being so mean to poor Veda, but the woman gets on my nerves worse than chaffed thighs.

But courtesy came first at the Jacobs Mercantile. The customer was always right, and Veda was a good customer—paid her bills on time and didn't complain when a sugar shipment came in late.

"I can't stay long, John. Eudora and I are hanging new curtains this afternoon, but I had to see if you'd had any further news. Don't think I'm nosy, now."

Veda nosy? Never.

"News?"

"Regarding your fiancée."

"No news—I'm expecting her any day now." Even as he defended Hope Kallahan, he knew he was grasping at straws. If Hope were coming, she'd have been here by now. He had to face up to the fact that she'd gotten cold feet and wasn't coming. Dear Lord. How could he face Veda and the town in his despair?

"Oh. That's a pity." John could see it was all she could do to keep from turning handsprings. Veda tried to hide her joy. "Now, John. You wouldn't be trying to fool the town, would you? You've told everyone that Miss Hope Kallahan is arriving any day, but we've not seen hide nor hair of her."

"I haven't told everyone," John corrected.

"You've told me. And Edna and Louise."

Medford has three ways of surefire communication: telegram, tell Veda, or tell Louise.

"Just where is this woman?"

John was wondering the same thing. Where was Hope Kallahan? And why, indeed, hadn't she sent word if she'd been fortuitously delayed?

"I don't know where she is," he admitted.

He'd diligently met each stage that managed to get through. He'd had no further correspondence from Miss Kallahan. She wasn't coming. She'd simply decided she didn't want to marry him. Her letters had sounded as if the arrangement pleased her. But women change their minds.

He could forgive her for changing her mind; what he couldn't tolerate was neglect. Neglecting to inform him of a change in heart was unforgivable.

"Is it possible your fiancée got cold feet?" Veda asked, coyly lifting the cloth on the basket.

John caught a whiff of chicken.

"Miss Kallahan said she was coming. Something undoubtedly has delayed her, but I trust that she is still coming. Now, if you don't mind, Veda, I have an appointment with Edgar."

Veda's brow arched. "The tailor? Your fiancée hasn't even arrived, and you're about to be fitted for a wedding suit?"

"That is precisely what I'm about to do." Jerking his vest coat into place, he stepped around the counter. He'd had just about enough of this inquisition. He wasn't meeting her niece, Ginger, and that was that. "If you'll excuse me."

Veda trailed him out the front door. "My niece, Ginger, arrived on yesterday's stage. Have you seen her yet?"

Only two women got off that stage yesterday. The statuesque young woman with dark hair and ivory porcelain skin who'd turned more than her share of men's heads must have been Freeman Hide's granddaughter. Freeman's whole family was good-looking. Were John not already contracted, he'd be sorely tempted to ask Freeman for introductions.

The other woman was as homely as sin.

"Yes, I did. Lovely young woman."

"You did!" Veda glowed. "Pretty as a picture, isn't she? Didn't I tell you she was a jewel?"

"Yes, ma'am, you did." *At least once a day for the past four months.*

"She's most delicate you know, fragile as china. The long trip from San Francisco wore her out, so she's taken to bed for a few days. Once she's up and around, I'll bring her over to the Mercantile."

Wonderful. She's trying to marry me off to a sickly girl with the constitution of fine china. He stepped off the porch and started across the street.

"John!" Veda hurried after him. "You're going to the box supper, aren't you?"

Box supper? That was a misnomer if there ever was one. It was a man trap. Snares in a basket—albeit bait dressed in an interesting fashion and offered up for auction, but snares nonetheless. The bidder wasn't supposed to know whose box he was bidding on, but one generally had a strong hint.

Every time he attended one of those infernal box suppers, every eligible woman in town dropped clues on which box was hers. The town matchmakers had put him in an impossible situation.

If he dared bid on a certain basket, other women were hurt or angry, and either they or their daughters gave him most unpleasant looks during the course of the long evening.

If he didn't bid, he went without supper.

Enjoying a carefree meal in the comfort of his home above the store wasn't an option for that night. In a town the size of Medford, every absence was noted and unduly speculated upon. He'd tried to get out of going once, and the flood of chicken soup the next day had created such a tizzy for him that he vowed to never try that again.

John picked up his stride, hoping Veda would take the hint. When he glanced over his shoulder, he saw she was still close on his heels. Oliver trotted along behind her.

"You have to eat, John, affianced or not. Just say you'll

come to the box supper Friday night. By then, my Ginger will be feeling up to entertaining callers."

He set his jaw and kept walking. "I won't be calling on your niece, Veda."

Veda hurried to keep pace with his long-legged stride. "I'm not talking about calling on her—I know you're not at liberty to do that—not at the moment, but it won't hurt you to be sociable, will it?"

The woman was a bulldog. There'd be no peace until he agreed. "All right, Veda. I'll come."

She paused, grinning. "Now, see. That wasn't so difficult, was it? Ginger's entering a box, you know. I'll make certain you know which one."

John's new suit awaited him. Cut from the finest Italian cloth, the dark blue wool fit him to perfection.

"Excellent job, Edgar."

Edgar was overjoyed with his handiwork. "You're going to make a splendid bridegroom!"

Indeed he was. Examining his mirrored image, he twirled his mustache, wishing anew that Miss Kallahan would get here. Shame to spend all this money and not have it appreciated by the fairer sex.

John toted the apparel back to the Mercantile, smiling to all he passed. Miss Kallahan was coming, he told himself. When she arrived, she would have a suitable explanation for her tardiness. Pity that Medford's nearest telegraph was at Winchester, the other side of the Basin River. Come to think about it, it was quite easy to see why she couldn't let him know of her belated arrival. Nor could he send a telegram to inquire of her whereabouts until the spring rains let up. The river was over its banks, and the Melhume boys had set the one bridge linking Medford to Winchester afire two weeks previous. He brightened, feeling considerably better with that revelation.

The evening of the box supper arrived. Shortly after seven o'clock that night, John walked into the one-room schoolhouse that doubled as the community meeting hall.

Everyone who could attend was here tonight. Floralee Thomas had shoved her teacher's desk to one side, and a long table had been erected between two sawhorses. Cloths borrowed from the ladies of the planning committee made a colorful background for the boxed suppers. His eyes searched for a glimpse of Freeman's granddaughter. Now if the town wanted to play Cupid, why couldn't Freeman be as eager to introduce his granddaughter as Veda was her niece?

Veda was in charge of the festivities. There was an intent clear on her face tonight. John sighed. For the briefest of moments, he wondered which box contained Freeman's granddaughter's offering, then decided he didn't want to know. *Temptation, get thee aside.*

He glanced around the room, wishing that Hope were here so he could introduce her to the doubting Thomases and end the town's annoying speculation.

Threading his way across the floor, he paused to speak to his regular customers. He smiled, nodding to the widows who had taken up court in the long row of chairs lining the east wall. Their particular, odd ceremony puzzled him. Widows separated themselves in such a way that they seemed out of sync with others. The same bizarre ritual occurred at church socials; "Widow's Row" they called it. A woman over forty habitually went there within weeks of her husband's death. Companionship, he'd decided, was the reason. Wasn't it the same sense of aloneness that had led him to place that ad in the journal?

"There you are, John!" Veda sailed across the room, flapping a hand in the air to get his attention.

John whirled and tried to lose himself in the crowd, but Veda had already nailed him. Her shrill voice was drawing attention, the last thing he wanted.

She docked, breathless. Looping her arm through his, she smiled. "There you are. I was worried that you wouldn't come tonight."

John stiffened. "I'm a man of my word, Veda. I said I would be here, and here I am."

"Here you are, and I'm just sick. Ginger is still feeling a little under the weather, and she's asked me to make her apologies for her absence."

John's knees buckled with relief. A reprieve. The good Lord had granted him a reprieve!

"I'm sorry to hear that. I trust your niece will be up and about very soon."

"She will be—I'm having Doc come by in the morning. I'm hoping he will prescribe a tonic for her."

"Yes—a tonic would be just the thing."

Veda straightened when she saw the church elder's wife sailing in their direction. The tall, stout woman resembled a Scandinavian Viking with her shock of steel-colored hair and breastplate of flouncing lace.

"Heavens. Here comes that overbearing Pearl Eddings. She's going to insist that you purchase Cordella's box supper." John winced as Veda painfully tightened her grip on his arm.

"Let me do the talking," she ordered from the corner of her mouth. She smiled as the matronly woman approached. "Good evening, Pearl."

"Veda." Pearl's beady eyes flew over the couple, then landed on John. "Cordella's box is the one with the blue bow."

Stepping in front of John, Veda crossed her arms. "John's affianced, Pearl. He can't be buying your daughter's boxed supper."

Pearl's eyes narrowed, and John edged closer to peer over Veda's shoulder. He'd never seen eyes pulsate this way.

Pearl and Veda faced off.

"He's not married yet, Veda Fletcher."

"He will be, Pearl Eddings."

"And soon," John added, then closed his mouth. He located Cordella standing on the sidelines. The tall, bucktoothed girl wasn't exactly a head turner.

"Hummpt." Pearl leveled a finger at John. "Blue bow. You'll not regret it."

When Pearl departed, Veda patted John's arm. "The very idea of Pearl thinking you'd be interested in Cordella."

"Thank you for coming to my rescue, Veda." Praise God, he was finally getting through to her!

"You're welcome, dear." Veda gave his arm another matronly pat, then absently tidied her hair before merging with the crowd. "Can't imagine what Pearl is thinking," John heard her mumble as she walked away. "Why, you've not even met my Ginger."

Chapter Nine

Don't ask questions—run!" Dan caught Hope's hand, and they bolted across the barnyard. Shots rang out. Water flew up from Luther Bennett's rain barrel sitting next to the feed trough.

They ducked into the barn as a hail of bullets riddled the outside walls. Striding toward a stall, Dan seized a horse and quickly threw his saddle on it.

"We can't take Luther's horse! That's stealing!"

"Luther's nephews mean business this time, Hope. I'll send money later. Get on!" Swinging Hope on behind him, he flanked the horse, and it galloped out of the barn. Bullets ricocheted off the trees as Dan rode toward the lane.

"Keep low!"

"I am! Ride faster!"

Lead whined overhead; Hope bent close to Dan's back, hiding her face in his thick shirt.

The Bennett boys stepped from the stand of trees and fired until the bullets were hitting thin air.

The horse galloped for what seemed like miles to Hope before Dan gradually slowed the pace. The horse was lathered, its sides heaving with exertion.

She gradually loosened her grip around Dan's middle, sick with fright when she saw the bright, moist, red stain on her arm. Blood.

"You're hurt!" she cried.

Favoring his left side, he slid off the horse and sank to the ground. The effort brought a fresh surge of red stain to his shirt. "Nothing to worry about . . . it's just a flesh wound."

She slid off and knelt beside him. "We've got to treat it!"

"We have to keep moving." He stood and took a handkerchief from his pocket, folded it into a triangle, and wedged it between his shoulder and shirt. Gaining his bearings, he climbed back on the horse. With his right arm, he hefted her astride.

Throughout the rest of the day, despite Hope's repeated protests, Dan refused to stop; he insisted through clenched teeth that they had to keep moving. By nightfall, he was beyond decision making. Barely conscious, he hung on to the saddle horn with one hand.

The distant rumble of thunder worried Hope. A spring storm was brewing, and she didn't want them to be caught out in it. "We've got to stop," she insisted. *Please, Father. Help us find shelter.*

You can't put God on demand! Papa's voice echoed in Hope's mind. But right now God was her only hope.

They rode on until she spied the mouth of a cave behind a bank of brush. Thunder was closer now, accompanied by sporadic lightning flashes. Dan didn't respond when she pointed to the shelter. Taking the reins out of his hand, she urged the horse through the thicket. Sliding off its back, she tied the animal to a low-hanging limb, then helped Dan off.

"I'm all right—just lost a little blood." His shirt was soaked and his features ashen. He'd lost a lot of blood; she didn't need medical knowledge to know that.

Stepping to the mouth of the cave, she peered inside. Wings fluttered in the black interior. Shuddering, she reached for Dan's arm and helped him through the narrow entrance.

Her strength was quickly overpowered by his weakness. It took all her might to get his considerable bulk through the cramped opening.

"Fire," Dan murmured. "Cold." He was shaking uncontrollably now.

"I'll get one started. Matches—"

"Find two flint stones—strike them together." Removing his coat, he lay down on it.

Once an old Indian had stopped by the parsonage. He'd shown Papa how to start a fire by using two flint stones, repeatedly striking them in a rapid fashion until a spark ignited the ember. But that had been so long ago. Could she remember how to do it?

Rain was falling when she emerged from the cave.

Quickly gathering handfuls of small sticks and leaves before they got too wet, she carried them into the cavern. It took awhile to locate the flint stones on the uneven ground, and even longer to get the hang of generating a spark. But after repeated failed attempts, the tinder finally caught. Smoke pillared up.

She sat back on her heels, exhausted. She kept her fears at bay by concentrating on what had to be done. The bleeding must be stopped or Dan would . . . she couldn't voice the thought. *Please, Father. Grant me wisdom in this hour of need. I'm sorry I've been so doubtful lately. I'll do better—please don't let Dan die because of my foolishness.*

Grow up, Hope. She bit down on her lip until she tasted blood, recalling Dan's gruff admonition. "I'm trying," she whispered. "I'm trying."

The cave was shallow but deep enough for shelter, the ceiling low but high enough for the fire to draw well.

Fighting panic, Hope piled more sticks on the fire. Dan was attempting to shrug out of his shirt when she turned to check on him. His face was pale, his forehead glistening with sweat.

Her heart was drawn to him, and her mind traveled back to less than a week ago when he had cared so diligently for her. If it were possible, she would take part of his pain. "Wait, let me do that."

Her stomach pitched at the sight of the angry wound in his left shoulder. Too weak to argue, he allowed her to peel the last of the bloody fabric away.

"Don't you die on me," she pleaded, her hands shaking as

she probed the injury. She checked him front and back. "The bullet went through, so I won't have to dig it out."

Dan grunted. "Do you have the feeling we make a bad team?"

She grinned, laying her head on his good shoulder for a blissful moment. "It would seem our luck isn't the best." Straightening, she wiped the moisture out of her eyes. "Lie still. I need to clean the wound."

He winced. "This is going to hurt, isn't it?"

She didn't have the heart to tell him how much. "I'll need your hat."

His eyes gave her permission to remove it.

She left the cave and returned momentarily with water. Ripping his shirt into pieces, she dipped the cloth into the rainwater, her hand pausing above the injury. "Ready?"

"Be gentle." As painful as the injury was, he was still able to tease. She took small solace in that. "The bullet must have hit something as it went through—it's still bleeding hard."

Touching the cloth to the wound, she recoiled as he sucked in his breath. "Now, Grunt," she chided, trying to disguise her terror, "were you gentle with me when I ran away?"

"No . . . not overly."

"I remember that." How well she remembered how scared she'd been when he'd physically dragged her back to the cabin. He'd not been gentle at all that day.

The water in the hat turned bright red as she continued to cleanse the area.

Catching her arm, he gazed at her. "I was afraid for your life that day. Do you know what would have happened—"

She gently laid her finger across his lips. "Shush, you're making the bleeding worse. I know what you did that day, Dan." She looked away for fear her eyes would reveal more of her feelings than she wanted. "Thank you."

He held tightly to her hand, even when he could have released it.

She shook her head, fear crowding her throat. The wound was bleeding heavily now. "I don't know how to stop the bleeding."

"Cauterize it," he gritted between clenched teeth.

"How?"

"My knife . . . in the fire . . . get the blade red-hot."

"Oh, Dan." She closed her eyes, faint. Could she do such a thing? The pain would be unbearable.

His grip tightened. "Do it, Hope. I'll bleed to death if you don't."

She wouldn't allow him to bleed to death. No matter how vile the cure, she had to do it. Rising, her eyes searched the dim interior. She needed more wood. "I'll be right back."

"Don't take all night," he murmured.

She returned breathless, her hair falling down from its pins. Dropping to her knees, she heaped more sticks on the fire.

"Knife . . . sheath, left side. Hurry, Hope . . ."

"I'm hurrying." Rolling him gently to his right side, she

located the knife and removed it. She quickly wiped the blade on a piece of petticoat, then laid it over the flames.

"I can't do this." The mere thought of laying that red-hot brand across his tender flesh made her dizzy.

Rolling to his back, Dan closed his eyes. "Any woman who can make Joe Davidson clean house can do anything."

Smiling between her tears, she reached for the knife. The blade glowed bright red. Closing her eyes, she willed her hands steady.

Dear God, let him lose consciousness. Don't make him go through this pain awake.

"Do it," he whispered. "Now!" Blood gushed from the wound, drenching him and her dress.

Bringing the tip of the blade down, she mashed it to the lesion. Dan's agonized scream as the blade singed the open flesh tore at her heart. The stench of burning flesh filled her nose, and she fought the tide of dizziness that threatened to overcome her. Struggling for breath, she bit her bottom lip until she tasted blood. She sobbed openly now.

When his scream became a low moan, she dared to look down. The wound barely oozed now. With a cry of relief, she flung the knife aside and collapsed on his now unconscious form. "I'm so sorry, darling . . . so sorry."

Her prayer had been answered.

She tended the fire all night, watching Dan sleep, checking every few moments to see if the steady rise and fall of his chest abated. He would live—the bleeding had stopped. She'd changed the bandage only twice in an hour.

From the moment they'd met, she'd caused him nothing but trouble; he'd done nothing but try to help her. And now he lay near death, his face pale and lifeless, all because of her. She'd tried to settle a feud that had gone on for years, and in the process, she'd hurt this wonderful man.

Blinking back hot tears, she listened to the rain spatter on the ground outside the cavern, staring at the small fire that gave off a little warmth. She'd never been more miserable, more alone, in her life. Once her life had been simple, secure. What had gone wrong? Was God punishing her for ignoring Aunt Thalia's wishes? Thalia hadn't wanted her or her sisters to be mail-order brides. Why hadn't they listened—why hadn't she listened? Now, because of her, a man was wounded.

Why does Dan have to suffer when all he's done is try to protect me? I don't understand, and I don't know that I've got enough faith to accept this change in my life without knowing the reason.

She threw more wood on the fire, glancing up when she saw Dan's eyes flicker, then open. He spoke, his voice thick with pain. "I hope you harbor no thoughts of ever being a doctor."

Dropping to his side, she threw her arms around his neck, careful not to disturb the wound. "I know the pain was awful, but the bleeding's stopped now."

"Careful . . . ," he warned.

She gingerly hugged him to her chest. "I thought you were never going to wake up."

"What time is it?"

"I'm not sure, somewhere near daybreak, I think." The night had been the longest of her life.

"Is there any water?"

"It's still raining—I'll catch some in the hat. When it's light, I'll look for a stream."

Outside, she washed the blood from the hat, then caught fresh rainfall and was back within minutes. Cradling his head, she helped him drink, tenderly blotting water that spilled from his mouth.

"Did you get my saddle off the horse?"

"No . . . but I will."

He nodded, licking his dry lips.

"Is the saddle special?"

"Brother gave it to me . . ."

"Sleep," she whispered when his eyes shut with pain. If only there was more she could do.

She moved back to the fire and began to doze, her dreams filled with images of dirty men who stealthily crept toward the mouth of the cave. Animals lured by the scent of blood.

Dan's feverish mumbling brought her out of her confused state.

Though the air was cool, he was sweating profusely. She laid her hand against his forehead. He was so warm. Drawing her coat up to his chin, her mind raced. He was feverish. Infection! She had no means to treat infection. What would Aunt Thalia do? Break the fever—make certain that he drank lots of water.

Stepping out of her petticoat, she used the knife to split it apart. The fabric was soiled, but she'd scrub it in rainwater and use it for fresh bandages and a sling.

When the laundry was drying near the fire, she bathed Dan's hot face, chest, and arms, repeating the process throughout the day as his fever continued to rise.

"Lie still," she whispered as he thrashed about on the bed pallet.

When he shoved her coat aside, Hope patiently drew it back over him, knowing a chill at this point could mean death. Late in the afternoon, she broke sticks from the bushes at the mouth of the cave and wedged them into crevices in the cave wall. She patiently washed more of the petticoat and hung the strips to dry. Unsaddling the horse, she gave it water out of the hat, then lugged the heavy hand-tooled leather saddle into the cave.

When darkness fell, she was able to cleanse Dan's wounds again and apply fresh bandages.

A couple of times he opened his eyes, but she wasn't sure he recognized her. Was she doing enough? Sitting beside him, she studied his features in the firelight. He had a strong face, well defined, ruggedly handsome. He knew what he was about—a man with a purpose in life. What had he told her? He wanted to buy some land in Virginia and farm it. Farming sounded very nice.

Dan Sullivan was exactly the kind of man Aunt Thalia would approve of: a good man, a godly man. Hope had seen his faith, experienced it. In many ways he was making her stronger in her own beliefs. At least he made her stop and think; that was something.

Her thoughts turned to the man she'd promised to marry. Somewhere tonight, he was waiting for her, wondering about her. Poor John. If only she was able to send a note, explain why she hadn't arrived on the stage more than four weeks ago. Did he know about the stagecoach robbery? Had he wired Aunt Thalia and inquired about his intended bride's whereabouts?

Her gaze focused on the man lying beside the fire. *Oh, God, I'm not questioning your wisdom—truly I'm not.*

If only she'd met Dan before—no. Events happened for a reason. Papa had taught her that. But if she was going to start relying on her own faith instead of Papa's, she must trust that God watched over her.

"Grow up, Hope. It's time you took responsibility for your life," she murmured, getting up to bathe Dan's face again.

Why would she think Dan would even want her after all the trouble she'd caused? At this point he probably prayed for the hour when he could hand her over to another man.

The thought stung. She gently smacked his sleeping form. "How dare you think that. I'd make you a good wife. You'd see, I'd be everything you ever wanted and more."

Outside, darkness covered the earth. A gray drizzle replaced the earlier downpour. Toward daybreak even the drizzle gave way to watery sunshine.

Dan was resting easier now. Hope bathed his face and arms, coaxing him to drink from the hat between parched lips. When he was restless, she soothed him in low tones, reassuring him everything was all right.

She told him stories of when she was young—of the time Papa cut the wrong Christmas tree and brought it home. She and her sisters, Faith and June, had popped corn and made colorful paper chains to hang on the fragrant cedar boughs. But the tree that year was so small Hope had cried. She'd had her heart set on a tall, rather splendid pine that was twice the height of the parsonage ceiling. Papa had dried her eyes and promised that next year they'd either get a taller ceiling or he'd let her have whatever tree she wanted, provided he could get it through the door.

Her thoughts drifted aimlessly. Luther and Harriet. What were they doing tonight? Had they retaliated by stealing something from Lyndon? Were they mad as hatters at Dan and her?

Well, *she* hadn't given the pig back. And she certainly wouldn't have given Fawn permission to let it loose if she'd known what the girl was planning.

Had the world gone mad?

Weren't Christians supposed to be different from unbelievers? Fawn had said her family believed in God, yet Lyndon stole from his own brother. Papa had contended that a Christian wasn't perfect, sinned just as hard as the next person, but a Christian was bothered by the fact and tried harder not to sin. Would Lyndon realize that family was far more important than a pig?

During the long hours in the cave, she read from Dan's Bible. She had part of Genesis memorized, except for all the begets. Dan would be proud of her.

The sun shined warm as Hope moved to the mouth of

the cave, her face lifted toward the heavens. Her strength was ebbing; she hadn't slept in two nights, and she didn't think she could go on.

"I can't do this, Lord," she whispered. "I haven't enough faith—I try, try so hard, but I can't hold on to you. You just keep slipping through my fingers. Please strengthen me, Father; grant me powerful faith—like David's faith as he faced Goliath—so I can be of benefit to this injured man."

Resentment swelled within her. Papa had always said to expect the unexpected. She'd gotten on that stage full of hopes and dreams, her thoughts only of John. Her future had seemed rosy and bright. Today she was falling in love with another man and wondering if she or he would live to see another day.

Toward dawn the third day, Hope was startled awake by the horse. Her eyes flew open, and she wondered what had disturbed it. A wild animal?

The horse neighed softly.

Reaching for the rifle, she crept to the mouth of the cave and peered out. Daylight illuminated the small clearing. The horse, definitely upset about something, suddenly reared. Hope heard the rein snap. Seconds later, she heard the animal thrashing off through the underbrush.

Bounding to her feet, she ran outside, foolishly thinking she could somehow catch it. A twig snapped, and she whirled.

A cougar, the size of Aunt Thalia's fainting couch, crouched near the mouth of the cave. Its yellow-eyed gaze held hers captive, its tail slowly twitching.

Dan was in that cave—unprotected, alone.

Helpless.

Swallowing against her rising hysteria, Hope lifted the rifle and took careful aim. She fired twice. When she dared to open her eyes, she saw the tail end of the cat bounding off through the underbrush.

Sinking to her knees, she dropped the gun and stared at the spot where the cougar had been not two minutes ago.

Throwing her head back, she addressed God in a way that would have sent Papa in search of the biggest hickory switch he could find.

"I can't stand anymore of this! Faith! I need faith!"

When she came back into the cave, Dan was sitting up. He glanced at her, his face flushed, his hair tousled, a heavy growth of beard covering his face.

"You look nice."

Cradling his head in his arms, he muttered, "Why are you yelling at God?"

She propped the rifle against the cave wall. "I've tried talking. He isn't listening."

Lying back down, Dan closed his eyes. "Come here."

She moseyed closer, feeling ashamed of herself. Reaching for her hand, he gently pulled her down beside him. Holding her close, he said softly, "God doesn't respond to shouts."

Emotions overcame her, and she broke into tears, sobbing against his good shoulder. It felt so wonderfully good to have someone hold her, someone to help worry for a moment.

"I'm sorry—it's just that you're so sick, and I had to hurt you so badly, and then there was this big cat that scared off the horse—"

"Cat?" He stopped her, his voice guarded now. "Big cat?"

"Yes—cougar. I shot at it. It's gone."

"That's what woke me—where's the horse?"

"Gone." She cried harder at his frustrated groan. "I'm no good at anything; I'm just a mess."

"No," he said, patting her back tenderly. "You're not a mess."

She cried harder, allowing the fear and frustration to pour from her eyes.

"Think we should pray about this?"

She nodded, snuggling closer to his warmth. He always knew the right thing to do.

In a voice weak in energy but strong in conviction, he softly asked for God's help. "Father, forgive us when we don't rely on you. It's been a rough week, God, and our faith has been tested to the limits. Watch over us, make us ever mindful you're still here running the show."

"And, Father, I'm really sorry I yelled at you," Hope whispered. "I'm just a mess."

Drawing her closer, Dan buried his face in her hair. "He knows you're sorry, but he likes to hear it."

"How did you get so nice?"

"Practice."

She felt his weak grin.

"Well, I'm going to practice harder."

"Go to sleep. Unless I'm mistaken, it's still very early."

Right now, leaving the comfort of his arms was unthinkable, but he needed rest.

"I'll be close by if you need me."

"Hope?"

"Yes?"

"Try to keep out of trouble until I can get over this . . ." His voice trailed as sleep once again claimed him.

She moved away, settling where she would be close if he needed her. She had plenty to keep her busy—there was always Genesis . . .

The fire burned low. Outside, a new dawn was breaking. Finches chirped in nearby trees; tender shoots of new grass pushed their heads through the damp soil. God's world woke to a new day.

Inside, Bible folded across her chest, Hope slept, feeling safe in God's love for the first time in a long time.

Chapter Ten

By the fourth night Dan was well enough to travel. Hope wasn't convinced that his strength was sufficient for the long walk ahead of them, but the meager rations she'd been able to supply had dwindled to nothing. If they didn't move on, some lone hermit would one day discover their remains in the cave.

"What should we do about the saddle?"

The look on Dan's face confirmed her fears: the beautiful, hand-tooled leather saddle was one of his prized possessions—perhaps his only prized possession.

"My brother made it for me. Gave it to me on my sixteenth birthday." His eyes caressed the worn hide that must have held memories too numerous to count. Days of idyllic youth; months, even years, served in the war. Hope wanted to hold him, cry out at the injustice of it all. He was too weak to carry the saddle, and she didn't have the strength to oblige.

"I'll carry it," she said. She couldn't bear to see it left behind because of her. If it took everything in her, she would carry it.

"You can't carry it. Help me get it on my right shoulder. I'll carry it."

With considerable effort, they got the heavy saddle on his back. Hope hurt just looking at him. "You can't carry that all the way to Medford."

"I'll carry it as far as I can. It's the best we can do."

Was he hoping for a miracle—someone to come along and carry the saddle for him?

Hope wasn't. She was about to give up on miracles. God was putting every obstacle imaginable in front of them, and for what purpose?

"Do you have any idea where we are?" she asked as they started off. Twilight settled over the verdant hillsides, and a warm breeze ruffled bare tree branches. Daffodils pushed their heads up through the ground, and crocuses bloomed by the roadside.

"The map's in my saddlebag."

And the saddlebag was at Luther's. Dan hadn't had time to go back and retrieve it in their hasty getaway.

"So what are we going to do? We have no money, no means to buy either a horse or a map. We don't know where we are or how far we still have to travel."

"We're not more than three or four miles from the Bennetts'. I looked at the map shortly before we met up with

Luther and Harriet. Medford is to the east, maybe another thirty miles."

"Thirty miles!" Hope's heart sank. "That's a long way to walk."

"It could be less, Hope. I'm just not sure."

He bent low as the weight of the saddle sapped his strength. Men had it worse than women, Hope decided. They had to act strong, no matter how they felt. Women, on the other hand, could whine.

"How are you?" she ventured, keeping an eye on his pace.

"Top of the world. How about you?"

"Same."

They traveled by back roads, hoping to go unnoticed. Hope halfway hoped that someone would come along; Dan could put the saddle in the wagon and he could claim it later. It seemed like hours before she heard the welcome sounds of a stream.

"Water."

Dan forged the way through the undergrowth, trampling a path to the water. Throwing the saddle aside, he dropped to the ground and flattened himself to the bank, drinking in the cold, clear water.

Hope quickly joined him. She drank until she had to come up for air. "I've never, ever tasted anything so good." She dunked her face beneath the water and emerged, sputtering.

Dan was sitting up, trying to remove his right boot with his right hand.

"Here." She leaned over and removed it for him. Her eyes located the holes in his socks. The cloth had rubbed away, and blood oozed onto the fabric. "Blisters."

That's all he needed—blisters *and* a gunshot wound.

"I wish I had some butter to rub on them."

He grunted. "If I had butter, it wouldn't go on my feet."

She lay down, rolling to her back. Overhead, stars twinkled in a cloudless sky.

Butter—and hot biscuits. Eggs and ham. Hotcakes and rich maple syrup. They hadn't eaten a decent meal in days. Dan refused to admit it, but he was weak, half starved. The heavy saddle was taking its toll on his energy. How much longer before he was forced to leave it behind?

"I'll carry the saddle for a while."

"You can't lift the saddle, let alone carry it." He lay back, easing his shoulder into a comfortable position.

"I'm hungry," she admitted, more to herself than as a complaint.

"I'll see if I can scare up some game."

"No, tell me what to do, and I'll do it."

"My darling Miss Kallahan. I would let you, but I'd like to eat sometime tonight."

She blushed, recalling the inordinately long waits he'd endured between meals lately. But if he recalled, he'd always eaten; she'd not let him go hungry. Acorns and nuts gathered near the mouth of the cave. She tried running a rabbit down on foot once, but that had consumed all her energy. She wasn't fast or clever enough to best nature.

Toward morning, they finally met a wagon. Hope sat

beside Dan on the side of the road; both were too fatigued to go on. Dan had carried the saddle all night; he couldn't walk another step.

Hope sprang up when she spotted a young man who looked no more than fifteen wielding the buckboard. Sawing back on the reins, he brought the wagon to a halt. A goat was tied to the back. "Havin' trouble?" the youth said.

It would take all day to tell him how much trouble they'd had, so Hope came right to the point.

"A cougar spooked our horse, and it ran off. My brother is injured and needs medical care. Can we catch a ride with you to the next town?" When she saw hesitancy in his eyes, she rushed on. "Could you at least haul his saddle in the wagon for us? As soon as my brother's able, he'll be back to get it."

The boy eyed her suspiciously. They must look a fright—clothes torn and dirty, Dan unshaven, her hair wild as a March hare.

"Muddy Flats is five miles down the road. I spent the night with a friend there, and I'm on my way home to do chores. I'm an hour late; Ma would have my hide if I was to take you all the way back into Muddy Flats and leave those heifers bawling to be milked."

Hope sagged against the wagon. "We really do need your help." Their feet were in bad shape, but they could take it slower, walk the remaining distance to Muddy Flats; but Dan couldn't carry the saddle, and she couldn't bear to see him leave it behind. "If you'll just take the saddle—"

"Ma wouldn't hold for that. Says we ain't to take anything that we don't earn."

"I'm not giving you the saddle; I'm only asking you to keep it for us until we return to claim it."

The boy shook his head. "Cain't. I don't know you folks, and that'd be like taking something that wasn't mine."

Dan slowly got to his feet and walked toward the wagon. The blisters caused his gait to be slow and uneven. Leaning on the wagon's side, he took a deep breath. "Would you make a trade? My saddle for whatever you offer."

"Dan," Hope murmured.

Dan repeated the proposition. "My saddle for whatever you got."

The boy eyed the fine-looking saddle, breaking into a youthful grin. "It's a fine saddle. How 'bout I trade you . . . a goat for it?"

"Yeah—how about that," Dan grumbled.

"Oh, Dan! You can't trade your saddle for a goat." Hope eyed the mangy critter tied to the back of the wagon. It was worse than the pig.

The goat bleated in protest.

Dan turned away. "The goat can walk; the saddle can't."

"It's a deal?" the boy cried.

"It's a deal, Son."

The boy hopped out of the wagon and made a beeline for his prize. Hope hurried along behind him. "We'll be back—will you trade back if we bring money instead of the goat?"

"Money?"

"Twenty-five dollars." It was all the money Hope had to her name, money she'd made sewing and looking after old Mrs. Johnson when she took ill a few years back. The money was in her missing bags, but when she got them back she'd have the money. And she'd use every bit of it to buy Dan's saddle back.

"Twenty-five dollars!" The boy clearly couldn't believe his luck. "I'll trade back for twenty-five dollars!"

Minutes later, the old wagon rumbled away with Dan's saddle lying on the front seat beside the boy. Before he left, Hope got his name.

"Take good care of that saddle!" she yelled as the buck-board rattled off.

"Yes, ma'am! You take good care of my goat!"

Her bottom lip curled with disgust. She'd take care of that goat—but she'd be back for Dan's saddle.

And Clifford Baker had better hand it over.

"How far did he say it was to the next town?"

Walking was easier now that Hope didn't have to worry about Dan and the saddle, but the sun was full up now. Birds flew overhead on their way to breakfast.

"The boy said five miles."

Five miles. It might as well be five hundred. Would she ever see Medford? or John Jacobs? Did she even care any longer? She was beginning to think her intended husband was a curse. As horrible as the past few weeks had been, she still wasn't in any hurry to reach her destination. She was in even less hurry to leave Dan's company. Once they reached Medford, she would never see him again.

"We'll come across a farm before much longer. Maybe we'll find a kind soul who'll offer us a hot meal."

So far, strangers had proved ruinous. She wasn't sure she would accept a meal from a Good Samaritan without serious thought. Still, the idea of a hot meal was delicious to think about. Hotcakes dripping with melted butter, fat sausage patties, cups of cold, spring-cooled milk. She'd taken food for granted in the past, but never again would she be gluttonous without the hurtful knowledge that somewhere, someone was terribly hungry.

Dan pulled the goat behind him, slowing their progress. The animal was stubborn, intent on eating everything she could snatch between steps. They had followed a riverbank for the last hour. The wet hem of Hope's dress slapped against her ankles, but she was barely aware of the discomfort.

Katie Morris, the woman Dan once loved, popped into her mind. Envy only added to her misery. Had Dan looked at Katie the way he had looked at her in the cave during his conscious moments, with helpless masculine vulnerability? Had he held Katie in his arms, whispered his love, and planned a future with her?

Think of more pleasant things, Hope. But there wasn't anything pleasant to think about. She was wet, tired, and hungry, and the goat was getting on her nerves. She couldn't imagine where Dan found the enthusiasm to push ahead when she knew he must be in fierce pain and probably willing to shoot the goat. During the night they milked the animal and drank the warm liquid for sustenance, but Hope's stomach demanded solid food.

"Can't we stop now?"

"Soon—there has to be a family living along the riverbank somewhere."

They walked on until Dan suddenly stopped. The goat plowed into him. Hope plowed into the goat.

Untangling herself from the animal, she pressed closer to Dan, peering around his shoulder. "What is it?" *Please, God. Let it be food and shelter.*

"A cabin."

"A cabin?" She cried out with relief when she spotted a fair-sized dwelling, barn, and outbuilding in a secluded grove. Two mules stood inside a small pen. Her eyes followed Dan's to a garden patch not yet plowed. There was no movement inside the house, no sign of life.

"What do you think?" she whispered.

"I don't know—looks like the place is occupied."

Someone lived here. Food. Warmth. Dry clothing. "Do we take a chance and see if they're friendly?" She held her breath as he studied the situation. His gaze shifted from the barn back to the cabin where a wisp of smoke curled from the chimney.

"We don't have a choice. You need clean clothes and hot food. Maybe we can buy both from whoever lives here."

"How? We have no money."

"I can give a promissory note that my agency will pay for anything we use."

She wanted to wring her hands. "What if no one's there?"

"Then we break down the door and help ourselves. We'll still pay for it later."

How could he be so calm when her heart was racing with anticipation?

She scrambled after him as Dan started down the gentle incline, dragging the goat behind him. She was encouraged when there was no visible sign of interest in their approach.

Red-and-white-checked curtains covered the front windows, but there was no sign of life behind them. Dan hauled the reticent goat up the steps, and Hope followed.

The two exchanged a resigned look, then Dan rapped on the door.

A faint sound penetrated the heavy wood.

"Did you hear that?" Hope whispered.

Dan nodded, then knocked again, harder this time. The faint cry came again.

"Hello?" Dan called, nudging the door open a crack. The old portal groaned on squeaky hinges.

Hope looked around Dan's shoulder, trying to see into the dim interior.

Someone—something, she couldn't make out who or what—was stretched out in a mammoth bed, beckoning them to enter.

Glancing up at Dan, she swallowed. "It wants us to come in."

"Then let's go in."

Hope took a deep breath. No telling what they were getting into this time.

Stepping back, she pointed to the goat. "She goes first."

Chapter Eleven

C ome in!" the figure in the bed yelled. "Been waiting for ya!"

Hope entered hesitantly. "Is anything wrong?" she asked.

Dan tied the bleating animal to the porch railing and strode inside.

Nudging her shoulder, Dan whispered, "Don't get involved. We're here for a day's rest; we move out tonight. Whoever this person is or whatever problems he or she is having, we aren't getting involved. Understand?"

"Oh, absolutely," she whispered back. "We're not getting involved."

It was obvious whoever—or whatever—was lying on that bed did have a problem. The cabin's state of disarray, the way the individual's hair looked as if he or she had thrown it in the air and jumped under it—something was wrong, all right.

Dan was right; they couldn't take on one more person's troubles. Every hour they tarried just caused more needless worry for John Jacobs.

Hope's eyes roamed the stale-smelling room. The log home was huge, with massive pieces of hand-hewn furniture crammed about the one enormous room.

"Come closer. Don't be afraid."

Hope crept toward the voice, holding tight to Dan's hand. "Are you ill?"

"Hurt my leg—been praying the Boss would send someone to help." The figure motioned her nearer. "Don't be shy; these old eyes cain't see as good as they once did. Come closer."

Though Hope would have complied, Dan's steely grip restrained her. Clearing his throat, he said, "We're just passing through. We saw your cabin and thought we might impose on your hospitality."

A cackle rent the air, startling Hope. Wide-eyed, she stepped back.

"You're welcome to anything I have, but you'll have to fix it!" the voice crowed. "Pete's sakes—come closer. I cain't see ya."

Wrenching free from Dan, Hope approached the bed. The voice sounded friendly enough. And it sure wasn't Big Joe or Frog trying to trick them. "How long have you been here?" Hope asked.

"Abed? Two days now. I was startin' to think I was a goner for sure."

Hope edged nearer, focusing on the lone figure. The dim

light revealed an old woman lying abed, her foot propped up on a stained pillow, her snow-white hair in wild confusion.

"Hello," she said as Hope bent closer. "That's better. Why, ain't you a pretty little thing. What brings you clean out this way?"

"Well—"

Dan intervened. "We're on our way to Medford, ma'am. We'd hoped to be there by now, but we've been delayed."

A pair of faded molasses-colored eyes looked him up and down. "You're welcome to stay the night with me. Hafta sleep on the floor; the bears are a real bother lately, comin' around at night looking for food. It won't be safe to sleep outside or in the barn."

Hope turned to look at the floor. Would she ever sleep in a real bed again?

Dan nodded. "Thank you for your hospitality. We'll be moving on tonight."

"Tonight! Why, land sakes. A body shouldn't be out there in the dark. You'll stay the night and strike off early in the mornin'."

Dan glanced at Hope.

The old woman smiled. She didn't have a tooth in her mouth. "Glad to have the company. Maybe your wife will take a look at my wound. Tried to clean it myself, but ain't had no luck."

"I'd be happy to." Hope located a bucket near the sink and filled it at the well in back of the house.

Dipping a cup of fresh water from the bucket, Hope held

the old woman's head as she drank thirstily. "Oh my, that tastes good. I've been makin' my peace with the Boss," she said, dropping weakly back to the pillow. "Not many folks come this way. I figured I was about to be called home."

"How did you hurt your leg?" Hope busied herself straightening the rumpled sheets. The bedclothes were a disgrace. They needed a good washing.

"Had a little mishap with the ax."

"You were chopping wood?"

"Choppin' at it. Charlie died last fall. Pneumonie fever, I'd say. My husband was a good man; had enough wood laid up for the whole winter. But now it's gone, and I'm forced to do somethin' about it." She lifted the injured leg, chuckling. "At least Charlie left the old ax sharp."

"Do you have any medicines?" Hope asked. She could cleanse the old woman's leg and apply salve, then properly care for Dan's shoulder.

The woman raised up on a frail arm, her eyes on the sling on Dan's left arm. "Are you feelin' poorly, Son? You're looking a mite peaked."

Before Dan could answer, Hope fielded the question. "We've been walking for days. I apologize for our appearance. We look a sight. I'm Hope, and this is Dan."

"Hope, huh? Well, you're aptly named, young'un. 'Cause that's sure what you've brought me. I'm Letty McGregor. Pleased to meet you. The Boss answered my prayer."

"The Boss?"

"The Big Man—the Almighty. He's my boss—" She

paused, her razor-sharp eyes pinning Hope. "Ain't he yours?"

"Oh yes, ma'am," Hope said. "He is." Papa would have switched her good if she'd ever called the Lord "Boss." Just didn't seem proper.

Letty pointed a bony finger at a shelf on the far wall. "See those jars and cups there? They've got herbs and such in them. Bring that biggest jar over here and a bowl to mix in." She glanced at Dan. "Son, would you mind checkin' on my mules? I fear they've not got a drop of water. Haven't been able to tend them since I got hurt. Might have rained, but I ain't heard it."

"Yes, ma'am."

"I'd appreciate that, young fellow. They've been faithful mules."

Hope picked up the big jar of herbs and carried it to the bed, then searched for a bowl in the messy kitchen, jumping back, startled, when her hand encountered a roach.

"You've got a mighty good-lookin' man there," Letty called. "My Charlie was powerful handsome, too."

Yes, Dan was powerful handsome. Any woman would be proud to claim him. But he wasn't hers. "How long were you and Mr. McGregor married?"

"Nigh on to sixty-seven years." Letty lay back on her pillow, staring at the ceiling. "Come from Missouri, you know. I was helpin' Papa farm when Charlie comes along lookin' for work. Papa hired him for room and board and a dollar a month. I was fifteen at the time. The first six dollars Charlie earned, we up and got married." She shook her head, her lined face pale and drawn. Hope suspected she hadn't eaten in two days. "Charlie was a fine man, God rest his soul. Buried out back—you'd see his grave if you was to look."

Hope brought the bowl and a wooden spoon to the bed.

"Take a couple spoonfuls of that powder and add about half as much water." Letty watched Hope's movements. "That's it—now, mix it up real good until it's thick as mud."

Hope wrinkled her nose as the vile smell permeated the area.

Letty chuckled. "Smells like the outhouse, but it works."

When the mixture met the approval of Letty's critical eye, the old woman uncovered her left leg.

Hope stepped back, sucking in a deep breath. The wound was bright red with the beginning of infection.

"It looks bad, but the salve will fix it right up. Spread it on the cut; by morning it'll be workin' on the poison."

Dan returned, carrying a few sticks of wood in his good arm. Hope jumped up to help him.

"You shouldn't be doing this," she scolded, taking the bundle from his arms.

"If you're going to fuss over me, do it by serving me a hot breakfast," he bantered lightly.

They pitched in and got a roaring fire going in the wood-stove. Hope set a kettle of fresh water to boil.

"Bless you young'uns' hearts." Letty watched the activity from the bed. "I sure could do with a cup of tea when you get the time."

"Yes, ma'am, hot tea coming right up." Hope eyed the sink piled high with dirty dishes. No one was drinking or eating a morsel until she did something about that.

"There's pork, beef, and deer in the smokehouse, Dan. And there's a hen or two in the chicken coop. There's plenty of eggs out there waitin' to be gathered. You'll find canned goods in the cellar. Land sakes, this couldn't have come at a worse time," Letty complained. "Spring comin' on and I haven't got nary a potato in the ground. Ain't even got the soil tilled. Looks like I'm not gonna be able to now."

"We'll find everything we need, Mrs. McGregor. You just rest." Hope moved about the small kitchen, moving quickly to restore cleanliness and order.

"While you're thinkin' on breakfast, maybe your man will come sit by me—let me have a look at that shoulder."

Dan's eyes darted to the green mass covering Letty's leg, then back to Hope.

"It ain't purty to look at, but this stuff'll fix the problem. Now come over here; let me see why you got that arm in a sling."

"He was shot." Hope pushed Dan toward the chair beside Letty's bed. He sat down, looking as if she'd thrown him before a firing squad.

Letty's brows went up. "Bullet wound, huh? You running from the law?"

"No, ma'am." Dan straightened defensively. "I am the law. I got this wound in the line of duty."

Grunting, the old woman leaned over the side of the bed,

peeling the bandage aside. Her eyes assessed the wound. "When Charlie built the house there was a small band of Comanches livin' nearby. They was a mean lot, causing all kinds of trouble. After a while they decided we meant them no harm, even began comin' by for a cup of coffee or a biscuit I'd hand out. They shore loved my strong coffee—said they could hunt for days without tirin' after drinkin' a cup. They're the ones that taught me about herbs and such." Dan winced as her fingers examined the wound. "I trust the Boss for healin', but I believe he helps us by providin' plants and such toward that healin'. Herbs have been all Charlie and I've had through the years." She grunted. "Worked real well till Charlie up and died on me."

Hope watched Letty tend the wounded shoulder, her eyes trying to tease Dan into a better mood.

Letty chuckled. "You two remind me of the way me and Charlie was when we first had eyes for each other. Couldn't git enough lookin'."

"Mrs. McGregor, we're not—," Hope began, compelled to explain the situation, but Dan stopped her.

"Hope would appreciate a bath, if you'd be so kind."

Letty cackled out loud. "And a comb wouldn't be too far amiss. Traveling without nary a thing, are you?" Her sharp-eyed gaze missed little. "Must not afigured on being gone long."

"No, ma'am. We didn't figure on being gone long." Hope quickly averted her gaze for fear of bursting out laughing. Neither had figured on being gone this long, and that was the complete truth.

"We've had to travel slowly because of the wound," Hope admitted, absently patting Dan's back.

"Well, the wound don't look good. You boil some water, and we'll get some hot compresses on it. You're lucky the bullet went clean through."

Hope nodded solemnly. "We have the Boss to thank for that."

"Yes, coulda lost your man. Take that pot there and fill it with water, heat it to a roiling boil. Might as well get more pots goin' so you can wash up before we eat. You'll enjoy your meal more with the tangles out of your hair."

Smiling, Hope wondered if the old woman had any idea what her own hair looked like.

Settling back against the pillow, Letty sighed. "There's a pile of Charlie's shirts in the chest there against the foot of the bed. Might even find a dress or two for you, Hope, and some clean undergarments, if you don't mind wearin' someone else's duds."

Pure joy filled Hope. Clean clothing! "I wouldn't mind at all, thank you!"

"Should be me thankin' you. I'd a-been a goner if the Boss hadn't sent you my way."

Hope carried in buckets of water, refusing Dan's help. Carrying water was something she could do. "You rest that shoulder."

Soon the smallest pot was steaming. Letty still fretted from her bed. "There's muslin in the chest for bandages. Get a poultice on that shoulder; should look better by mornin'."

Hope quickly readied the bandages; then amid vehement protest, she sat Dan down at the table.

He eyed the bandages and hot water. "This is going to hurt."

"Not much."

"I've heard that before."

"Pour some of that hot water in the bowl, dip in the cloth, and let it cool just enough for him to bear it," Letty directed.

Hope followed the old woman's instructions, flinching each time Dan's face contorted with pain.

"This is for your own good," she whispered.

The muscle in his jaw worked as she alternated hot compresses. She thought his shoulder looked even angrier with treatment, but Letty looked satisfied.

"Now, spread the herbs on, heavy-like, and leave off the bandage until we eat." She watched Hope work, her bird-like eyes intent on Hope's job. "Those pots hot enough for bath water?"

Hope glanced toward the stove. "I think so."

"There's a copper tub in the back room, what I call my bathin' room. There's plenty of soap in there—nothin' fancy, but it'll get you clean. Towels aplenty."

Hope jumped up to check the pans of boiling water. The steamy liquid bubbled away. "I'll bathe right after we eat, Mrs. McGregor."

"Letty, sugar. Call me Letty, and you go on and take your bath. Won't hurt us to wait breakfast a spell longer, and you'll feel better. Your man and I can sit and talk awhile."

Hope glanced at Dan, and he nodded, holding his smarting shoulder. "Go ahead. I'll keep Mrs. McGregor company."

Hope smiled, aware that it was the last thing he wanted to do, but he was a gentleman. She located the oversized tub, worn smooth by frequent use. A stand containing soap and towels sat nearby. She quickly filled the tub with hot water, tempering it with a bucket of cold, then stripped out of the tattered dress and underclothes. She sank into the water up to her chin and closed her eyes in ecstasy.

When she climbed out of the tub and toweled dry half an hour later, she whispered, "Bless you, Letty. And thank you, Boss."

Letty's dress hung on her slight frame like a feed sack, but it was clean and gloriously dry. Hope began to wonder if she'd ever wear her own clothes again.

Had the stage line shipped her things to John? If so, what must he be thinking? Even when she did reach him, would he accept her story of why she was so late, or would he think she'd been sullied? Her cheeks grew hot at the thought. Big Joe, Frog, and Boris were rude and disgusting louts, but they'd respected her privacy. And Dan . . . Dan had been a perfect gentleman during their times of enforced confinement.

Sullied indeed! *Shame on you, John Jacobs, if you even think such a thing!*

When she returned to the main room, Letty was resting. Dan was dozing by the fire. He glanced up when she entered the room, his gaze appreciatively skimming her fresh-scrubbed appearance. The look spoke more than words ever could. He obviously liked what he saw in a manly, most exciting way. Shivers inundated her. Did he find her beautiful? desirable? Someone he would fall in love with if only she wasn't promised to another man?

She hurried to the stove. "You must be starved. I'll fix us something to eat, then heat water for your bath."

"Your man's already got the water boiling, though I told him not to be movin' about. Needs to keep that poultice on his shoulder," Letty said in a voice thick with sleep.

"He can be stubborn." Hope risked a smile at Dan.

"Aren't you in charge of breakfast?"

"Yes, sir. Coming right up." His sudden gruffness didn't bother her; it meant he was getting better.

Letty opened her eyes. "Charlie hung those hams and smoked beef up high enough the bears can't reach them. You'll need to go with her."

"I can get them, Letty—"

"I'll go with you." Dan reached for the lantern, then preceded Hope out of the cabin. "The smokehouse is behind the barn."

"How do you know where it is?"

"I scouted around while you were taking your bath." He frowned when he saw the goat chewing on the porch railing. "Fool pest."

Hope hurried to catch up. "Think Letty might be a criminal? Maybe she's harboring a band of miscreants on the property?"

He was unaffected by her feisty banter. "You're too trusting, Hope. Never take a stranger at his word, even if it is a kindly old woman bearing food and hot baths."

Hope nodded, sobering. He was far more experienced than she at these matters. Until now, she'd never traveled farther than a few miles from home. She trusted everyone, expecting them to be as honorable as she was. Having met men like Big Joe, Frog, Boris, and yes, even the Bennetts, she was learning that didn't hold true.

His smile made her warm inside. "You've done well. I'm not complaining."

She matched his long strides as they walked toward the smokehouse. "I don't feel as if I've done well. It's as if I've been put to a test and failed."

Dan opened the door to the narrow shed and hung the lantern on a nail. Hope pressed close, straining to see around him. "Be careful . . . there could be a bear in there."

"The only bear you have to worry about is me, Miss Kallahan."

She whacked his back playfully.

"Ouch."

Inside, the smokehouse was dark, the air pungent with smoked meat.

"Even you getting shot was my fault," she reminded him.

Dan paused in the doorway, his right hand catching her upper arm in a gentle motion. His eyes locked with hers, and she thought she might die of love. Oh, dear God. She loved him! How could she have let that happen? "Don't be so hard on yourself. Without you, I would have been in real trouble in that cave—alone, wounded."

Despite her intention to avoid any impropriety, her hand reached out to touch his beard. "You look absolutely disgraceful."

"Yeah?"

A magnetism she was powerless to explain drew her closer. Her gaze focused on his mouth, and she wondered how many women he'd kissed.

"Well, you smell prettier than a woman ought to smell."

The feelings he raised were primitive, and new, and overwhelming. "I look awful. It'll take more than soap and water to repair this damage." She thought about the lemon verbena perfume in her valise and the lovely rose-scented talc Papa had given her one Christmas. She wished she had those things now to please Dan . . . but she shouldn't have such an improper desire. Why weren't her thoughts on John Jacobs?

Was it because she and Dan had been inseparable lately?

Of course she would have mixed feelings. Dan had been good to her; she'd entrusted her life to him. They had formed an indelible bond. Her feelings weren't improper; they were perfectly natural under the circumstances. Once she met John, all thoughts of Dan would recede—except those of profound gratitude.

His eyes skimmed her face, his voice low, deep, and disturbingly masculine. "John Jacobs is a lucky man."

She closed her eyes, about to cry. She wanted to kiss him—longed with every ounce of her will to draw him near, press her lips to his . . .

"Dan—"

He touched a finger to her lips. "I know," he said softly, gently moving her aside. "I'll get that meat now."

She was glad that he still had the sense to distinguish right from wrong. She lost the ability when he was this close. His voice penetrated her confusion.

"What'll it be, Miss Kallahan? Ham or beef?"

"How does ham sound?"

"Sounds good. I saw potatoes and dried peas in the cellar earlier."

Dan appeared a moment later carrying a medium-sized ham and a side of bacon. He pretended to throw the bacon at her.

Hope laughed. "Go ahead."

This time he threw it. The side of pork smacked into her middle.

She threw it back, and he caught it with one arm.

"No fair, I'm injured."

"You're not injured enough to keep you from throwing it at me."

He threw it back.

She faked a throw, and he fell for it. Straightening, he grinned, then staggered backward, catching the bacon before it slammed into his midsection.

The war was on.

Bacon flew back and forth until Hope collapsed in a heap on the ground, breathless with laughter. "Stop! You're going to ruin our breakfast and hurt yourself!"

Dropping the meat, Dan pretended to be in pain. She immediately flew to his side.

He reached down and threw the bacon back at her.

She squealed, running from him as he chased her to the house.

Letty raised herself up on her pillow as a giggling Hope burst through the front door. "Land-o'-the-mighty. Thought you two got lost."

Blood rushed to Hope's cheeks, and she realized how she must look. Cheeks pink, eyes sparkling. Mrs. McGregor would think she had been—no telling what she'd think!

Letty cackled. "Now don't be feeling all guilty. The Boss meant young'uns to fall in love. Charlie and me did our fair share of sparkin', I'll tell you. Now, I could eat a polecat. How about you startin' breakfast?"

Soon the aroma of sizzling ham and potatoes cooking in the oven filled the cabin.

Dan helped Hope set the table. Her cheeks were hot, and she refused to meet his gaze. Hope took a plate over to Letty in bed. As Hope and Dan sat down to eat, Letty prayed from the bed.

"Thank you, Boss, for this good food and for these fine folks who came to rescue me. I'm sure much obliged."

Later, Hope refilled the copper tub and laid a towel and washcloth nearby. Rummaging through the old trunk, she found several pairs of trousers and shirts. She selected a blue shirt and dark pants and laid them beside the tub.

Dan was sitting at the table reading the Bible when she finished. Letty's soft snores filled the old cabin.

"Tub's ready."

"I suppose it would be totally improper to ask that you wash my back?"

"Totally," she agreed. "I'd sooner drown you," she whispered against his ear as she passed him.

"You do smell good," he whispered back.

"You will, too, once you bathe."

"Is that a hint that I smell bad?"

"A strong suggestion."

When he moved to the back room, she reached for the Bible and curled up beside the fire.

She'd finished Genesis when he emerged from the wash room, still drying his hair with a towel. Charlie's trousers were too short in the legs, and the blue shirt was too tight for the width of his shoulders.

"You look breathtaking."

He grinned. "At least I'm clean for the first time in weeks."

Mixing up another batch of herbs, Hope applied the mixture to Dan's wound, then bound the injury in soft white muslin that Letty provided. His dark, damp hair curled over his shoulders and forehead.

Locating a comb, she gently groomed his damp mop. "You need a haircut."

"I'm waiting for you to offer."

She sat down in front of the fire and worked the comb through her matted tangles. Dan sat at the table watching her.

"Dan, I don't feel right about leaving so soon. Letty's virtually helpless. What kind of people are we to just ride off and leave her to fend for herself?"

He sighed, studying his hands. "I know. I was going to talk to you about that. I know you need to reach Medford as quickly as possible, but we can't leave for a while. Letty needs help, someone to look after the animals, plow that garden, lay up a good supply of cordwood."

She wasn't surprised by his answer; she'd been expecting it. It was clear they couldn't leave Letty, not until she was up and about on her own.

"Your shoulder won't permit you to plow and cut wood."

"The mule will do most of the work, and you can help." His eyes met hers. "I'd welcome the company."

She'd welcome his company—more time to be near him. "Of course, and I don't mind the delay. I'll help Letty with housework, and I can plant a garden—I'm very good at planting. Papa always had a large garden—biggest one in Cold Water."

Dan seemed pleased that she didn't put up an argument. "Letty should be up and around in a few days. By then, my shoulder will be well on the way to mending. Medford should be only a couple of days' ride from here."

Hope nodded, laying the comb aside. "I wonder if Letty shouldn't think about moving closer to a town. What if we hadn't come along?" She looked up when he didn't answer.

"You look almost like you did the first day I saw you," he said softly.

"I hope that's a compliment." She was afraid to have him look closely at her, afraid her love was written so vividly on her face that he would see it.

"It's a compliment," he said quietly. "Hope, if I could . . ." He didn't finish the thought.

Disappointed, she got up to tend the fire. "When we get to Medford, I'm not sure I want people to know what's really happened."

He was so quiet, she wasn't sure he'd heard. Then, "Why not? You're not responsible for anything that's happened."

She shrugged. "I'll tell John, of course, but Aunt Thalia would only be concerned about . . ." She paused, unable to express her anxiety.

"Your reputation? Hope, I'll talk to John. Explain to him that you've been in my custody." His gaze drew hers again and held it. "No one will question your character. I won't allow it."

The days at Letty McGregor's flew by. Dan's shoulder began to heal, and Letty's leg was coming along nicely. By the end of the week, the old woman moved about the cabin with the assistance of a wooden cane Dan made for her.

The goat ate three shirts and two petticoats off the clothesline, and was now busy at work on the front yard.

Dan hitched a mule to the single plow and turned the garden. Hope raked the rich black soil and planted potatoes, onions, and radishes. At night, the "young'uns" fell onto their quilt pallets, exhausted.

At the end of the week as Dan finished the last bite of egg on Sunday morning, he shoved back from the table. Meet-

ing Hope's expectant look, he announced, "Letty, we hate
to leave you, but Hope and I have to go."

Nodding, the old woman looked lonelier than any soul
ought to look. "Breaks my heart to see you young'uns go,
but of course I understand. You take the other mule," she
insisted. "Dandy's fine for plowing, but Cinder's not cut
out for harness. He's a good riding mule. He'll get you to
Medford."

"Oh, Letty, we can't take your mule," Hope said.
"You've done so much for us already."

"Well, I could sure use the goat, if you were a mind to
leave it. I'm right partial to the milk, and she could keep the
front lawn eat down."

"Letty, you have the goat with my most sincere blessing."
Dan swallowed the last of his coffee and stood up.

"I suppose you'll be leavin' today?"

"Yes, we have to be on our way."

"Then you better go to the smokehouse and get another
ham. Hope can make sandwiches for the road."

Under Letty's watchful eye, Hope spread bread with
golden butter and added thick slices of ham; she filled can-
teens with fresh water.

When it came time to leave, Dan and Hope stood near
Letty, who was seated in a chair, while Dan offered a brief
prayer. "Lord, thank you for bringing us to Letty. Please
heal her leg completely, and watch over her. Watch over us
also, as we travel. Protect us from harm, and speed us to our
destination. Amen."

Letty got up, leaning on her cane. Dan hugged her.

"Good-bye, Mrs. McGregor. Thank you, and God bless you."

When he stepped back and it was Hope's turn, she couldn't stop hugging Letty. "I'll think about you every day of my life," Hope said.

Awkwardly thumping Hope on the back, the old woman replied in a voice choked with emotion. "I'll be mentioning you to the Boss, myself, young'un. You take care, now. You hear?"

"Yes, ma'am." Hope wiped her eyes and blew her nose.

"Oh, wait. I've got something for you. You'll be needing a hat." Letty crossed the room and took off a peg a flat straw hat with cloth flowers around the crown.

Hope set it atop her head, then scrambled onto the mule behind Dan.

"Good-bye, Letty!" Hope yelled as Dan nudged the mule's flanks and they trotted off down the lane.

"Bye, young'uns! God speed!"

Hope watched over her shoulder until the cabin and Letty faded from sight. Melancholy assailed her.

"Are you going to cry?" Dan called over his shoulder.

Nodding, she bit her lip.

He covered her hand with his. The gesture touched her deeply. "Don't worry; the worst is over."

Biting her lip harder, she took comfort in the simple statement.

The worst was over.

Nothing else could possibly happen to delay their arrival in Medford.

Chapter Twelve

John ran his index finger around the inside of his collar, looking around to see if anyone had thought to open the windows. It was the second box social in a month. Didn't these women ever give up?

"A little warm under the collar, John?"

John looked up to see Jack Vance sipping a glass of punch. The town barber smiled as if he knew a secret John didn't.

"It's a little warm tonight."

"Oh? Thought it might be the idea of getting hitched." The older man chuckled.

"No." John smiled. "I'm looking forward to that."

"From what I hear, the bride might not be quite so anxious to tie the knot."

"Oh? And who might have formed that opinion?"

"The town. We all think she's not coming."

"Well, the town is wrong. Excuse me, Jack, my cup needs replenishing." John walked away before Jack could respond, but he didn't make the punch bowl before Lawrence Grant stopped him.

"Heard from that bride yet?"

"No, I haven't," John said, determined to be pleasant if it killed him. "How are things at the livery, Larry?"

"Busy, real busy. Got that new buggy in. You still in the market?"

"I'll be over tomorrow to take a look."

First thing tomorrow morning he'd march down to that river and insist Eldon Jacks ferry him across to the other side, where he could wire Thalia Grayson about Hope's whereabouts.

Had Hope even gotten on that blasted stage as planned? He didn't want to alarm the old aunt if Hope had set about on her own adventure, yet if something was amiss, someone needed to know. If Mrs. Grayson knew why Hope chose not to honor her commitment to him, would she feel comfortable revealing the reason? It was a troubling predicament, to be sure.

Disappointment beset him. Anyone who had the least consideration for him would have found a way to spare him this embarrassment. Perhaps he'd been wrong about Hope. Could that be? Could he have been so anxious to acquire a wife that he had been taken in by a hard-hearted woman?

Martin Gray clapped John heartily on the shoulder. "John, how's everything at the store?" The Gray family lived five

miles outside of town and were among John's best customers.

"Everything is fine. Had a fine winter. New families moving in means good business for me."

"Hear you're about to start your own family."

"I'm hoping to."

"Sort of left at the altar, were ya?"

John bristled. "Who told you that?"

"Well?" Martin laughed apologetically. "Did I get the
story wrong?"

"Yes. My intended is a bit late in arriving—"

Martin held up his hand. "Didn't mean to offend, John.
Maybe the little lady can't bring herself to leave her family.
She got brothers and sisters in Michigan?"

"An aunt." Perhaps that was the reason for her absence.
John felt almost faint with relief. Hope didn't want to leave
her family—but she could have told him. He was compas-
sionate; he'd understand her hesitancy—but wait. Hope's
sisters were leaving, too, also to become mail-order brides.

"Well, there you have it. Women like their families
around 'em. Could be she's decided she doesn't want to
move clear to Kentucky."

"No . . . I feel confident that she would contact me if that
were the case. She's just been delayed."

Martin glanced past John. "Mercy. Who's that pretty
young thing?"

John turned to see Freeman Hide's granddaughter standing near the punch bowl, chatting with Jed Lane. Her slen-
der fingers worked a black lace fan back and forth, stirring

the humid air. He detected the scent of her perfume even at this distance. His pulse accelerated. By George! Never had he beheld anyone so breathtakingly lovely.

Uncommonly tall, she was dressed in midnight blue lace, her raven black hair piled high atop her head with a delicate lace mantilla falling around her shoulders. The young woman was exquisite.

John approached the punch bowl, searching for a proper introduction. Something neighborly, he told himself, appropriately friendly without being overly solicitous.

"I see your cup has run dry. May I refill it for you?"

Now that was a real conversation stopper, he berated himself.

The lovely young creature turned, and John's knees buckled when confronted with dark-lashed, intelligent eyes the color of thick honey. "Thank you, but I've had quite enough." She gently fanned herself as she gazed at him.

John's tongue whiplashed into a bowknot. For the first time in his life, words failed him. His eyes darted about the room for Freeman. He should be here to make proper introductions.

"Lovely party," he said, absently dipping another cup of punch. The liquid spilled over the sides and onto the white tablecloth. Grabbing for a napkin, he upturned a vase of flowers. Water dribbled off the sides onto his newly polished shoes. When he sprang back, his heel slipped and he grabbed for support. The whole table went down with him in the middle.

The ensuing crash caught every eye and ear in the room. Every woman in attendance rushed to his rescue.

Crawling to his feet, John mopped at the front of his jacket, grinning at the striking beauty. "I'm fine, thank you. Lovely party."

The young woman frowned. "Yes . . . lovely. I'm new in town, and I haven't met many—"

Veda shouldered in with a mop and bucket. The crowd stepped back as the table was set back in place.

John seized the moment. Reaching for the young woman's hand, he turned her toward the front of the room. "Permit me to do the honors. Over there's Mose Foreman. He raises chickens. And Aaron Caldwell sitting in the corner? He's the mayor of Medford, owns two stores on Main Street. Good man, Aaron. And Lynn Baker, the one with the fiddle? He's retired. All he does is fiddle around." John smiled. He wiped at the front of his suit, his mind searching for a new topic of conversation.

"How do you find the weather here?"

"I find it fine," she said. "And you?"

"Spring is my favorite time of the year."

"Mine too. I'm looking forward to investigating the woods surrounding the town. So many lovely wildflowers are starting to bloom."

"You are? Well perhaps—"

John spotted Veda coming back through the crowd, and his smile faded.

The young woman turned to follow his gaze, her eyes searching the room. "Is something wrong?"

"Veda Fletcher." The name was a pox on his lips.

"Who?"

He dropped his voice. "Veda Fletcher, the woman coming toward us in the yellow dress."

She turned. "What about her?"

"I want to avoid her."

"Avoid her?"

"Like a case of hives."

Amusement showed in the woman's smile. "May I ask why?"

"She's intent on introducing me to her niece."

"And you don't want to meet the niece?"

"No."

John's gaze darted to the back door. It was now or never. "Would you care to join me for a stroll in the moonlight?"

John held his breath as she considered the invitation. *Please, a simple walk in the moonlight,* he prayed.

"A breath of air might be nice."

"Come with me." Taking her by the arm, he ushered her quickly out the back door. Several others had taken the opportunity to gain a breath of fresh air and stood talking in small groups around the school yard. At John's direction, they made their way toward a low wall that ran along one side of the school yard.

"It's a beautiful night."

"Yes, it is," he said, taking off his jacket to spread it atop the wall for her to sit on. The air was cooler than inside, and he felt he could breathe again. Moonlight illuminated the young woman's features. Her beauty was almost unearthly.

"Thank you, you're very kind."

"Completely nonthreatening." He smiled.

"But you're threatened by that woman—Veda Fletcher."

Settling beside her on the wall, he drew a deep breath. "Well, Veda is a little intimidating, especially when she's on a mission."

"A mission?"

"Of matrimony."

Her eyes widened. "Veda Fletcher wants to marry you?"

"Not Veda. She wants me to marry her niece."

"Oh . . ." After a moment, she said, "You've met this niece and find her unappealing?"

"No, no, I haven't met Veda's niece. That's what I'm hoping to avoid."

Snapping open her fan, she murmured, "Interesting."

"I know I must sound overly suspicious, but it's the truth. Veda has targeted me for her niece, and I don't intend to oblige her. When I marry, it will be the woman of my own choosing."

"I can imagine your aggravation. One must wonder what sort of woman the niece is if her aunt has to secure a husband for her."

"Yes, that has crossed my mind." John was surprised to discover how much he enjoyed this woman's company. It had been years, if ever, since he'd been this comfortable with a member of the opposite sex. "I fear the niece is exactly like Veda."

"And that would be bad?"

"Well, yes. Veda is a lovely woman, very warm and caring. Unfortunately, she's a hopeless matchmaker, and she makes the worst chicken casserole I've ever tasted. Believe me, I've eaten her casserole enough to make an unbiased judgment."

She smiled. "You can't find it in yourself to tell her you don't like the dish?"

"No! I wouldn't hurt her for the world."

"You're far too nice," she suggested.

"I don't know about that. It's just that Veda is so all-consuming. One can hardly have a thought of his own, much less express it. I worry this compulsion to run everything is a family trait."

The young woman hid the lower half of her face behind her fan, and John had the distinct impression she was laughing as she slid off the wall and took a few steps away from him.

"I'm glad you find it amusing. I assure you, having Veda come into the store every day to arrange my marriage isn't funny."

"Oh, but it is." She turned, dropping the fan from her face. She was smiling. "You see, I am Ginger Gonzales, and I can assure you that I haven't the slightest intentions of trapping you, John Jacobs."

John was struck dumb. This was Veda's niece! This unspeakably lovely creature was the woman with the constitution of fine china?

He'd never felt so foolish in his whole life.

He grappled for something intelligent to say, some graceful way out of his faux pas, but his mind abandoned him. "I—well, I—"

Her smile widened impishly. "Yes, John? Is there something you want to say?"

"I wish I could," he finally managed. He slid off the wall, mortified. He'd managed to insult the most beautiful woman he'd met in his entire life—not only insult and embarrass her but also alienate her from him forever!

Wonderful, John.

Suddenly her laughter penetrated his fog. She was laughing! The woman was laughing at him! He'd need to be as tough as a twenty-cent steak to get out of this one.

"Miss Gonzales. Is it possible for me to convince you that I'm John Jacobs's evil twin?"

"Umm, how does the real John feel about Aunt Veda?"

"Well," he said, "I'm sorry to say that he doesn't care any more for chicken casserole than I do."

She lowered the fan, flipping it closed with a soft snip. "Frankly, I don't care for Aunt Veda's chicken casseroles either. They're too dry, and every time I eat one, I'm up half the night drinking soda water."

"Soda water?" He hoped his eyes weren't bulging right out of his head. "I have to drink soda water every time I eat one!"

"Well, then, John Jacobs, perhaps we might think about meeting after all." She smiled, a smile so pretty it just about knocked him off his feet. "It seems we have much in common." She cocked an ear toward a mounting commotion inside. "I think they're about to start the bidding for the box dinners. Shall we go in?"

Eternally grateful for her graciously releasing him from

utter mortification, John escorted her back inside the school building. He was shaking from the whole experience.

Fred McArthur was trying to get everyone's attention. "Ladies and gentlemen, it's time to get down to what we came here for. Box suppers!"

The crowd clapped and cheered him on.

"You know it's for a good cause, so be generous!"

Veda was helping sort boxes, handing each to Fred as he worked up the crowd, encouraging a wild and furious spate of bidding. As each offering sold, the buyer claimed the box from Veda, passed the money to Fred, then waited for the lady who had prepared the supper to claim it. Depending on whose box supper it was, loud and teasing comments ebbed and flowed from the audience, along with laughter and good-natured jesting.

Since he'd already made a fool of himself, John dispensed with etiquette and looked down at Ginger.

"Which box is yours?"

The fan flipped open again, and she fanned herself, her eyes coy behind the fan. "I can't tell you which box is mine. That would be cheating."

He grinned. Veda had schooled her well.

"Every man in this room knows whose box he's bidding on."

"You don't." Her eyes twinkled merrily behind the fan.

He leaned closer. "Which box, Miss Gonzales?"

"Am I to assume you'd like to spend the evening with me, or is your query merely curiosity?"

He was a little taken aback by her directness, but he liked

it. "What if I said I wanted to have supper with you at any cost?"

The fan ceased its movement.

"Then I would say, yellow is my favorite color, and the daisy looks especially inviting."

John's gaze quickly scanned the table. A large woven basket, wrapped in a blue-checked cloth secured with a wide yellow ribbon holding a clutch of daisies to the handle, presided at the end of the table.

"Isn't that a coincidence? I'm rather partial to yellow myself. And I've always had a deep appreciation for daisies."

"Amazing coincidence," she murmured, her gaze capturing his over the open fan she now held to her cheek.

". . . and the red-ribbon box goes to Jefferson Mason. Jeff, better hope Miranda put that supper together."

Laughter rewarded Fred as Veda pushed the yellow-ribboned basket containing Ginger's contribution to the edge of the table. She located John in the crowd and pointed to the offering. Pearl Eddings yelled out.

"No fair, Veda Fletcher!"

"Now here's a fine box. Yellow ribbon, daisies." Fred leaned over to sniff. "And unless my nose is wrong, there's fried chicken in there." He sniffed again. "And chocolate cake."

The crowd laughed. Fred couldn't smell a skunk if it sprayed him.

"Chicken?" John mused softly. "Let me see. Do I want chicken, or should I hold out for a box with roast beef?"

"Fried chicken, best around." Ginger edged closer. "And

biscuits and honey, fresh butter, and some of Aunt Veda's special sweet pickles."

Well, Veda could make a mean pickle. John never doubted that.

"Pickles," he swooned, his hand over his heart in mock seriousness. He winked. "And chocolate cake?"

"Apple pie with cheese."

"Ah, a woman with superb taste." He raised his hand. "Five dollars for the yellow-ribboned basket."

"Five dollars from John Jacobs, mercy me! Do I hear five and a quarter?"

"Five and a quarter," someone shouted from the back of the room.

Ginger was watching from the corner of her eye, resting the fan against her cheek.

"Five-fifty," John bid, hoping he had enough money in his pocket.

"Do I hear five seventy-five?" Fred asked expectantly. "I've got five-fifty; do I hear five seventy-five?"

John held his breath.

"Five seventy-five!" someone yelled from the back of the room.

"Six," Ginger urged from behind the fan. "I'll chip in the extra twenty-five cents."

"Seven-fifty!" John yelled, then leaned over to whisper. "Keep your money. I'll pay fifty if I have to."

"Seven-fifty! Sold to John Jacobs for seven dollars and fifty cents! Come claim your supper, John."

John parted his way through the crowd, accepting congratulations as he reached up to take possession of the basket.

Veda looked unforgivably smug. "Enjoy your meal, John."

Handing over the money, he threaded his way back to Ginger. But she wasn't there. His eyes frantically searched the room before he detected a movement toward the back door. Hurrying in that direction, he was relieved to see Ginger casually strolling across the yard to the wall where he'd made such a fool of himself earlier.

He shot out the door and followed her.

"I thought we could picnic out here," Ginger said as he caught up.

"A perfect place," he agreed.

Ginger untied the ribbon and loosened the checked cloth, then spread it across the top of the stone ledge. Handing John the daisies, she opened the basket. The tantalizing aroma of fried chicken wafted upward, and John smiled.

"You are a temptress," he accused.

Ginger laughed, and the charming sound coursed through John's veins like wildfire.

"Biscuits, chicken, Aunt Veda's pickles, baked beans with sorghum, apple pie."

John reached to help extract a round plate. Their hands touched, and he felt as if he'd been hit by lightning.

"And cheese." Their eyes met and held in the moonlight. "A beautiful woman, a warm spring night. Life is good."

"You're a romantic, John Jacobs."

"I like to think so, Miss Gonzales."

Later, they packed the remnants of the meal back into the basket, and John escorted Ginger back into the school building. Excusing herself, Ginger went to gather her things.

"There you are! Yoo-hoo, John!" Veda stood on tiptoe, vying for his attention. "How was the meal?"

Striding toward her, John reached out to take her pudgy hand in his. "Mrs. Fletcher, I owe you my heartfelt apologies."

Veda blushed prettily. "What on earth for?"

"Because you tried to tell me how completely lovely your niece was, and I was reluctant to take your word." He leaned close and whispered into her ear, "Indulgent aunts and parents tend to be a bit prejudiced, you know."

Veda tittered. "I was so pleased when you bid on Ginger's basket," she confessed. "And I didn't even have to tell you which one it was. Could this mean you no longer consider yourself engaged? Have you finally come to your senses and realized Miss Kallahan isn't coming?"

He hadn't thought that far yet, but he supposed he must. And soon. He couldn't go on this way forever. Hope wasn't coming; he'd only been fooling himself. As bad as he hated to admit it, she'd stood him up.

"I'd rather your niece doesn't know anything about my engagement until I think it through."

"Of course, but John—" Veda squeezed his hand affectionately—"I only want the best for you. I know you've thought me pushy and overbearing at times, always on you to meet my niece, and I admit I've been overly anxious. I'm a selfish woman. I want you in the family. You're a fine man, and my niece couldn't be more blessed were the two of you to fall in love."

John's gaze located Ginger across the room. She was chatting with Idella Merriweather, her animated laughter drifting to him. Three hours ago he would have found Veda's thoughts ludicrous. At the moment they didn't seem at all out of place.

"If you don't mind, I would like to walk Ginger and you home."

"Of course, dear. And you can take your time. It's a lovely night. I'll be with you in a minute."

Veda zeroed in on Pearl Eddings. "Oh, Pearl!" she warbled. "Wait up. I have something to tell you."

Chapter Thirteen

The old mule, Cinder, was a pest. The cantankerous beast of burden nipped at Dan's dangling legs with its big teeth, making a real nuisance of herself.

"If we didn't need the transportation so badly, I'd shoot this thing!" Dan groused, swatting the critter's rump when she bit him a third time.

Even Hope's newfound positive attitude was flagging. She was beginning to feel as if everything was against her, even the mule. What had her life become? What would Aunt Thalia think if she could see her now—riding a mule, wearing Letty's ridiculous-looking straw hat?

But no matter. She would be in Medford before much longer, and her troubles would be over. By this time next week, she would be serving John Jacobs dinner.

The thought didn't do much to lift her spirits.

She spent the day trying to revel in her final hours of freedom, glorying in the spring flowers blooming along the hillsides, the call of meadowlarks, and the occasional glimpse of
a deer through the thick foliage. She sang songs, inviting
Dan to join in. To her delight, he did, his rich baritone
blending harmoniously with her alto as they rode through
the greening countryside.

Hope waved to occasional passersby, though Dan barely
noticed them. He seemed preoccupied, deep in thought.
Hope wondered if his thoughts included her. At times, she
was certain that he was attracted to her; but at others she
realized he was a man with a duty and she was only a part of
that duty.

Her feelings for Dan had deepened with lightning swift-
ness. During the idyllic days at Letty's, they had been
inseparable, working side by side during the day, talking late
into the night over popcorn and sugared tea at the table
while Letty snored in her bed.

Yet at other times, they seemed continents apart.

She knew what her problem was—love. But other than
the one time at the smokehouse, she'd fought the feeling
because there was John to consider.

There was always John.

Her resentment bloomed. What sort of man put an ad for
a wife in a journal, anyway? How could she possibly explain
to her husband-to-be everything that had happened to her
since she'd kissed Aunt Thalia good-bye and boarded the
stage in Cold Water?

Had that been almost two months ago? She'd lost track of time.

Would John believe that Dan had been only her protector? Or would he have qualms about her respectability, requesting that she leave? Her spirits lifted at the prospect, then plummeted back to earth. John Jacobs was an honorable man. If he had misgivings about her reputation, she doubted that he would openly voice them.

If God had put these trials upon her to test her faith, then she had most certainly failed. She wasn't even sure God loved her. How could she believe this man she didn't know but was consigned to marry could love her?

"Muddy Flats straight ahead." Dan indicated the silhouette of buildings against the distant horizon.

A few miles back, a passerby had told them the small crossroads settlement had a general store. Letty had insisted that they take fifteen dollars for necessities. Dan assured her the money would be repaid the moment he contacted his commander. When they reached Muddy Flats, they would have to purchase food. The sandwiches would last for one more meal.

"If only there was time to buy a dress that fits me." She lifted the baggy waist of the dress Letty had given her. It was going to be embarrassing to meet John looking like a beggar. "And a bath would be nice."

"We'll see if the town can accommodate your wishes, miss."

"A bath isn't a necessity," she reminded him. "But it sure would be nice."

Dan's hand rested on hers for a brief moment. The artless touch set her heart rate into double time. "We'll make you presentable to meet John. Another couple of hours isn't going to make a difference. You can buy a pretty dress and have a long soak in a hot tub. Come to think about it, a bath sounds good. We'll each have one."

Hope felt like she was going to explode with all the emotions boiling up inside her. "Thank you." She squeezed his waist, and he squeezed her hand back.

Muddy Flats wasn't large, but Hope was happy to see a mercantile, a small livery, a saloon, a blacksmith, and a boardinghouse that promised bathing facilities.

"We might even stay the night," Dan decided as they rode the mule down Main Street. "Probably do you good to sleep in your own bed, stay in your own room for the first time in weeks. We can start out early in the morning, be in Medford by noon. What would you say to that?"

"Sleep in a clean bed with real sheets? I'd say yes!"

"I'll leave you at the Mercantile. You pick out a pretty dress and buy some matching shoes. I want John Jacobs's bride to be the talk of the town."

She did too; she just wished she wasn't that bride. She poked her foot out and studied her once-fashionable foot attire. During the weeks since she'd left Michigan, she'd plowed through wet grass, forded streams, and walked untold miles. Her shoes weren't a pretty sight.

"What will you do while I shop?"

"I'm going to sell this ornery critter. Or bury it." He jumped when the mule turned, trying to take a chunk out of his leg. He boxed the animal's ears. "Either way, Lucifer, here, and I are parting company."

Dan stopped the animal in front of the Mercantile, and Hope slid off the mule's back. "Stay out of trouble." He winked at her.

"I'll try." It was her heart, not her feet, that needed to stay out of trouble.

She felt like a street urchin as she opened the door to the Mercantile and stepped inside.

"Afternoon!" A short, round older man behind the counter greeted her, his gaze sweeping her appearance.

"I need a new dress," she explained.

The clerk's mouth turned up in a half smile. "That right? Right pert hat you've got there."

"Well," she admitted, "it keeps the sun off, thank you."

"I see that. Hiram Burk, clerk, at your service."

"Hope Kallahan, battered traveler, at yours." She extended a soiled hand and they shook.

"I suppose you'd like to look at some ready-mades?"

"Yes, and shoes. Comfortable ones—inexpensive, comfortable ones. I don't have much money."

She had no idea what a mule would bring. Not much, she ventured to guess, and they would need all they could get to buy a horse to replace it. She needed to be thrifty, even though they also had Letty's fifteen dollars.

"Dresses to the right, bonnets three aisles back. You'll find everything you need."

Hope easily located the rack of ready-made gowns. Most were too large for her, but she eventually decided on a pink-and-white calico. Browsing through the rack of bonnets, she found a pretty white one; then she selected a few simple undergarments and carried them to the counter.

"How much?" she asked, anxiously watching the clerk tally the apparel.

"Well, let's see." The old gentleman figured on a piece of brown paper, his pencil flying. "Three dollars."

"Three?" She worried her teeth on her lower lip. "Dan and I both need comfortable walking shoes."

"Three dollars includes two pairs of shoes," he said with a friendly smile. "I'd throw in a brush and comb for three and a quarter." He leaned forward slightly. "Got some fine bathing facilities up at the boardinghouse."

"Thank you," Hope said, heartened by his generosity. As Papa would say, the world needed more men like Hiram Burk. "You're so very kind."

"The Lord's been good to me; I like to pass it on." Straightening, he picked up his duster and tidied the counter. "Looks to me like you've had a time of it. You slip off one of those shoes and I'll see if I can match the size. Meanwhile, there's some finely milled soap, sweetest smelling thing this side of heaven, right over there near the window. You pick out a bar, and I'll sell it to you for a penny."

Hope unlaced her shoes and handed them over the counter, then went to see about the soap. She smelled each and every bar before she selected one that smelled like the roses that vined along Aunt Thalia's backyard fence.

"Now let's see, little lady. Think these will fit?" Mr. Burk held a sturdy brown pair of shoes aloft for her inspection.

"They look as if they might."

Sitting on a stool Mr. Burk provided, Hope slipped her feet into the shoes and stood up, testing their length.

"They look mighty fetching on you."

"They're perfect." She sat down and pulled them off.

"Don't you want to wear them? I could wrap up this old pair—"

"No, I won't wear them until I have a bath," Hope said.

Mr. Burk smiled, nodding with understanding. "Just what my wife, Beulah, would say."

Reaching for her parcels, Hope smiled. Sometimes a person just knew when she was in the presence of angels. This was one of those times. "God bless you, Mr. Burk."

The old clerk looked almost angelic. "It's mighty nice to be of service. You send your man in, and I'll fix him up too."

Hope didn't bother to correct Mr. Burk's assumption that Dan was her husband. She rather fancied the idea herself.

Hurrying out of the store, she anticipated the hot bath, rose-scented soap, shampoo for her hair, clean, new clothes, and a night's rest in a real bed with clean sheets and feather pillows.

Not looking where she was going, she ran smack into a tall man just exiting the mouth of the alley. She opened her mouth to apologize.

"I'm so—no!" She shrieked as Joe Davidson's filthy hand clamped over her mouth.

"Thought ya could escape Big Joe, huh? Well, think again, missy."

Hope's heart hammered wildly in her chest as the outlaw hooked an arm around her waist and hauled her into the alleyway. Her packages scattered. Struggling, she pawed at his hand, but Big Joe's grip was far superior. He stifled her cries by stuffing a dirty bandanna into her mouth.

"Now, hush up!"

Manhandling her onto a waiting horse, he stepped into the saddle, digging his spurs into the horse's flanks.

The gelding burst from the alleyway and headed east.

Dan emerged from the boardinghouse and strode toward the Mercantile, whistling.

Stepping onto the porch, he cupped his hands, peeking through the store window. His gaze swept the empty store, and he frowned. A moment later he entered through the front door.

The portly man behind the counter glanced up. "Can I help you?"

Dan's eyes scanned the empty aisles. "I'm looking for a woman. Dark hair, wearing a yellow dress, silly hat?"

"Mrs. Kallahan! You must be the mister."

Dan smiled. "Is she still here?"

"No, she left a moment ago—you must have passed her on the way in." The friendly clerk stepped to the front window and looked out. "Now that's odd. She couldn't have gone far."

Dan joined him to look out. "I didn't pass her on the way over. I'd have noticed that."

The clerk walked outside, and Dan followed him. The two men stood on the porch, their eyes searching the street.

"I think she was heading over to the boardinghouse. Said something about wanting a bath."

Dan suddenly bounded off the porch and started running.

"Mister! Hey, mister!" the clerk called. "I'm sure she's all right—"

Dan dodged the packages spilled in the dirt—a dress box, a pair of brown shoes. A small bar of feminine-looking soap.

"Hope!" He ran faster, his breath coming in bursts, his eyes searching the sidewalks and walkways.

"Did anyone see anything?" he shouted as a crowd started to form.

Serious expressions stared back. Not a man, woman, or child indicated they'd seen anything peculiar.

His eyes swung to an old-timer dozing in a chair propped against the saloon wall on the opposite side of the street. Dan sprinted across the road.

"Did you see a young woman come out of the Mercantile a few minutes ago?"

The old man cracked a sleepy eye, peering up at him. "Eh?"

"A young, pretty woman. Coming out of the store—just a few minutes ago."

"Young woman?"

"Yes."

"Pretty?"

"Tall, slim, dark hair, wearing a silly straw hat."

"Oh, that woman." The old fellow stroked his bristling jaw. "Yes, sir, I did see that little filly. Wearing a dirty yeller dress, leastwise it looked yeller—could have been white. Can't even say it wasn't faded brown; could even have been coffee-colored—knew a woman once who had a coffee-colored dress. It was real pretty. Or it could have been—"

Dan cut him off. "Where did she go?"

"Rode out of town."

"Rode out?" Dan whirled to look down the road.

"Yep. On th' back of a horse . . . with a big ol' fella."

Dan grabbed the front of the old-timer's vest. "How long ago?"

The old man showed surprising strength. He struggled to break Dan's grip. "Now hold on, you young whippersnapper—"

Relaxing the clench, Dan stepped back. He swiped a hand over his face. "This is important. What did the man look like?"

Frowning, the old man shook his head. "Big—tall, hat pulled low. Beard. Ridin' a big gelding. That one's trouble, I tell you. Why any woman would want to—"

"Joe Davidson," Dan muttered. "Which way did he go?"

"Thataway." The man pointed up the street. "If you want to catch him, you better lasso yourself a cyclone, Sonny. That feller was in a powerful big hurry."

Leaping off the porch, Dan sprang aboard a big roan standing at the saloon hitching post.

A cowpoke just coming out from the watering hole threw his arms in the air, yelling, "Hey! That's my horse!"

"I'll return it later!" Wheeling the mare, Dan spurred the animal's flanks and galloped out of town.

Chapter Fourteen

Well. This is getting out of hand, Lord! Is there a particular lesson you want me to learn from this insanity?

Hope huddled beside the fire, glaring at her captors—Big Joe, Boris, and Frog. Why hadn't she been more cautious? In her eagerness for clean clothing and a hot bath, she had been careless, thinking only of herself. Now once again, an oafish lout and his two similarly oafish sidekicks were holding her prisoner. If there was a lesson to be learned, she didn't have the slightest notion what it was.

She had no idea where they were. They had ridden for what seemed like hours. Dan would be hunting for her, trying to determine who had taken her, and where—or at least she hoped he would. He'd have a fair idea of who was responsible for the nefarious act, but how would he find her? They could have taken her anywhere.

Lord, I don't know how you'll work it, but guide Dan's steps—lead him to me, Father. "God, please be here," she murmured.

Lo, I am with you always, the wind seemed to whisper.

Big Joe, Frog, and Boris sat around the campfire, bandannas tucked into their collars, slurping pork and beans from tin bowls.

"Want some?" Boris asked when he caught her staring.

She shook her head, averting her gaze. "No."

"Still snooty, huh? Well, good. Jest more for me." The bandit leaned over and dipped his bowl back into the iron pot hung over the fire.

Their manners were still atrocious. They'd forgotten everything she'd taught them.

Boris grinned as if he'd read her thought. "Aw, she don't like our ettin' skills, gentlemen." He winked at the others. "We're jest a bunch of heathens—but right fine-lookin' ones, right, Joe?"

Big Joe nodded. "Right fine." He belched, loud enough to wake the dead.

Boris sopped up stew broth with a cold biscuit. "Ain't changin' the way I eat for her again. Iffin it's good enough for Ma, it's good enough for Miss Snooty here."

"Animals," Hope murmured.

Big Joe glanced up. "What was that?"

"I said you are like animals, eating like pigs, dripping broth down your front, slurping, burping. I've met pigs with better behavior."

At least the Bennett pig didn't have slop dripping off its chin.

"She ain't happy with us," Big Joe said, falling over Boris's shoulder to sob mock tears. "Don't that jest break yore hearts, boys?"

"Aw, let up on her, Joe. Cain't you see she's what she is, and she ain't gonna change?"

Heads pivoted to stare at Frog.

Boris swallowed, his Adam's apple bobbing. "What'd ya mean, 'let up on her'? You goin' soft on us, Frog?"

"No. But you do et like a pig, Boris. You got drippin's on yore face. Wipe 'em off."

Boris took a swipe at his mouth with his shirtsleeve. Big Joe leaned over to swat him. "You don't hafta do what she says!"

Hope looked away. *Where are you, Dan? Please hurry. Please, Lord, give him wisdom and a strong sense of direction.*

The men went back to eating. Big Joe crammed a wad of biscuit into his mouth, talking to Boris at the same time. Crumbs flew in Boris's face and sprayed out on the front of the outlaw's chest.

"Et with some manners, Joe!" hollered Frog.

Big Joe scowled as he whirled to face Frog.

Frog looked down at his plate, refusing to meet Joe's glare. "Don't jaw with yore mouth full—it ain't appetizin'."

The ruffian gestured to Hope with his spoon, slinging beans. "You sidin' with her? She's a troublemaker. Has been from the minute we took her off that stage. Nothin' but trouble. And now, she's gonna be more trouble until we git rid of her, which we gotta do right off. She can identify ever' last one of us, and don't you fergit it, Frog."

"No I can't," Hope said. "I mean, I won't, if that's what you're worried about. If you'll let me go, I'll lose my memory—I won't be able to identity myself, let alone you, I promise."

Big Joe scooped up another bite. "Like I'm gonna believe that."

"I won't," she contended. "And Dan—" Realizing she'd just given them Grunt's real name, she bit her tongue.

"Dan?" Big Joe's eyes narrowed. "You talkin' about that low-down, connivin', yeller-bellied dog, Grunt?"

"No, I don't know why I said Dan—I meant—"

"Dan, huh? So that's the polecat's name. Well, you kin jest tell *Dan* for me that when he shows up to git you—which I figure he's tryin' his best to do right now—we'll have a little present waitin' for 'im." He patted the Colt revolver at his side.

"He isn't looking for me; he couldn't care less what happens to me. He's happy as a tick at a dog fair that I'm your problem now and not his. I'm nothing but a headache, honest. And mean, real mean-spirited."

She prayed Dan didn't feel that way about her, but if they thought for a moment that Dan cared about her welfare, she would endanger him more.

Big Joe scoffed. "Mean? You ain't mean, little missy. I've met women meaner than a scalded cat."

Her temper flared, and she struggled against the ropes

binding her wrists. "You untie these ropes and I'll show you mean, Mr. Davidson."

"Ooowee. You scarin' the puddin' right outta me."

"What are we gonna do with her?" Boris grunted. "Her and her highfalutin ways are gettin' on my nerves."

"Gonna git rid of her, and the sooner the better."

"No!" Hope cried.

"Wadda ya mean, no. You ain't talkin', I am. Now pipe down." Big Joe rammed another wad of bread into his mouth.

"Maybe that ain't so smart, Joe." Frog set his bowl aside.

"What're you talkin' about, Frog?" Joe said, talking with his mouth full.

"We're jest wanted for robbery. I don't hold with no killin'."

"Too bad. I'm still not convinced Ferry ain't her pa. Maybe he had that newspaper article planted so's to catch us."

Not my father, Hope mouthed in astonishment. And no ransom money.

Didn't he get it?

The three men tossed their bowls in a pile and swigged down the last of their coffee. Hope watched the appalling exhibition, wondering what would happen to her. She hoped Dan was trying frantically to find her. He'd have seen her scattered parcels and put two and two together. Any moment, he would come bursting into camp and save her.

But what if he didn't? What if he didn't have an inkling

who had taken her or in what direction they had ridden?
Joe said they had to do away with her and soon.

How soon?

She focused on Frog, who was quiet now. Of the three
outlaws, Frog seemed the most—what? Certainly not intelligent, but perhaps the one most open to suggestion. He sat
beside the fire, staring into the flames, apparently removing
himself from the fray. In an odd way, her heart went out to
him. Perhaps it was the innate sympathy one felt for a
weaker brother. Had anyone ever told Frog about God and
his love? "The rain falls on the just and unjust," Papa used
to say. It was hard to convince herself that God loved Joe
and Boris and Frog as much as he loved her. But his Word
said that he did.

Could it be that simple? If these men knew someone
cared about them, really cared about them, would they
change?

Warming to the thought, her mind ricocheted in lightning fashion. If these men—Boris, Frog, and Big Joe—were
to experience God's saving grace, their lives would change
forever. And if their lives changed, it would be because of
God's unending love.

What if she told them about God's mercy? She, Hope
Kallahan, daughter of Thomas Kallahan, preacher. What
harm could it do? They couldn't get any madder at her;
they were already furious. She'd not witnessed before; Papa
was the preacher in the family, not her. But Papa was dead,
and she was here. Poor manners or unpardonable belching
wouldn't put off God.

Straightening, Hope squared her shoulders. God loves these numbskulls—she was going to tell them so.

She shrank back. How should she start? She could see Papa with the Bible in his hand, preaching, urging sinners to repent. But she didn't have a calling, and she sure wasn't Papa with his solid convictions and impeccable Scripture knowledge. She made a real mess of things when she tried to quote anything. Why, she was barely an adequate talker. How could she be a witness for God?

Ye have not chosen me, but I have chosen you, that ye should bring forth fruit, and that your fruit should remain. . . .

Oh, Lord! Why me? She pondered the problem.

. . . Whatsoever ye shall ask the Father in my name, he will give to you. These things I command you, that ye love one another. She couldn't believe she was remembering the Scriptures—though she still would be hard-pressed to cite chapter and verse. Drawing a deep breath, she muttered, "Why do you steal?"

The men looked up. Big Joe's eyes tapered into venomous slits. "I told you to pipe down."

Clearing her throat, she continued, willing authority into her voice. "As soon as you tell me why you steal."

"'Cause we want to."

"Why?"

"Why?"

"Why."

"We steal, Miss Snooty," Boris said, "'cause . . . well, 'cause . . ." He glanced at Joe. "Tell her why we steal, Big Joe."

"We steal 'cause we feel like it," Big Joe said. He elbowed Boris, laughing. "We like to take other folks' things, ain't that right?"

Boris nodded emphatically. "That's right."

Hope noticed Frog wasn't joining in the conversation.

"You take other people's things, live in filthy cabins, wear foul-smelling clothes, eat out of dirty dishes, sleep on the hard ground, forsake the love of family and home because you like it?"

Big Joe nodded. "We like it."

"That's nuts," she said. "Your life could be so different."

The men exchanged glances, then went back to talking among themselves.

"Hey!"

Their eyes shot back to her.

"Did you hear what I said?"

"We heered; we jest ain't interested in anythin' you got to say."

"Don't you want to be different?"

They swapped another set of impatient looks.

"Wadda you mean, different?" Frog finally said. "Like we'd ought to hit banks instead of stages? Different like that?"

"No, nothing like that."

Frog was the only one who took the censure to heart. In a while, he snorted. "What? Workin' for wages, havin' somebody tell us what to do all the time?"

"Quit eggin' her on, Frog," Joe snapped. "She's trying to

confuse us with talk about livin' different. Ain't no way we can live different. We are what we are."

"Wrong."

Joe rewarded her with an acid look. "Don't say 'wrong.'"

"But you are wrong. There's a better way to live, and you're not too old, or too mean, or too set in your ways to change. Not even you, Joe."

Frog seemed uncomfortable with the subject. "I agree with Joe. You oughtta stop talking."

"All right. Can I read?"

"Read?" Joe shook his head as if she was trying him beyond his limits. "Yore a nuisance, ya know that? You ain't got nothin' to read."

"I have a Bible. It's in my pocket."

"Good for you. Now shut up." He leaned back, tipping his hat over his eyes.

"OK, I won't read. Can I recite out loud?"

"Recite all you want. Just don't bother me." Boris chuckled, getting up to move around. Frog sat by the fire, whittling on a piece of wood.

"For God so loved the world, that he gave his only begotten Son, that whosoever believeth in him should not perish, but have everlasting life." Hope sighed, proud of herself. All that Bible reading was paying off. "John 3:16."

Big Joe and Boris acted as if they hadn't heard. Frog looked up, catching Hope's eye. "My ma read that to me once."

Hope quelled her fear. The Lord was with her; she could feel it. "Do you understand what it means, Frog?"

He shook his head. "Not really."

"It means that God loved you so much that he allowed his Son, Jesus Christ, to die a most shocking death on a cross. For your sins, and my sins, and Joe's sins, and Boris's sins. Christ was buried and rose on the third day. Before he left this earth, he promised that he would prepare a place in heaven for those who believed in his name, and someday he will return for his children. He wants you to be his child."

A strained silence fell over the camp. Overhead, a full moon rose higher. A lone coyote called to its mate. The men stood around the fire cradling cups of coffee in their hands.

"He gonna build a bigger fire, give us better blankets, better food?" Joe scoffed.

"He can, if you ask. He's not in the business of catering to our whims, but he has the ability to move a mountain, if he wants to."

"That's the stupidest thing I ever heered. Move a mountain—no one can do that. And why would God's Son die for me? I ain't even met the man." Boris kicked dirt into the fire.

"That I can't say. I certainly wouldn't. I can only tell you, he did die for your sins, and mine. That's the joy of his love. No one asked him to die; he did it because he loved us. And we have no way of saving ourselves but through him."

"That's jest stupid," Joe pronounced. "I'm going ta bed."

Hope looked at Frog, who refused to meet her eyes now. Was she reaching him?

"Guess I'll turn in too," Frog said. He walked past Hope, pausing in front of her. He dropped his voice. "Iffin I was to git that book . . . the Bible. Where would I find that stuff yore yammerin' about?"

"You can have this one."

"Cain't read," he whispered gruffly.

"You can have someone read it to you."

Nodding, he glanced over his shoulder. "You jest keep the Bible for now, and don't go tellin' Joe 'bout this."

"Don't worry." Hope's eyes traced Frog's. "He wouldn't listen if I did."

Later, she lay gazing up at the moon. Was Frog thinking about the plan of salvation? She prayed that God would open the outlaw's eyes and his heart.

Oh, Dan, maybe there is a reason why we've been thrown together. God loves Frog so much he sent someone to tell him so.

Somewhere, Dan was under the same sky, searching for her. She closed her eyes, trying to remember his smell, the way his eyes lit when he smiled. Hot tears burned behind her lids. Would she ever see him again?

"Miss Kallahan?"

Hope wasn't sure she heard her name spoken, but she opened her eyes. Frog was leaning over her. Her heart sprang to her throat.

"What is it?"

Kneeling beside her, he lay a hand across her mouth. "Don't wake the others. I need to talk to you."

She nodded, her eyes making a silent promise.

Untying her hands, he helped her up. She nearly cried out from relief. Flexing her fingers, she tried to revive the circulation.

"Come with me."

He led her away from the fire where the other men's snores clogged the chilly night air.

They sat down on a carpet of moss beneath an oak tree. Moonlight streamed through the branches, illuminating the setting. Frog suddenly got back up and started to pace.

"I want to know what you was talkin' about earlier."

"John 3:16?"

"Yeah," he said. "Was it the truth, or are you jest tryin' to pull our legs?"

"It's the truth. I was talking about the power of Jesus Christ to save us—each of us—from the consequences of our sin."

"He cain't do nothin' 'bout me. I'm too far gone . . . he cain't help me."

"Oh, Frog. I know it sounds like wishful thinking. We've all sinned and fallen short of God's glory. But when we confess our sins and ask for forgiveness, the Lord is swift to pardon us. But we—you and I—have to surrender our life to the Almighty. He'll settle for nothing less."

"Surrender?" Frog shook his head. "I ain't never surrendered to no one."

"Well, it isn't easy," she granted. "To die to our own will is hard. But once we do, the Lord can come into our heart and bless us in such a mighty way we can only fall on our knees and thank him for his unbelievable love."

She smiled, aware that she was talking to herself as well as to Frog. "I struggle with placing my whole trust in the Lord. To trust him with my life, and my thoughts, and my future—most of all my future—is difficult."

Exceptionally hard. She had to work at it every day; but it was getting easier. She still didn't understand why God would choose to place her in the path of Big Joe and his gang, or why she met Dan after she agreed to marry John. Or why she'd gotten so sick, and Dan had been shot and had to surrender his fine, leather-tooled saddle for a mangy old goat. Why Letty wanted to trade that old mean mule for that scruffy old goat that'd eat the clothes off a person's back if they'd let it. She couldn't explain any of those things; she just chalked it up to the fact that God in his infinite wisdom knew what he was doing.

"You see, Frog, we have a choice, a simple choice, actually. We choose to live for Jesus Christ or for Satan. Has anyone ever told you about God's love for you?"

Frog nodded, sheepish now. "Ma tried; it jest never got through my thick noggin."

"God loves you. He loves you more than I can ever make you understand." She pressed Dan's Bible into his hands. "I know you can't read this, but hold it close to your heart and talk to God. He can hear our deepest needs. We don't have to see words to apply them to our hearts. We only have to know that they're there and believe them."

Nodding, Frog said quietly, "Thank you, ma'am. I'm gonna think real hard on this."

"How long has it been since you've seen your papa?"

Tears welled in his eyes. "A long time."

"God's your heavenly Father. Our heavenly Father. He'll listen and understand your problems just as your earthly father would. Even more so. And he'll remember those sins no more. You can't hide from God, Frog. There's nowhere to go; he's with us every moment. Once you've confessed your sins and asked Jesus to come into your heart, no one can ever separate you from his wondrous love."

Frog glanced toward Big Joe, whose snores were lifting the bedroll.

"Nobody?"

"Nobody."

Hope leaned closer. "Nobody."

He looked at her, his eyes dark with need. "It sounds mighty simple."

"It is simple. Living for him is harder, but the Scriptures are there to guide us. We may step away, but he doesn't."

He pressed the Bible to his heart, then squeezed her hand.

"We gotta git back. It'd be real hard on you if Joe was to catch us talkin'."

"Frog?"

"Yes, ma'am?"

"I'll pray for you every night."

"Yes, ma'am—I'm much obliged."

They crept back to camp. Hope held up her wrists, and Frog secured them with the rope. He obviously took pains, making sure the cord wasn't too tight. His touch was gentle.

"Thank ya again, ma'am," he whispered. "I won't let them hurt ya."

"Thank you, Frog. God bless you."

The rain falls on the just and unjust, she thought as she watched him walk away. Her eyes shifted to Big Joe and Boris, where funny-sounding whistles were coming from their gaping mouths. *He also takes care of fools and children.*

How did a man turn to crime and violence when his mama prayed for his salvation every night? She guessed she just might ask God that when she met him. But she hoped that tonight, God might have answered Frog's mama's prayers.

Thank you, Father. We all fall into the category of fools and children, don't we?

Somehow, through his grace, the terror of this long day had turned into a blessing.

"You're right as usual, Papa," she murmured as she huddled beneath a thin blanket to stave off the chill wind. "God is good."

Chapter Fifteen

Darkness was closing in as Dan topped a rise, drawing the heavily lathered roan to a halt. In the distance, a tuft of campfire smoke spiraled toward the early evening sky.

Clicking his tongue, he nudged the horse down a steep incline. With the edge of the forest as cover, he rode the fringe of the pines until he picked up a set of new tracks. He urged the horse up a steep bluff, then slowed as the aroma of side pork, beans, and coffee reached him. He studied the terrain.

Up ahead, a line of cedars stretched across the rugged landscape. The thick, prickly growth provided what he needed. Minutes later, he stepped out of the saddle, letting the horse graze as he squatted behind the cover. And waited.

One hour. Two hours. One by one, the men rolled into their blankets for the night. Dan kept his eyes on Hope, who was lying at the edge of the campfire, her wrists bound tightly behind her back. When the camp settled down, Dan began to carefully plan his approach. Then a movement caught his eye. Frog! He was untying Hope's wrists. Leading her away from the camp. If he dared touch her . . . Dan felt his blood begin to boil.

Frog led Hope to a spot under an oak tree. They seemed to be talking, from what Dan could make out in the moonlight. Frog was pacing. After a while, Frog led Hope back to camp, retied her wrists, and settled down on his bedroll. What had that been about? Relief flooded Dan; Frog hadn't hurt her.

A little longer; wait until the camp is quiet again before you make your approach.

Big Joe's snores overrode the crackling fire as Dan crept toward the sleeping encampment.

Creeping silently around the sleeping forms, he made his way to Hope. Slipping his hand over her mouth, he pulled her upright. Predictably, her eyes popped wide open. When her eyes registered recognition, he removed his hand and cut the rawhide cord binding her wrists.

He pressed his mouth close to her ear. "Move quickly."

Every rustle of clothing, every footfall sounded like a gunshot as they crawled out of the circle of firelight and disappeared into the shadows. When they were in the clear, Hope threw herself into his arms.

"I knew you would come," she whispered, throwing her

arms around his neck. "I don't know how you found me, but I prayed that you would."

"You don't think you could get away from me that easily, do you?"

Her hold on him tightened. "I didn't want to get away from you at all."

Dan held her close, smoothing her hair. "Are you all right?"

"I'm fine. They didn't hurt me." She stepped back, grinning. "Frog accepted the Lord—at least I think he has!"

Dan frowned. "Frog?"

"Frog—our Frog. I think that he's accepted Jesus!"

"Our Frog?"

"It's true, Dan. Frog is thinking about things of the Lord. It's nothing short of a miracle. I'm so thankful God brought me here to witness to him. It's been a real blessing."

"Our Frog?" Dan repeated.

"Our Frog. For the first time I know, really know, what Papa meant when he said leading a person to Christ is the most exciting thing in the world."

Dan chuckled, pulling her closer.

"What?"

"You're amazing, you know that? You're the only woman I know who could get herself kidnapped twice and consider it a blessing."

She laughed. "Well, not the kidnapping, but the conversion is, and I want to experience it again. And again, and again. Now what?"

Dan drew a deep breath. "I have to arrest Joe and Frog and Boris, Hope."

Her face fell. "Do you have to arrest Frog?"

"He's part of the gang. I was sent to do a job, and I'm bound by duty to finish it. I haven't been able to find out where the gang gets its information, but the Davidson gang has stolen their last payroll."

She glanced at the sleeping camp. He was right; Frog was a part of the gang, but how she prayed that tonight he had felt the touch of God's hand. "All right . . . I'll help. Tell me what to do."

"You aren't to do anything. It's too dangerous. With any luck, I'll have them arrested before they know what's happening. Stay here and keep quiet. I can handle this. All right?"

She bit her lower lip. "I—"

Dan finished the thought for her. "Will do as I'm told, Dan. Thank you." Bending down, he kissed her.

She looked up, eyes wide.

"All right?"

Reaching out, she hurriedly drew him back into an embrace.

"All right?" she whispered.

"More than all right." He kissed her once more, lightly, then set her aside. He was about to walk off when she reached out again and latched on to his arm. When he saw the look in her eye he mentally groaned.

"I really want to help."

"No. You'll only be in the way."

"I won't get in the way, I promise. It's only fair that you let me help; I have a stake in seeing Big Joe and Boris behind bars. I wish Frog didn't have to be, but with God's help he'll serve his time and come out a new man." Her eyes plaintively beseeched him. "Please, Dan, let me help."

She smiled, blinking violet-colored eyes at him prettily. "Please?"

"All right, but you're to do what I say, when I say it."

"I promise." She wiggled closer, her eyes bright with excitement. "What's our plan?"

Dan's eyes scanned the sleeping outlaws. "Do you know anything about a gun?"

"Only that you point it and pull the trigger."

"That should work."

"I don't want to shoot anyone. Not even Big Joe, although the thought is tempting."

Dan quickly outlined what he wanted to do, and they crept back into the clearing.

Moving silently, they approached the sleeping men. Big Joe had his back to the fire. Frog lay facing it. Boris angled on his right side, his head burrowed under a matted blanket. Moving on hands and knees, Dan reached out and struck Boris behind his left ear, rendering him unconscious without a sound. Unbuckling the outlaw's holster, Dan pitched the gun to Hope.

Hope remained at the edge of the firelight, gripping the gun in both hands as Dan crept to Big Joe.

"Hey, Davidson."

Big Joe woke with a start, his eyes unfocused. Spotting Dan, he sprang to his feet with a snarl.

Dan pinned the rifle on him. "Guess who. You're under arrest."

Big Joe's gaze swept the campsite. Swallowing, Hope steadied the gun, her eyes locked with the outlaw's.

Joe's eyes switched to an unconscious Boris. On the opposite side of the fire, Frog began to stir.

"Don't anybody move," Dan warned, loud enough for Frog to hear. "Frog, get over here."

Eyes on Hope, Frog got slowly to his feet and moved toward Dan.

Handing Frog a strip of rawhide he'd taken off the saddle-bags, Dan motioned to Joe. "Tie his hands, Frog, and do it right."

Frog's eyes flew to Joe's. Joe snarled, "Take him, Frog. I'll back ya up!"

Dan calmly leveled the rifle at Frog. "Tie Joe's hands. It will go easier on you."

Emotions warred on Frog's face. Finally, the outlaw reluctantly wound the rope around Joe's wrists.

"Polecat," the leader hissed. "Turncoat."

"Shut up, Joe."

Dan glanced toward Hope. "Come over here. Easy now."

Hope skirted the fire, staying clear of the two outlaws. When she reached Dan, he handed her a strip of leather.

"Tie Frog's hands."

Nodding, she handed Dan the gun. "I'm sorry," she

apologized to Frog a moment later. "I wish I didn't have to do this."

He refused to look at her. "We do what we gotta do."

She secured the knot, then leaned closer to whisper, "You've got a new friend watching over you now. Put your trust in his hands."

"Yes, ma'am. I'm tryin' real hard to do that."

Giving his bound wrists a supportive squeeze, she stepped back to Dan and reclaimed the gun.

Dan quickly secured Boris's hands as the outlaw groaned, regaining consciousness. He set him on his feet. Lining the outlaws in front of the fire, he glanced at Hope. "Good job."

Sinking to the ground, she let the gun fall out of her hand. Burying her face in her hands, she asked in a shaky voice, "What now?"

"Now?" Dan came over to sit down beside her. "We wait for dawn."

As the eastern sky brightened, Dan instructed the three outlaws at gunpoint to mount their waiting horses. Pulling Hope onto his horse behind him, they started back to Muddy Flats.

The strange ensemble rode into town by late afternoon. A storm was brewing; dark clouds scudded overhead, and the wind whipped dust across Main Street.

When Dan marched the three prisoners into the one-room jail, he found the sheriff reared back in his chair, boots propped on the desk, sawing logs.

Leaning close, Dan rapped smartly. "You got company."

Sheriff Ettes's boots thumped to the floor. The portly, balding man blinked up at them sleepily. "Yes, sir. What can I do for you?"

Dan nodded toward the outlaws. "I need you to keep these men for me until I come back."

The sheriff eyed the scruffy-looking bunch. "The Davidson gang?"

Big Joe smirked. "That's right, Sheriff, the Davidson gang." He stepped closer. "Boo!"

The old man frowned. "Well, well. Big Joe Davidson, not an ornerier polecat around. Someone finally caught up with you, huh?"

Joe's eyes narrowed. "No one caught me, Sheriff. This here is Grunt Lawson. He's tryin' to pull a fast one on ya. Used to ride with us, but all of a sudden, him and his woman decided they wanted more than their fair share, so they're tryin' to pull a slick one on ya, Sheriff."

The sheriff turned to look at Dan. "You don't say?"

"I'm Dan Sullivan, and I work for the government. These men are under arrest. I need you to keep them for me until I deliver Miss Kallahan to Medford."

"He's lyin'. He's Grunt Lawson; been our lookout on the last four robberies."

Dan shot Joe a quelling look. "Davidson, pipe down."

"He's lyin', Sheriff. Don't fall for it."

"Well, this is easy enough to settle." The lawman turned back to Dan. "Let's see your credentials, Son."

Dan's hand went to his pocket. "Right here . . ." He looked up sheepishly. "In my saddlebags."

Hope mentally groaned. And the saddlebags were with the Bennetts.

"Joe Davidson, you stop this lying!" She struck out, smacking Joe in the middle of his chest. The outlaw staggered, fixing her with a sullen look.

The sheriff's gaze swung from the three bound men to Dan. Then to Hope.

"Frog," Hope said. "Tell the sheriff the truth."

Frog opened his mouth to speak, but Big Joe's look silenced him.

Dan frowned. "Now look, Sheriff. I'm—"

"Just hold on," the sheriff interrupted. He turned to assess Hope, his eyes skimming her mangy appearance. "What do you have to say for yourself, young lady?"

"He is Dan Sullivan, Sheriff. He's a government agent sent to infiltrate the Davidson gang and learn how they're able to know what stages to—"

"A government agent?" The sheriff frowned. "In Muddy Flats?"

"In Washington," Dan said.

"Then what are you doin' here?"

"I'm trying to get Miss Kallahan to her fiancé."

The sheriff turned back to give Hope another once-over. His eyes fixed on her stringy hair and filthy dress.

"I'm getting married." Hope smiled lamely.

"And I'm trying to deliver her to her future husband—in Medford," Dan added.

Sheriff Ettes frowned. "Thought you said you were working for the government."

"I am; I'm also trying to get Miss Kallahan to Medford to meet her fiancé!"

Big Joe snickered. "A likely tale. He's makin' a fool of you, Sheriff. We ain't done nothin'. He's jest sore 'cause he thinks we cheated him outta wages."

"Wages, huh?" The lawman stroked his chin.

Boris nodded. "He's lyin', Sheriff. Grunt's a sorehead."

"You big oaf!" Hope reached out to smack Boris; Dan caught her arm.

"This is bunk! I work for the government, and these men are under arrest. I demand that you house them until I can transport them back to Washington on federal charges."

The sheriff's brows lifted. "You demand, huh?"

"That's right. I demand."

Heaving himself to his feet, the sheriff fished a ring of keys off a hook just above the desk.

Dan sent Hope a satisfied glance.

"Put your pistol on the desk," he told Dan. "You're all in jail until I can sort this out."

"Jail!" Hope exclaimed. "You can't—"

"Sheriff—," Dan protested.

"I can, and I am, little lady," the sheriff said emphatically, gesturing toward the cells with his gun. "Now git! All of you."

Dan laid his rifle on the desk, motioning for Hope to do the same with her pistol. She did, scowling at Joe.

Sheriff Ettes herded the three outlaws into one cell and Dan and Hope into the another.

"Look, Sheriff, wire Frank Talsman in the Department of

Justice. He'll verify who I am," Dan called as the cell door slammed shut and the lock turned.

"Can't until the river goes down."

"River goes down—what?" Dan winced as a clap of thunder shook the jail.

"It's outta banks—with all this rain we ain't been able to cross it for days."

"Good grief—how long will it take to go down?" Hope said.

"Don't know. Depends how much new rain this storm dumps on us." Another thunderous boom rattled the windowpane. "River's predicted to go down by mornin', but who knows? Could be days. But soon as she lets up, I'll wire Washington."

Sinking onto the cot, Hope stared glumly through the bars. "It won't stop. It'll rain cats and dogs, and we'll have to build an ark to get out of here."

"You folks just make yourself at home," the sheriff said. "I'll have the missus round up some grub. Every last one of you looks as if you could use a square meal."

Dan rattled the bars. "You can't leave Miss Kallahan in here!"

The old man swung the key back over the hook. "Now, Son, I suppose that I can do pretty well what I want. The little lady chose the company she's keepin'. Shouldn't be too much of a strain to endure it awhile longer until we can get this thing straightened out."

The sheriff walked back to his desk and sat down. In a few moments, he was dozing again.

"Well, well. Look at the big government man and his woman now," Big Joe taunted from the other cell. "How do you like them fixin's?"

"Cut it out, Joe!" Frog bowed his head, staring at his boots. "Miss Kallahan don't deserve to be in here with th' likes of us, and you know it."

"Shut your trap." Big Joe started pacing his cell like a caged animal. Boris sat on the floor, his back to the iron barrier.

Frog edged closer to the bars, his eyes on Hope. "It's not right. You don't belong in here. Don't you worry. The sheriff will have you out in no time atall."

"Shut up, Frog," Joe repeated.

Hope sat on the narrow bunk, looking at Dan. "Do you think the sheriff will send a wire?"

"I don't know." Dan sat down beside her. "Hope, I'm sorry."

"It's not your fault. The sheriff's just doing his duty. When he wires your commander, everything will be fine . . ." Her voice trailed off. "What?"

"Nothing. I just hope Frank's in town."

She shot off the cot. "He might be gone?"

"No—I don't know! He's in and out—I can't recall his saying anything about leaving, but that's been months ago. This job was supposed to take two weeks—three at the most."

"Wish the missus would get here with the grub," Boris complained. "Hope she brings corn bread—I love corn bread."

Frog sank to a bunk, closing his eyes. Big Joe kicked his foot. "What are you doin', Judas?"

"Praying," Frog murmured, refusing to look up.

Dan glanced at Hope and she smiled. "Didn't I tell you he'd changed? It's a miracle."

"Well, we need another one," Dan said softly. "And soon."

She slipped her hand into his. "Thank you for rescuing me," she said softly.

"I should have been with you. It wouldn't have happened a second time—"

"But it did, and I'm all right. We'll be fine. The Lord will deliver us."

Leaning back against the wall, Dan stared at the stained ceiling. "I don't know—I'm beginning to wonder. I'm supposed to be in charge of this, arrest the Davidson gang, and get you safely to Medford. Every day there's a new problem."

"Don't blame yourself. You've only tried to help me."

Pulling her to him, he whispered, "I will get you there, Hope. I give you my word."

Hope smiled, burying her face in his chest. "I'm not worried."

"Try to get some rest," he said, holding her tighter. Streaks of lightning lit the cell, followed by thunderous booms. Rain pelted the sides of the jail.

"The river will be down in the morning, and the sheriff will wire Franklin. We'll be out of here by noon."

"Breakfast," the sheriff called out. Unlocking the cell door, he handed Dan a tray of food. "Eat up! The missus went to a lot of trouble to cook for you."

Joe eyed the food piteously. "Slop."

"Eat it anyway."

Hope was on her feet in a flash. "Is the river down enough to cross it?"

"Don't know; ain't checked yet. Soon as I get you fed, I'll go have a look."

Hope sank back to the cot.

The day dragged by. Afternoon came, and there was still no sign of the sheriff. Dan alternately paced the small cell and kept Hope company. Frog sat on a bunk, praying.

Big Joe complained about the food and the lack of room. Boris slept.

The sun was an orange glow when Sheriff Ettes finally returned. "Evenin', folks. Trust you've had a fine day?"

Dan straightened from where he leaned against the wall. "Did you contact Washington?"

"Yes, sir, shore did. God's lookin' after you. It's a miracle, but last night's rain didn't interfere with gettin' across the river—"

"Did you reach Franklin?"

"Yep. And you're clear." The sheriff pinned Joe with a stern look. "Now, Big Joe," he began patiently, "you ought not to lie like that. You've caused me a whole heap of trouble."

Big Joe sat down on his cot, a scowl on his face.

The door to Dan and Hope's cell swung open. "Son, you and the little lady are free to go. Sorry about the mix-up, but no self-respectin' federal man would let his credentials out of his possession."

"There's a story behind that, Sheriff." Dan settled his hat on his head and reached for Hope's hand. "I have to deliver Miss Kallahan to Medford. I'll be back in a day."

"Guess you been after these three a long time, huh?"

"A long time."

Frog slipped off his cot. "Can I talk to Miss Kallahan a minute afore she leaves?"

"No you cain't," Big Joe growled.

"Sheriff?" Frog frowned. "It's real important."

Sheriff Ettes glanced at Dan. Dan shrugged.

"Well," the sheriff said, scratching his chin, "I suppose I could let you, but not alone."

"Frog!" Big Joe was on his feet, staring down the other prisoner. "You keep yore mouth shut!"

Frog ignored him. "That's all right, Sheriff. I kin say what I got to say in front of ya."

The sheriff opened the cell and motioned him out.

"What is it you want to say?" Hope asked as they walked to the desk.

"Judas!" Joe yelled. "Yellow-bellied coward!"

The outlaw cleared his throat, hanging his head. "I jest want to say thank you for talkin' to me the other night. I've never felt so free, though I know I'm going to spend the next several years in jail."

Hope smiled. "I'm happy for you. Knowing Jesus Christ is liberating. I'll pray for you every day."

"Well, I need to clear my conscience," he said, lifting his eyes to meet hers.

"About what?"

"You want to know where the money is," Frog said softly, glancing at Joe.

"Turncoat!"

Dan straightened. "The army payrolls? Can you tell me?"

"There's a cave not far from the cabin."

"Frog!" Joe bellowed.

Dan frowned. "Three miles or so, off to the right?"

"Yes."

"Dan, that's where we stayed the first—" Dan stopped Hope.

"The money is buried toward the back. Big Joe and me hid it there."

"We were right on top of it!" Hope exclaimed.

"You were there?" Frog asked.

"The night Dan took me from the cabin. I was sick, and we took refuge in the cave."

They ignored Big Joe's rantings from the other cell.

A roguish smile played about Frog's mouth. "Big Joe don't like it, but I don't care. That's where the money is, almost all of it. Spent a few dollars on grub, but the rest is there."

Dan stuck out his hand. "Thank you."

"Ain't nothin'. Miss Kallahan said I had to turn my sins over to God, and I figure I might as well turn Joe's over too, 'cause there's not much chance he ever will. The good Lord's forgiven me, but I still got things to settle. This is the first one."

"God bless you," Dan murmured.

Tears swelled to the outlaw's eyes. "He has already."

The sheriff shoved his hat to the back of his head. "Well, Frog, guess you're gettin' a little cramped in that cell?"

"It's tighter than Grannie's corset in here!" Big Joe shouted. "Move me to the empty one! Git me away from that dirty, low-down double-crosser!"

"Nope, the empty cell goes to this gentleman." Sheriff winked at Frog. "Liars never win."

Chapter Sixteen

Sheriff Ettes insisted that Hope and Dan stay the night. He rounded up new clothes and arranged for hot baths and two rooms at the hotel.

"Can't meet your new husband looking like that!" the old law officer teased.

Hope stared at her image in the mirror over the washstand. She hardly recognized herself anymore. Gone was the young, naive girl who got on the stage in Michigan. The likeness she saw reflected was a woman's—a woman who had survived adversity and a crisis of faith. She'd changed inside, a good change, a change more to her liking.

Leading Frog to an acceptance of Jesus Christ as his Savior had brought a renewal of her own commitment and a revelation of what she needed to do to deepen her own spirituality. It would require a great deal more Bible study and prayer, but she was ready now. Ready to rely on her own faith, not Papa's.

And somewhere along the way to her spiritual awakening, she'd fallen in love. She sank onto the edge of the bed she'd recently vacated.

Dan Sullivan.

Hope sighed. They'd been through so much together, and she couldn't imagine life without him. They'd overcome fear and misfortune, put up with a temperamental goat, a vile-smelling pig, a hungry cougar, inept outlaws, and a sweet, helpless old woman, managing to laugh in spite of it all.

Oddly enough, the times they'd been drawn together by danger or illness had been the best. Times when there had been no one to depend upon but God and themselves.

Hope smiled. Dan Sullivan was a man to be reckoned with. He'd gone from a dangerous outlaw to a dear friend tenderly protective of her. He'd literally snatched her from the jaws of death, not once but twice. Three times, if she counted this last kidnapping.

Dan. From outlaw to tough undercover government agent. A rugged man with protective instincts, a man who respected her commitment to another man but whose kiss evoked such a myriad of feelings and emotions that it made her head spin.

But their time together was coming to an end. In a few moments she would be on her way to Medford to become wife to John Jacobs. The certainty of it caused an ache in her heart.

A knock on the door roused Hope from her reflections. When she opened the door, she found Dan, freshly shaved and dressed in clean clothes that fit his sturdy frame. Love overflowed in her heart.

"Hungry?"

"Famished," she said, tossing her hairbrush on the bed.

The light touch of his hand in the center of her back was like a brand, his brand, on her heart. She savored every moment of his company as if it were the last, because soon it would be, and she didn't want to waste a single minute. One day, when she was an old woman, she would tell her grandchildren about her great adventure on her way to marry their grandfather, and she would tell them about Dan Sullivan, a man she had deeply and irrevocably loved with all of her heart.

No, she couldn't tell them about Dan, but she would tell them about how important it was to follow the heart in matters of love. But she couldn't follow her heart; she must fulfill a promise, a covenant to marry a man she didn't even know.

When Dan and Hope arrived in the hotel dining room, the other guests looked up in expectation. Judging by the curiosity on their faces, they'd heard about the kidnapping, the rescue, the arrest, and the Davidson gang now securely locked away in Sheriff Ettes's jail.

Hope wasn't inclined to share what had actually happened, and Dan couldn't reveal any facts. Once the gang was transported to Washington, Dan would still have an obligation to fulfill. Big Joe, Frog, and Boris would be held for trial, and Dan would be called to testify, so any inquiries were now passed over with polite apologies.

Hope realized they lingered over breakfast far longer than was fashionable. Neither seemed eager to leave. The accidental touches and the lingering conversation only prolonged the inevitable.

"I should have wired John," Hope said, as Dan saddled their horse. "Let him know I'll be arriving today."

"Ettes tells me that someone will have to take the wire across the river and deliver it to John. By the time he gets it, you'll be there."

"Yes . . . I suppose." She sighed. "What if he doesn't want me?" She'd never considered that possibility. She brightened. What if after all this trouble to get there, he'd changed his mind? Her hopes rocketed. She would be free to marry anyone she chose!

Dan's hands paused on the cinch. "He's figured out you've run into problems getting there. Maybe he's been in touch with your aunt, sent her a telegram."

She frowned. "Oh, I hope not. Aunt Thalia would be worried sick if she were to learn that I hadn't reached Medford. She must be fretting as it is, wondering why I haven't written."

"You can write her a long letter when you reach Medford and tell her all about your trials and your new husband."

"Yes. She'll enjoy that." Aunt Thalia might enjoy it, but Hope sure didn't relish the prospect.

All the way to Medford, Hope wished that things were

different. But she could wish all she wanted, and nothing would change.

Why, oh why, God, did I answer that ad?

Dan would buy that piece of land in Virginia he loved. She liked Virginia—well, she'd never actually been there, but she knew she could love it. She'd love anywhere Dan resided.

They rode in silence, Medford drawing ever closer. Should she be telling Dan the things that were in her heart? It would only make their parting more difficult.

Did he have anything he wanted to tell her?

God, if he does, let him find the courage to speak.

When Dan finally drew the horse to a halt on a small rise, she was so deep in her thoughts she didn't realize the journey was over.

"Why have you stopped?"

"There's the Basin River. Medford's on the other side. It looks as if there's a ferry to take you across."

"Yes, I see it."

Her heart ached. How could she say good-bye to the man she loved so much it hurt? Should she beg him not to leave, throw herself on his mercy?

She'd die. There was no doubt about it; she was going to expire if she had to leave him.

"Ready?" he asked quietly.

"Ready."

He urged the horse down the slope and hailed the boatman. Hope waited as the two men talked, her heart heavy as Dan negotiated their passage.

"He'll take us," Dan said when he returned.

She couldn't look at him. "You don't have to come with me. I can make it on my own now."

"I want to go with you, Hope."

She lifted her head. Their eyes held, unspoken words clouding their gazes.

"I want to speak to John, explain what's happened."

"No, that won't be necessary." She would explain and trust that he understood. If he didn't, then she couldn't marry him. Marriage was built on trust and respect. Anything less was unacceptable.

He helped her off the horse, and Hope, Dan, and the boatman stepped onto the small flatboat a short while later.

"So, you're going to Medford," the boatman said.

"Yes." Hope smiled, trying to get a glimpse of her new home. She spotted a few buildings and a hotel sign. The town looked small.

"Nice place. Nice people."

"So I've heard."

The closer they got to shore, the more anxious she became. She was doing the right thing. She had to believe that if God had brought her this far, he meant for her to be with John. She'd prayed, recommitting the problem into God's hands. She had to accept his answer, though it most certainly wasn't hers.

No, her heart cried. *I love Dan!*

She had to face the truth. She had made her commitment to John and she had to honor it, no matter how strongly she felt about Dan. John would be good to her; God wouldn't throw her to the lions, would he?

The boat bumped into the shore, and Dan reached out to steady her. His touch was confident, unlike her chaotic reservations.

The boatman lent a hand as she disembarked. Dan followed with the horse. They walked several yards to the edge of the road and stood looking at the hill that led into Medford.

"Are you uneasy?"

She glanced up, willing him to stop her from going. "Yes."

"Why? John will understand, Hope."

"I'll . . . I'll explain why I'm so late, and yes, he'll understand. I've decided to tell him everything that's happened. After that, if he still wants me, then . . . I suppose we'll begin to build our life together."

A muscle worked tightly in Dan's jaw. "I don't want it to end this way. Let me go with you."

Yes, yes, her heart cried. *Go with me, never leave me again.* "No, there's no need. You've done so much already."

She tried to memorize everything about him. The way he wore his hat, the way his eyes softened to a rich cinnamon when he looked at her, the way his hair fell in soft waves around his shoulders.

"I'll . . . miss you."

"Miss you, too." She longed to reach out, take his hand and never let it go.

The silence stretched.

Drawing a deep breath, she willed herself not to cry. "I wish I could thank you for everything, but there aren't enough words to express my gratitude." Pausing, she took another breath, swallowing against the tight knot that suddenly crowded her throat. "Truth is, I wish—"

"I know," he said gruffly. "I wish it too."

She blinked back hot tears, biting down hard on her lower lip. "I know I shouldn't say it, but I love you more than I could ever love John Jacobs."

There, she'd said it. The admission that haunted her day and night. She could never love any other man the way she loved Dan.

"Hope—"

"Well . . . I'd best be going. Happiness is only a few feet away." She tried to laugh to lighten the mood, but it didn't come out right.

He nodded. "If you ever need anything . . ."

"Thanks. You too. Anything."

Walk away, Hope. Now, while you still can.

"Well, I'll be going now."

She started off, refusing to look back. Tears rolled down her cheeks, blinding her vision.

Don't let me go, Dan. Please. Don't let me go.

Turning around, she called over her shoulder, "I'm trying hard to grow up, Dan Sullivan! But it's not easy!"

"You're doing a fine job, Hope Kallahan," he called back.

She could feel his eyes on her as she walked up the long hill leading to town.

Medford was just as John had described it. A small, friendly town. Folks smiled as Hope stepped onto the wooden porch and tried to glimpse through the plate-glass window the man she was about to marry. A tall, rather ordinary-looking man with a handlebar mustache stood behind the counter, handing a wrapped package to a customer.

John Jacobs, future husband and father of her children.

She waited until the customer left before going inside. A bell over the door sounded as she entered the Mercantile. The store was roomy, well stocked, and smelled of coffee and spices.

John's back was to her. Smiling, he turned from replacing a jar of candies on the shelf.

"Afterno—" His greeting died, his jaw dropping when he recognized her. "Oh . . . oh, my goodness."

Summoning a timid smile, Hope said softly, "Hello, Mr. Jacobs."

"Hope Kallahan?"

"John." She drew a long, suffering breath. "I know I'm late, but I can explain."

"Late?" His eyes darted to the back of the store. "Yes—yes, you are . . . quite late. Uh, I'd given up—"

"I know you must have thought I wasn't coming," she apologized, approaching the counter.

Dear God, let me be able to do this. I trust your will for my life, but this is so very hard.

John backed off as if an apparition was about to confront him.

"I understand your consternation," she said, worried that he might faint. The color had drained from his angular features. "I was so afraid you'd think horrible things of me, but I can explain. You see, I was kidnapped off the coach—"

"Believe me, I . . . I had no way of knowing . . . what with the river up, and I couldn't wire . . ."

"Oh, I know. I wouldn't blame you for thinking that I'd decided not to come, but things got very complicated." She smoothed her skirts, trying not to cry. *Lord, I don't want to do this; I want to be with Dan.* "It was impossible to send a wire—though I thought about it, thought about it a lot, actually. But I couldn't; I was kidnapped three times."

John was apparently having a hard time grasping the explanation. "Three times?"

She nodded. "I know it sounds absurd. You see, I'm not Thomas Ferry's daughter." She edged closer to the counter as he continued to back away. "Luckily, there was this handsome undercover agent who knew I wasn't the senator's daughter, and so in order to rescue me from this horrible gang, he had to kidnap me. Then I got terribly sick, he got shot; then we had to carry his favorite saddle until he just couldn't tote it another mile. Do you know, we swapped that perfectly good saddle—Dan's prized possession—for a goat. Well. That goat ate everything in sight." Rolling her eyes, she continued.

"We walked for days, well, actually it seemed more like weeks, off and on. Oh—did I say we stopped to have breakfast with an old couple, and they were fighting with kin over this stolen pig, and we nearly got shot our-selves—well, Dan did get shot when we tried to escape—but I think I've already said that, haven't I?"

John nodded mutely.

"Well, I had to nurse Dan back to health because he came down with a fever. Just when he got to feeling better and we were on our way to Medford again, we stopped to help an old woman who'd hurt her leg with an ax. She was chopping wood when she shouldn't have been. We intended to leave right away, but we couldn't—Letty was down in bed and couldn't see after the farm, so don't you see, we had to stay on for a few days. By the time we got to Muddy Flats, we were wearing clothes way too big for us—why, we both looked like roosters wearing socks—we were riding that awful old mule, Cinder. Well, the moment we thought we were safe again, who should show up but that horrible Joe Davidson! Lo and behold, he kidnapped me again. Can you believe it?" She circled her ear with a finger, frowning. "Nutty as a squirrel, that one.

"Fortunately, Grunt—who's really Dan, the government agent—rescued me again, bless his heart. And this time he arrested the gang and put them behind bars where they belong. Big Joe, Boris, and Frog are this moment in Muddy Flats awaiting Dan's return. He'll have to transport them back to Washington because they're his prisoners—federal prisoners, you understand. The only good thing about all of this is that Frog made a commitment to Christ, which makes the whole ridiculous episode worthwhile, I guess.

And so, here I am. Finally." She pasted on a brave grin. "Ready to get married."

John opened his mouth, but nothing came out.

"I know," she soothed. "It sounds like a dime novel, doesn't it? But I swear—no, I don't swear anymore because the past few weeks have taught me a valuable lesson. I depended on Papa's faith, not mine. I'll not be doing that again, thank you very much. I was too lax with my beliefs—actually I didn't know what I believed until now—but I know I believe in the Lord and his teachings. Did you know I can recite two chapters of Genesis by heart—almost?"

John shook his head lamely.

"Well, I can, and all because of Dan—and the Lord, of course. You know—Grunt?" She smiled lamely. "He's just wonderful . . . but I think I might have said that."

Hope glanced up as a beautiful dark-haired young woman emerged from the back room wiping her hands on her apron. "John, you'll need to put flour on the next order—" She paused, smiling. "Good afternoon."

Hope nodded. "Hello."

The young woman joined John behind the counter. "I don't believe we've met. Of course, I've not met everyone who comes to Medford to shop." Smiling, she extended her hand. "I'm Ginger Jacobs. Veda Fletcher's niece."

Hope's smile gradually faded. "Jacobs?"

"Yes, John's wife." She glanced up at her husband ador-ingly. "We married a week ago."

"A week ago?"

John's face turned cherry red. He was having trouble meeting Hope's apprehensive gaze.

"Ginger, uh—," John began.

Hope let the words sink in slowly, gloriously.

John was married. John was married? John was married!

Praise God! John was married!

Hope stuck her hand out. "Hope Kallahan. I'm so glad to meet you, Mrs. Jacobs."

Ginger's eyes widened. "Oh, dear—you're Hope?"

"I'm so sorry," John said. "I thought—" He cleared his throat. "Well, after weeks passed, and you hadn't arrived, I assumed—"

"Just what anyone would assume! That I'd changed my mind and wasn't coming. I'm not angry!"

The realization that she was free—free to marry anyone she chose—left her giddy. And the man she wanted to marry most in the world was about to get away.

"It's a long story. I'll write you both a letter and explain it all, soon, but right now I really have something I must do—congratulations! I hope you'll both be very happy."

She whirled, leaving the young couple staring after her as she ran out the door and back down the hill.

Running as if her life depended on it, Hope prayed. *Please, God, don't let Dan be gone. I know I don't deserve your mercy the way I've been acting and thinking, but please, don't take Dan away from me.*

Suddenly, events of the past few weeks became clear to her: She'd been accusing God of deserting her, blaming him for all her troubles, doubting that he loved her, when in fact he was only trying to help her!

When she got sick and Dan nursed her back to health in the cave, God had removed them from Big Joe's path long enough to convince the outlaw they'd gotten away. When Dan got shot, God tucked them safely in another cave where the Bennetts couldn't find them. If it weren't for that old goat they swapped for Dan's beautiful saddle, they couldn't have traded with Letty for the mule—

She came to a skidding halt in the road, thunderstruck by the enormity of the revelation.

If she hadn't been kidnapped, then she would have reached Medford and married John. John would have missed the love of his life, and she, most certainly, would have missed hers.

But best of all, if she hadn't met Frog, she couldn't have told him that God loves him—truly loves him.

Dear God! Can you ever forgive me for being such a dunder-head?

By the time she reached the boat landing, she had a stitch in her side and her hair had come loose from the pins.

Dan was standing beside his horse as she ran toward him. "Dan!" she shouted.

Dropping the reins, he ran toward her. His boots covered the uneven ground in long, impatient strides. "Hope?"

She raced toward him, her breath coming in painful gasps. It took an eternity to reach him.

Catching her in midstride, he held her tightly, the shelter

of his arms firm and strong. "What's wrong? What's happened?"

Hugging his neck, she laughed with pure joy. "Nothing. Absolutely nothing! For the first time in weeks, everything is fine!"

He let her slide to the ground, still holding on to her. "Where's John?"

"With his wife."

"With his—what?"

"John is married."

His eyes anxiously searched hers. "Married? But—"

"I know. It's crazy, but so is everything else that's happened lately! Her name is Ginger, and she's the most beautiful woman I've ever seen. She and John got married last week, and I just know that God's going to shine on their union." She hugged him so tightly he stepped backward, swaying with the force. "Oh, Dan, they look as if they absolutely adore each other."

Dan stiffened. "Wait a minute. Jacobs is married? How could he do that? He's engaged to you."

She laughed. This protective side of him thrilled her. "It's all right. I'll be forever grateful that he did! He thought I wasn't coming—and why wouldn't he?"

"You're not upset?"

"No. Relieved. Ever so much relieved."

Dan took a deep breath, then pulled her back into his arms and held her as if he'd never let her go. "That's good, because I was coming after you."

"You were?" Her heart sang. The Lord was just pouring out blessings! Dan Sullivan was coming after her!

His arms tightened possessively around her waist. "You bet I was. I'm not about to let another man have you, even if you had given your word. I tried—I prayed about it, and God and I came to an understanding. We agreed I had too much time invested in you to let you go. We belong to each other. Until we're old and gray and have fifteen grand-children."

"Fifteen!"

Picking her up, he threw her up in the air, catching her about the waist, laughing and kissing her. "I was on my way to get you when you came flying back down the hill."

"Rescuing me again?" She grinned down at him.

"No, loving you." The devotion in his eyes overwhelmed her. "If John could make you happy, then maybe you might have made me go away—but I doubt it. I love you, Hope. I have from the first moment I set eyes on you."

"John couldn't make me happy," she said softly.

"No?"

"Not the way you can. You make me happy. I've known that for weeks, and I didn't know how I could ever marry John when I loved you so much." She tilted her head to one side. "Well, I'm a free woman, Mr. Sullivan. Will you marry me?"

Aunt Thalia wouldn't approve of her boldness, but then, what Aunt Thalia didn't know couldn't hurt her.

Dan grinned, his eyes dancing with laughter. "You're asking me to permanently hook up with a woman with your kind of luck?"

She sobered. "I know that you don't want any commitments, but I'll try real hard to make you happy, and I would never break your heart like Katie Morris did. And ordinarily, my luck isn't that bad. It brought us together, didn't it?"

"No," he said softly, tilting her face up to meet his. "God brought us together. Haven't you figured it out yet? It was his plan all along."

She nodded, breathless from his nearness. "I know—I have so much to tell you." Later, she would tell him of her revelation and of how God had been working in her life all the while she'd been yelling at him.

Brushing a tendril of loose hair away from her face, he smiled down at her. "How do you feel about moving to Virginia?"

She nodded solemnly. "I'd feel real good about it. Thank you."

"Then I guess we ought to get married just about as quick as we can find a preacher."

"Muddy Flats!" they chorused.

"Let's hurry before trouble can find us again." Hope hooked her arm into Dan's, and they set off for the ferry.

"Dan?"

"Yes?"

"How far is Virginia from Michigan?"

"A long way. Why?"

She held on to his arm tightly, afraid he might get away. She'd been through too much to get him; she wasn't about to lose him now. "I want to see my sisters, Faith and June. Faith's in Texas, and June will be living in Seattle, but we could all travel to Aunt Thalia's for Christmas. Would that be impossible?"

She longed to show off her handsome government agent and meet Faith's and June's new husbands, share her exciting adventure. Why, Faith and June wouldn't believe what she'd gone through to get her husband!

"My love, we can go anywhere you want." He bent over to kiss her. "A Kallahan Christmas family reunion. I like the idea." When she would have walked on, he caught her back to him, and they tarried in the middle of the road exchanging long kisses.

Three horses galloped out of Medford and blew past them on their way down the hill. Jerking apart, Dan started to yell at the inconsiderate horsemen when Hope quickly slapped a hand over his mouth.

"Mhdidhgy?"

Shaking her head, she pointed to the fleeing riders. The lead horseman had a chicken coop wedged between him and the saddle horn. Feathers flew as they galloped toward town.

"More trouble," they murmured.

Dan and Hope swapped a silent look, then locked hands and bolted off in the opposite direction.

"Is this what our life is going to be like?" Hope puffed as they raced down the hill to the ferry. It didn't matter, but she'd just like to be prepared for disasters on a daily basis.

"I hope not!"

Their feet flew over the ground in record fashion.

Throwing her arms in the air, Hope couldn't contain herself any longer. She shouted and whooped, making a powerful noise. She was going to marry the man she loved! "I love you, Dan Sullivan!"

"I love you, Hope Kallahan!"

The boatman looked up, waving.

And somewhere above, their heavenly Father smiled down and said, "I love you, too."

A Note to Readers

Dear Reader,

I hope you've had as much fun with the Kallahan sisters—Faith, June, and Hope—as I have had writing about them.

When God called me to write Christian romances, I reacted with trepidation. Maybe I felt I wasn't worthy enough to minister through the written word; there are certainly others more qualified. Also, I'm a person who resists change, even though I believe that God will uphold his children wherever he puts them, if only they will follow him. A Scripture verse that means a lot to me is Matthew 8:26, where Jesus calms the storm: "And he saith unto them, Why are ye fearful, O ye of little faith? Then he arose, and rebuked the winds and the sea; and there was a great calm."

I'm happy to say my earlier trepidation quickly vanished, replaced with absolute certainty of God's will. I'm thankful that God heard the desires of my heart. Writing Brides of the West has been an unparalleled blessing for me. What joy I've found in "letting go and letting God" do his work! Today I write with a smile and a song in my heart for my Savior, honoring the Lord Jesus Christ. How blessed can one person be?

I thank you so very much for accepting Brides of the West in such an overwhelming manner. If you haven't read *Faith* or *June* yet, I hope you will put them on your "must read" list.

In his name,

Lori Copeland

About the Author

Lori Copeland has published more than fifty romance novels and has won numerous awards for her books. Publishing with HeartQuest allows her the freedom to write stories that express her love of God and her personal convictions.

Lori lives with her wonderful husband, Lance, in Springfield, Missouri. She has three incredibly handsome grown sons, three absolutely gorgeous daughters-in-law, and three exceptionally bright grandchildren—but then, she freely admits to being partial when it comes to her family. Lori enjoys reading biographies, attending book discussion groups, participating in morning water-aerobic exercises at the local YMCA, and she is presently trying very hard to learn to play bridge. She loves to travel and is always thrilled to meet her readers.

When asked what one thing Lori would like others to know about her, she readily says, "I'm not perfect, just forgiven by the grace of God." Christianity to Lori means peace, joy, and the knowledge that she has a Friend, a Savior, who never leaves her side. Through her books, she hopes to share this wondrous assurance with others.

Lori welcomes letters written to her in care of Tyndale House Author Relations, P.O. Box 80, Wheaton, IL 60189-0080.

HEART
QUEST.

Current HeartQuest Releases

- *Magnolia*, Ginny Aiken
- *Lark*, Ginny Aiken
- *Camellia*, Ginny Aiken
- *Dream Vacation*, Ginny Aiken, Jeri Odell, and Elizabeth White

- *Sweet Delights*, Terri Blackstock, Ranee McCollum, and Elizabeth White

- *Awakening Mercy*, Angela Benson
- *Abiding Hope*, Angela Benson

- *Faith*, Lori Copeland
- *Hope*, Lori Copeland
- *June*, Lori Copeland
- *Glory*, Lori Copeland

- *Freedom's Promise*, Dianna Crawford
- *Freedom's Hope*, Dianna Crawford
- *Freedom's Belle*, Dianna Crawford

- *Prairie Rose*, Catherine Palmer
- *Prairie Fire*, Catherine Palmer
- *Prairie Storm*, Catherine Palmer
- *Prairie Christmas*, Catherine Palmer, Elizabeth White, and Peggy Stoks

- *Finders Keepers*, Catherine Palmer
- *Hide and Seek*, Catherine Palmer
- *A Kiss of Adventure*, Catherine Palmer (original title: *The Treasure of Timbuktu*)
- *A Whisper of Danger*, Catherine Palmer (original title: *The Treasure of Zanzibar*)
- *A Touch of Betrayal*, Catherine Palmer
- *A Victorian Christmas Cottage*, Catherine Palmer, Debra White Smith, Jeri Odell, and Peggy Stoks
- *A Victorian Christmas Quilt*, Catherine Palmer, Debra White Smith, Ginny Aiken, and Peggy Stoks
- *A Victorian Christmas Tea*, Catherine Palmer, Dianna Crawford, Peggy Stoks, and Katherine Chute

- *Olivia's Touch*, Peggy Stoks
- *Romy's Walk*, Peggy Stoks

Coming Soon (Fall 2001)

- *A Victorian Christmas Keepsake*,
Catherine Palmer, Kristin Billerbeck, and Ginny Aiken

Visit www.HeartQuest.com for lots of info on
HeartQuest books and authors and more!

www.HeartQuest.com

Other Great Tyndale House Fiction

- *Jenny's Story*, Judy Baer
- *Libby's Story*, Judy Baer

- *Out of the Shadows*, Sigmund Brouwer

- *Ashes and Lace*, B. J. Hoff
- *Cloth of Heaven*, B. J. Hoff

- *The Price*, Jim and Terri Kraus
- *The Treasure*, Jim and Terri Kraus
- *The Promise*, Jim and Terri Kraus

- *Winter Passing*, Cindy McCormick Martinusen

- *Rift in Time*, Michael Phillips
- *Hidden in Time*, Michael Phillips

- *Unveiled*, Francine Rivers
- *Unashamed*, Francine Rivers
- *Unshaken*, Francine Rivers
- *A Voice in the Wind*, Francine Rivers
- *An Echo in the Darkness*, Francine Rivers
- *As Sure As the Dawn*, Francine Rivers
- *The Last Sin Eater*, Francine Rivers
- *Leota's Garden*, Francine Rivers
- *The Scarlet Thread*, Francine Rivers
- *The Atonement Child*, Francine Rivers

- *The Promise Remains*, Travis Thrasher

HeartQuest Books by Lori Copeland

Faith—Book 1 in the exciting new series Brides of the West, which follows three sisters as they become mail-order brides. Faith leaves her Michigan home for a husband on a Texas ranch in a lighthearted story that reminds readers of the importance of growing in their faith. Nicholas did not know what to expect from his mail-order bride. What he found in Faith changed his life forever.

June—The second book in Lori Copeland's historical romance series about three sisters who become mail-order brides. June leaves her home in Michigan to become the mail-order bride of a preacher in Washington State. A lighthearted, easy-to-read story that teaches the important theme of God's faithfulness even during times when we don't know what his plan or purposes are.

Heartwarming Anthologies from HeartQuest

A Victorian Christmas Cottage—Four novellas centering around hearth and home at Christmastime. Stories by Catherine Palmer, Jeri Odell, Debra White Smith, and Peggy Stoks.

A Victorian Christmas Tea—Four novellas about life and love at Christmastime. Stories by Catherine Palmer, Dianna Crawford, Peggy Stoks, and Katherine Chute.

A Victorian Christmas Quilt—A patchwork of four novellas about love and joy at Christmastime. Stories by Catherine Palmer, Ginny Aiken, Peggy Stoks, and Debra White Smith.